FALSE DIAMOND

An Abbot Agency Mystery

Veronica Heley

severn
House

This first world edition published 2013
in Great Britain and the USA by
SEVERN HOUSE PUBLISHERS LTD of
9–15 High Street, Sutton, Surrey, England, SM1 1DF.

Trade paperback edition first published 2017
In Great Britain and the USA by
SEVERN HOUSE PUBLISHERS LTD
Eardley House, 4 Uxbridge Street, London W8 7SY

British Library Cataloguing in Publication Data
A CIP catalogue record for this title is available from the British Library.

ISBN-13: 978-0-7278-8298-1 (cased)
ISBN-13: 978-1-84751-798-2 (trade paper)
ISBN-13: 978-1-78010-484-3 (e-book)

ONE

Bea Abbot ran a domestic agency whose watchword was discretion and whose clients did not wear fake diamonds . . . until, that is, the Holland family crashed into her busy day.

Wednesday afternoon

It took a lot to rile Bea Abbot.

The woman in the mink coat succeeded. She burst into Bea's office, pushing someone before her. 'Mrs Abbot? Right! We need your help!'

Bea said, 'I'm afraid I don't—'

The mink coat swung a young woman into a chair and stood over her. 'Mrs Abbot will set you right!'

'Who . . .?' said Bea. Out of the corner of her eye she was aware of a third person hovering in the doorway . . . until he was pushed aside by Carrie, her office manageress.

Carrie, arms akimbo, was not amused at the intrusion. 'I'm sorry, Mrs Abbot. They asked if you were in and swept right past me. Shall I . . .?'

Bea had belatedly recognized the young woman in the chair. 'No, Carrie. It's all right.'

Carrie hesitated. She was no fool and could sense trouble.

Bea was firm. 'I'll deal with it.' She waited till the door had closed behind her office manageress to say, 'Dilys? Are you all right?'

Obviously, the girl was very far from all right. Her hair was all over the place, her lipstick was smeared, the handbag over her arm was open and her coat was awry. 'It's not true! He loves me!'

'Humph!' said the mink coat, seating herself, unasked. 'Let me introduce myself. I am Dilys's aunt, Sybil Holland. I do not visit London often, and I do not normally concern myself with what the family gets up to. The dividends I receive from Holland and Butcher are not my only source of income, and I have never questioned my brother's ability to run his companies until now. It is true that I expressed some concern when I heard that his only daughter was marrying a salesman with a dubious background but he would not be warned, not he! Little pig-head, we used to call him when we were young, and the years have done nothing to compensate for his lack of common sense. So what do I find when I return to this distressingly run-down country where bad manners seem to be the norm? My niece has allied herself to a charlatan who gave her a piece of glass for an engagement ring! Typical!'

Bea looked at the mink coat, recognizing intelligence and the easy assumption of command possessed by those accustomed to wealth. Yes, the woman must be seventy if she was a day, but her mink coat – it showed a disregard for popular opinion that she should wear one – was superb, and she was wearing the biggest, most sparkly diamond rings Bea had seen in a long while. Her hair was a doubtful red, her eyes were outlined in black and she wore a bright blue eyeshadow, the sort which had been popular in the sixties. Was she out of date? Yes. But those same eyes glittered as brightly as her diamonds.

'It's not true!' screamed Dilys, throwing her legs about. 'It's not! He loves me!'

Sybil Holland sniffed. 'Chucking your toys out of the pram will get you nowhere.'

'I'm twenty-eight years old! I'm a married woman with three children!' Dilys tried to hit her aunt, and missed. 'I won't listen, I won't listen, I won't—'

Bea shouted, 'Enough!'

Silence.

Sybil Holland snapped her mouth shut.

Dilys overflowed with tears, but was also quiet.

Bea leaned back in her chair and told herself to relax. It was not at all like her to shout. Even when provoked, she took pride in presenting a civilized exterior to the world. She reminded herself that she was a successful businesswoman, that she ran a first-class domestic agency from the basement of her Georgian house in Kensington, that her only son was a member of parliament, that she paid her bills on time and that she looked pretty good for her age.

She swung her chair round to her computer and saved the document she'd been working on. 'Now –' turning back to her visitors – 'I do not in the least understand why you have come to see me and, let me add, I have no wish to be involved with the firm of Holland and Butcher in any way. Yes: at one time there was a suggestion that that firm – responsible as it is for training people for high-class domestic work – might merge with my agency, which specializes in finding such people jobs. But I decided against it. End of.'

'I can see you're no fool,' said Sybil, 'but this development changes everything.'

Bea sent her a look designed to quell. 'May I call you a cab?'

Dilys started to hiccup. 'I . . . oh, hic! . . . You must . . . hic! . . . It's not—'

'Stupid girl!' said Sybil, pulling a gold cigarette case and lighter out of her enormous handbag. Prada, of course.

'No smoking, if you please,' said Bea. Cigarettes and a mink coat? The harridan lived in a time warp.

Sybil ignored Bea to light up, sending a stream of smoke down both nostrils. A dragon in action?

Bea averted her eyes. 'Dilys, I'll fetch you a glass of water.' Ignoring the third member of the party who was still standing by the door, she stepped out into the busy main office.

Carrie half rose from her seat. 'Shall I send for backup, Mrs Abbot?'

'No, thanks. I can cope.' She ran the cold water tap in the cloakroom and took a glassful back to her office. The man – and who on earth might he be? – had taken a seat by the window. He smiled at her as she returned. Smiling was cheap. Helping someone in distress costs energy.

'There you are,' said Bea, handing the glass to the hiccuping girl. 'Now, I'll call you a cab, shall I.' She made it a statement and not a question.

The mink coat was having none of it. 'Don't be obtuse. We need an expert opinion on that fake diamond of my niece's before we go anywhere. I knew it was a zircon, a poor man's substitute, as soon as I laid eyes on it. I offered to take her to the nearest jeweller's to have it valued, and she refused. My younger brother here said he'd do it, and she said we'd take it off her finger over her dead body.'

Bea observed that Dilys was wearing a gold wedding band, but no diamond ring.

Sybil said, 'She said she'd swallow it rather than let us have it appraised.'

Bea wanted to laugh, but stifled the impulse. 'Retrieving it might be, um, uncomfortable.'

The harridan took a pull on her cigarette and looked around for a non-existent ashtray.

Bea thought of opening a window to let out the smoke but they were having a bitterly cold winter and she wasn't keen on catching her death of cold.

Sybil said, 'We'd been talking about you over lunch, discussing your refusal to merge with H & B, and considering how best to make you change your mind. Of course, I understand why you turned us down. Only an idiot would have allied herself to the cretin my brother appointed to run it.'

'I don't think calling people names—'

'I never liked the look of him,' said Sybil, 'but there was never any arguing with my brother when he'd made up his mind. Appointing Benton managing director of one of the jewels in the crown of Holland Holdings . . .! A child could have foreseen . . .! What a disaster! The man talks like a PR machine and acts like an elephant, trampling upon the sensibilities of the workforce. I told my brother that Benton needed to be got rid of, but would he listen? No. In spite of . . . well, never mind that. Then at lunch today my eye was caught by the fake diamond which my niece was displaying to all and sundry. The Hollands have never stooped to glass before. I was devastated.' She didn't look devastated. She looked triumphant. 'It's clear that the man is as much a fake as his diamond, and that his removal from the company and from my niece's bed is a consummation devoutly to be wished.'

Bea leaned back in her chair. Almost, she applauded the old dear. 'Forgive me, but you cannot be aware of all the reasons why I decided against—'

Sybil raised one finger after the other. 'One: you think my brother is past running his business affairs in a sensible manner. I agree. Two: you disliked Benton on sight, thinking him a lightweight who'd been promoted beyond his capacity. Again, I agree. And three: you don't care to be pressured into a rash move by your ambitious member of parliament son.'

That last statement took Bea's breath away because it was true. Though how the woman had reached that conclusion . . .! With some reluctance, Bea nodded.

Sybil said, 'My brother ought to have retired some years ago, but he needed to have something to occupy himself with, and so long as he was bringing home the bacon, I was not disposed to interfere. However, when I was alerted to . . .' A frown and a dismissive gesture. 'No need for you to hear about that little problem, which I am sure can be sorted out quickly enough, no need for me to intervene, but in the matter of my niece and the affairs of Holland and Butcher, action needs to be taken at once. I am not about to sit back and see my dividends vanish. As far as you are concerned, you will wish to be involved since your son is in such dire need of money. In conclusion—'

Bea stiffened in her chair. Did Max need money? Really? Could it be true? How did this harridan know?

'It is clear we need you to save Holland and Butcher.'

Bea pushed back her chair. 'No.'

Sybil Holland grinned. 'Of course, you'll take some persuading, but you'll come round in the end. I like your style. You and I between us can sort this mess out, quietly and efficiently.'

Bea thought fast. Could Max really have got himself into a financial mess with H & B? When that firm had begun to make serious overtures to Bea concerning a merger, it was he who had arranged for Bea to dine out with Benton – the newly appointed managing director – and his wife Dilys. Max and Benton had sat next to one another, detailing Dilys off to entertain Bea. A bad move, as it was Bea who owned and ran the agency while Max merely swanned around being an important personage. Important in his own estimation, anyway.

What had Max hoped to gain by introducing them to one another? Well, Max had been aiming for non-executive but well-paid director-ships in both concerns. Max could talk big. Benton could talk big. Benton had a loud, braying laugh, which had made Bea shudder. Further observation had caused her to conclude that he was a Johnny-cum-lately: a backslapping, heavily-tipping, fully paid-up member of the chauvinist brigade. He'd ignored Bea and his wife throughout in order to discuss plans for a projected merger with Max.

Bea had been left to make conversation with his wife Dilys, who gave the impression of being a naive child, married too young to know what she was doing, and discouraged from thinking for herself ever since.

Something else of importance had happened that evening: Bea had gone down with food poisoning, and Dilys had been kind to her. Now that was the sort of thing which people remembered. Bea felt she owed Dilys something in return.

The girl shot a look at Bea from under shaggy eyebrows.

The child seems terrified! Why?

The mink coat lit another cigarette from her first and ground out the stub in the empty cup on Bea's desk. 'I admit I wouldn't have chosen to introduce myself to you with a naughty child in tow, but she seemed to have formed a good opinion of your abilities. So, when she starting having hysterics in the restaurant, I thought we'd give you a chance to show what you're made of. If you will accompany the silly girl along to the nearest reputable jeweller, ask for an appraisal and stand by her when she faints at the verdict, she'll have to believe us.'

Bea didn't know whether to be amused or indignant. 'The agency employs people who would be happy to—'

'The less outsiders know about this the better.' She looked at her watch, which was tiny and studded with more diamonds. Naturally. 'She's got to be home by four to fetch the children from school and prepare something for supper. Let's get this business dealt with here and now. Then she'll have to admit she's married a wrong 'un, and we can take steps to rectify the damage.'

Rectify the damage? This was the sort of woman who, during the French Revolution, whiled away the time on the steps of the guillotine by knitting.

Dilys wailed, and hiccuped. 'No, hic, no! He loves me! I won't go with you!'

'Benton,' said the mink coat, investing the word with the disdain of an aristocrat dealing with a turd deposited on the carpet by a visitor's dog, 'does not deserve consideration. He has foisted himself on to our family by fraud and, now that he has been found out, must be disposed of without delay.'

'He's my husband!'

'Who got you pregnant as a way to climb the ladder.'

'He loves me!'

'Humph!'

Bea shut down her computer and extended her hand to Dilys. 'Come. You'll want to visit the cloakroom and get yourself cleaned up, won't you?' To Sybil, 'Forgive us if we disappear for a while. I'll have a cup of tea sent in to you, shall I?'

Dilys put her hand in Bea's with the trust of a small child being rescued from a bully in the playground.

As they passed through the busy office, Bea smiled and nodded to Carrie, signalling that everything was under control. 'Tea for our guests, Carrie?'

Dilys was limping. The girl was wearing high-heeled boots which made walking difficult. Her black coat with a fake fur collar was not new and was too large for her. She'd probably bought it when she was pregnant. Underneath she wore a pink blouse which didn't fit properly, over black trousers which sagged around her bottom. Nothing was new and everything looked well worn, which made Bea wonder how much money Benton gave his wife for a dress allowance.

Dilys had worn a rather fussy, costly dress to the restaurant when they'd first met, but that hadn't been new, either. The girl had probably donned her best bib and tucker today to have lunch with her formidable aunt, and she had been hit with a piledriver instead of a custard pie.

Bea ushered Dilys into the cloakroom and said, 'When you've tidied yourself up we can have a talk, privately, just you and me.' Bea shut the door on Dilys and went to check whether or not Maggie's office was free. Maggie was not only Bea's sort-of adopted daughter, but also a project manager much in demand. Fortunately, she was out that afternoon. Good. Bea wanted to talk to Dilys in private and without interruption.

Dilys reappeared, with her coat over her arm. Not limping.

Bea ushered her into Maggie's office and showed her to a seat. 'Milk and sugar in your tea? Did you get to finish your lunch before the sky fell on you?'

The child sat, wary, wide-eyed. 'I wasn't hungry.' A tiny voice, barely audible.

Bea handed her a cup of tea and indicated the biscuit tin. 'You hid the ring in your boot? It must have been painful to walk on.'

Dilys twitched a smile. 'Yes, it was.'

'May I see it?'

Dilys placed it on the table. Bea gave it a cursory glance and decided the old terror next door knew what she'd been talking about. The colour was wrong. The cut was flashy but didn't convince. Zircon, definitely.

'Did you want a diamond for an engagement ring? Personally, diamond rings make my hands look dirty. I prefer sapphires.'

Dilys wriggled. 'Daddy introduced Ben to a jeweller friend of his and arranged for him to buy me a diamond ring. And he did. It was a beauty.'

Past tense. *Was* a beauty.

'You call your husband "Ben"?'

'His full name is Benjamin Benton, but most people just call him Benton.'

'You were not consulted about the ring?'

'No, it was a lovely surprise.'

'And a relief, too, if you were already pregnant?'

The girl ducked her head.

Bea wondered if the girl had been consulted about her options at that stage, either. As the aged Mr Holland's only child, she could have had the baby and been well looked after, without being pushed into marrying a man of doubtful quality.

Dilys breathed, 'He loved me to distraction. He begged me to marry him. He went down on one knee. It was wonderful. I'd never thought such a thing would ever happen to me.'

Bea diagnosed a terminal lack of self-worth. 'Your father was pleased?'

'Oh yes. Ben was head salesman of the company and it was as if it were meant. Daddy bought us the sweetest little town house and we had a lovely wedding at our country place, but we didn't go abroad for a honeymoon because I was being sick all the time.'

Bea could see it all. The men arranged everything to their satisfaction, and the girl – pregnancy sick and immature for her age – had gone along with it. 'When did you first notice something was wrong with the ring?'

A wriggle. 'Nothing's wrong with it.'

'Dilys, I can't help you if you don't come clean. Of course you noticed. Most young brides wear their engagement ring all the time—'

'Well, I didn't because I was being sick so much. I was worried about it slipping off my finger and going down the sink.'

'Let me guess. Ben said he'd get it altered for a better fit for you, but when it was returned from the jewellers you didn't wear it then, either, because it felt and looked slightly different.'

The girl recited, 'He loves me, he only thinks of what's best for me.'

Bea sighed. 'You keep saying that he loves you, but you don't say that you love him.'

A tinge of colour. 'Of course I do.' The wide eyes became wider. Terror loomed.

Bea said, in her softest tone, 'You're afraid of him. Does he hit you?'

'No, no, no!' Tears threatened. 'Of course not.'

A lie? 'Then what are you afraid of?'

'Nothing. He's just . . . He can be very sharp. If he knew that I'd let you see the ring, that you were trying to make me say awful things about him . . . I really do love him. Of course I do.'

'But . . .?'

Dilys gulped. 'It's not his fault. It's mine. He gets frustrated because I'm so stupid. I need to understand how silly I've been, so that I don't show him up in front of other people.'

'He criticizes you?'

'It's for my own good. I mean, I knew the business wasn't doing so well, and I thought that I might be able to help, because I used to go into the office and help out before I was married, but he made me see I'd be worse than useless.'

Ouch. Bea held on to her temper. She wanted to slap someone, and that someone wasn't Dilys. 'How is he with the children?'

'Oh, fine. At least, with the boys. They're so like him, take after him, he's so proud of them, you wouldn't believe how much he indulges them.'

'I seem to remember you have a little girl as well.'

'My little girl is like me, a bit stupid, you know? But he only tells her off for her own good.'

'Does he criticize you both in front of the boys?'

Dilys wrung her hands. 'The boys understand how silly we are. It's all in good part. They laugh, he tells them to laugh, and I don't like it much, but . . . I wish I were dead.' Dilys hung her head. Her arms went around her shoulders. Her hair hung over her face.

'Your dying won't help your children.'

'That's what I keep telling myself. I have to learn how to be a better wife and mother, I have to be honest with myself, and when I've done something awful, I must apologize and try to do better.' The girl's tears overflowed once more.

Bea was silent. Sybil's instincts were correct. Benton was a turd of the first water. Could you have a *turd* of the first water? No, that was for diamonds, wasn't it? Oh, forget it. 'Assuming that he did substitute a fake for the original diamond, have you any idea what he did with the money? Another woman?'

Dilys mumbled into her hankie. 'No, no! He wouldn't! He loves me.'

'Gambling debts?'

'Oh, no! How could you think that!' She seemed genuinely shocked at the idea.

It must have been another woman, then. Dilys would have guessed as soon as it happened, but not dared to do anything about it. She had no brothers, her father was a broken reed and her husband was a bully. What's more, Benton was now managing director of the firm which provided them all with a living.

All Dilys had on her side was an aunt. And what an aunt! Dilys ought to be grateful to Sybil, but probably wasn't.

Bea wondered what sort of mistress would have taken Benton's fancy. Someone blonde and full-bodied. A total opposite to the dumpy, badly-presented little girl he'd seduced and married.

'He took the money from the diamond and gave it to his mistress?'

Dilys blew her nose. 'You don't understand. It was a boy-girl thing from before we were married. He stopped seeing her when he met me but she'd got into debt and he wanted to help her out, so . . . Anyway, he told me all about it when I noticed about the ring, which I did straight away, and he said it was all right because everything he had was mine, and mine was his, and it had got him out of a terrible hole. Of course, I understood how it had been, and we agreed never to mention it again.'

'How do you know the affair's not still going on?'

'She died.'

'Really?'

'Oh, yes. She was run over late at night soon after that – in the October, just one year after we were married – in a quiet cul de sac. He was so shocked. He told me the next day, just gave me the facts, couldn't talk about it. He said he wasn't going to think any more about it and I shouldn't, either. He's very sensitive, you see. I have to remember that.'

'Of course,' said Bea, not believing a word of it. 'Now, shall we go and get that ring appraised?'

TWO

'We can't!' said Dilys, delving into her handbag with fingers that shook. Trying to find a hankie?

'Watch me!' said Bea, pushing a box of tissues towards the girl.

'You don't understand. I can't upset things or we'll all be ruined. Auntie—'

'What about Auntie?' said that redoubtable female, entering the room. Dilys stifled a scream. 'I'm bored, hanging around, waiting for you to see sense. Are you ready to have the ring appraised yet? Mrs Abbot, I was sure I could rely on you.'

Dilys said, 'Auntie, you startled me! We mustn't do anything to upset Ben or we'll all be out on the street.'

'Tell that to the birds!' The mink coat seated herself on a typing chair. She'd been followed in by the man in the shadows, but he still didn't seem interested in taking a hand in the game.

Dilys took a tissue and began to shred it. 'Daddy gave Ben some shares in the company when we got married. And he asked me to give him mine for his last birthday, to add to those he already had. So I did.'

'What!' Sybil Holland's face paled under the make-up. The blusher on her cheeks stood out by contrast.

'Yes,' whispered Dilys. 'So you see, Ben can't be touched. Daddy will always support Ben, you know that he will, and now he can outvote you so there's nothing you can do about it. I'm so afraid that if Ben gets bored with me, he'll sue me for divorce, and we'd lose our house and have to take the children away from their schools and live in a rented flat somewhere, and I'd have to go out to work which I know I wouldn't be any good at, and then the children would run wild and get into trouble and end up in prison and I can't bear the thought of it.'

The shadowy man laid his hand on Dilys's shoulder by way of comfort.

The harridan's face was a picture of shock, horror!

Bea looked from one stricken face to the other and wondered how much Max had known about all this.

'So you see,' said Dilys, sniffing, 'we can't query the ring, and we can't say anything to anybody about it.'

Sybil took a deep breath. Her colour was returning to normal though there was the very slightest suggestion that her head shook on her neck. 'I see that I have been remiss, involved as I have been in my own affairs, and living so far away.' She caught Bea's eye. 'Florida. The climate agrees with me, and the society in which I move is . . . But I ought not to have let things slide.'

Bea began to like the old dear.

Sybil's lips tightened. 'I only came over this time because my brother got into a panic about . . . Though I'm sure it's a storm in a teacup. But, added to the cut in my Holland and Butcher dividend, it caused me to cancel a cruise to the Bahamas. Looking back, I see I've been living in a fool's paradise. I hadn't bothered to keep abreast of developments.'

Dilys said, 'There's nothing whatever we can do about it. I begged you not to go on and on about the ring and—'

'Now, what on earth do we do? And don't say "nothing". I am not accustomed to sitting down when hit by a truck. Up and at 'em, I say.' She chewed on her lip, then turned to face Bea. 'Well, now you know how things stand, Mrs Abbot, your involvement becomes a matter not just of convenience but of life and death for everyone concerned.'

'No,' said Bea. 'Wouldn't touch it with a bargepole.'

'I dare say you *do* recoil from the prospect,' said the mink coat, getting to her feet and, incredibly, lighting another cigarette. 'I can quite see it would mean a move out of your comfort zone to come to our rescue, but there it is; it appears we've all got to take action if we're to survive. You'll want to speak to your son about this, no doubt. I'll leave you my card. Ring me tonight or tomorrow morning before ten. I have an appointment at the osteopath's at eleven and he lives in some far flung suburb which is probably inhabited solely by members of the third world living on benefits. And don't tell me I shouldn't say such things, because at my age I'll speak as I find. Now, you can get one of your girls to summon me a taxi, and I'll be out of your hair. Dilys, I'll drop you off on the way home, right?'

*   *   *

Bea saw the two women off into a taxi before returning to her office to open the window, despite the chilly air outside, and let herself relax into her chair. She passed her hand across her eyes.

What a mess!

Could Max really have got himself tangled with the affairs of H & B? So much so that he'd be in financial trouble if Bea refused to help them out? Sybil had hinted as much, but . . . No, surely Max wouldn't have been so naive. Or would he?

Perhaps the lady had been shading the truth – Bea wouldn't put it past her to do so – and Max was not heavily involved.

But if he was . . .?

Bea reached for the phone and paused with hand outstretched, for someone – a man – was sitting at the back of the room. The man who'd kept to the shadows throughout that difficult visit. He'd come in with the two women, but not left with them.

She stilled her breathing. He was no threat, was he?

He stood up, smiling. A tall man of about her own age. Solidly built, wearing an expensive camel-hair car coat over a good, grey pinstripe suit. A tan, a gold signet ring, an excellent haircut and shave. Mid to light brown hair and plenty of it, somewhat unruly. Dark brown eyes, smiling, smiling. A slightly crooked nose hinted that he was no pushover.

'May I congratulate you, Mrs Abbot, on your skill in dealing with my tiresome relatives? You are everything they said you were.'

She glared at him. 'And who might you be?'

'Leon, the black sheep of the Holland family. Much younger brother to Hector and Sybil. An afterthought, as you might say. In fact, a total shock to my parents. And before you jump down my throat, may I assure you that I have nothing whatever to do with the firm of Holland and Butcher or with the parent company, Holland Holdings. I have no money invested in H & B. What's more, I have no intention of pumping money into a sinking ship, and my reading of their balance sheet inclines me to think the company is going down as inevitably as the *Titanic*. My sister invited me to have lunch with her to meet my almost unknown niece, whom I had last seen when she was at school and monosyllabic about everything except some pop star or other. I accepted without realizing we were booked for melodramatics.'

He shook his sister's cigarette stubs – there were three of them

– out of the window, and closed it. 'That's enough fresh air for the time being, don't you think?'

He was charming, of course. And knew it. An interesting face, well-used, with sharp creases over his upper eyelids. He sat on a corner of her desk, smiling down at her. Always smiling, telling her without words how much he appreciated her looks and, well, everything about her.

She found herself smiling back, even while one part of her brain was waving a red flag. 'You do realize that I'm not going to get involved in their mess.'

'Neither am I.' He picked up one of the agency cards on her desk. 'This is your business phone number? Give me your mobile number as well, will you? It might be useful.'

She didn't see why it should be, but gave him one of her personal cards as well.

'Care to have dinner with me tonight?'

She had to laugh. She knew her colour had heightened. 'Certainly not.'

'I've sold my chain of dry-cleaners for a good price, I'm single with no dependants, I am buying a flat in the Barbican for weekends, and I promise I come with no strings attached.'

She shook her head. 'Even I can see you come with strings attached. Your powers of persuasion—'

'Equal yours? It would be interesting to discuss them over a decent meal. Our lunch was somewhat, er, curtailed, and I have an appetite for more.'

He didn't just mean an appetite for food. He was gazing at her cleavage with appreciation. She hadn't thought she had much of a cleavage when she'd pulled on a grey jersey wrap-around dress that morning, but he seemed to think she had. Her colour rose further, and she pushed back her chair. Hints of a good cologne wafted towards her. Better than cigarette smoke, of course, but . . . 'No, thank you. I have other plans for the evening.'

'Ah. You'll wish to speak to your son, Max. Of course.'

'You know him?'

'No. But the luncheon was informative. I admire Sybil, don't you?'

She said, 'Yes,' without thinking.

He made his way to the door. 'She doesn't give up easily, and neither do I. Tomorrow night, shall we say? I'll send a car for you at eight.'

'No, I . . .' But he'd disappeared.

'Bother,' said Bea. Then laughed. It occurred to her that she'd been working hard for a long time, that the cold, wet weather was depressing, and that she could do with being pampered for a change.

But. She reached out her hand to ring Max, and the phone trilled.

Snap! It was Max himself on the phone. 'Mother, how are you doing? Thought we might have a bite to eat together this evening. The wife and son are still up in the cold north, and I'm all by myself till Parliament reconvenes.'

'I'd like that. There's something I want to discuss with you.'

'Eight o'clock? There's a new restaurant opened in South Kensington. Thought we might try that. Capello's. I'll book a table now I know you're free.' He rang off.

Bea relaxed. Max was always one of the first to sniff out a new restaurant. He liked his food. In fact, his lean good looks were fast becoming a thing of the past, the outlines of his face and body becoming blurred with good living. It would be good to see him again and to hear news of her delightful little grandson. She missed him when he went up to the constituency in the holidays. Bea knew the other grandparents spoiled him to death, and that they had to have their turn at looking after him, but . . . Well, she was fortunate to have a son who wanted to take her out to dinner.

Now, back to work. A long-time client was complaining about the bill, saying the ingredients supplied for her supper party for twenty close friends were substandard. Now, who had been assigned to that event? The client usually asked for . . . Hadn't that particular chef been available for some reason?

She concentrated.

At a quarter to eight Bea checked to see if her skirt was revealing anything untoward. The current fashion for short skirts meant they were usually worn without a petticoat but she thought they hung better with one. Her new, moss-green skirt went well with an old but still fashionable beaded, cream silk top. So, yes, she looked all right.

She left a note for Maggie, who was out for the evening. She fed Winston, their overweight cat, shrugged on her dark-grey coat, collected her evening bag, summoned a taxi, set the alarm and let herself out of the house.

It wasn't far to the new restaurant, and it looked as if it were becoming popular since her cab drew up in a queue of idling motors, all waiting to deposit their passengers at the front door.

A man got out of the taxi immediately ahead. Bea, who'd been getting the fare ready, reached for the door handle and called out, 'Max!'

He hadn't heard her, of course.

Another man followed Max out of the taxi, and the two of them stood on the pavement, arguing in amicable fashion about who should pay the fare.

Benton.

Oh. How stupid she'd been to think Max would miss an opportunity to bring the two of them together! She did not look forward to an evening spent at the mercy of two bullies.

What to do? She said to the taxi driver, 'I'm so sorry. I forgot that I have to make a phone call before I go into the restaurant. Would you turn into the next street and find somewhere to park for a few minutes?'

She needed backup. For a moment she thought of Leon Holland and smiled. He'd alleviate the tension, but he hadn't taken any part in that difficult family interview in her office, and it might not be a good idea to rely on him. Besides which, whatever he might say to the contrary, he was tied to the fortunes of Holland and Butcher because he wouldn't want his sister and niece to be left in financial difficulty.

She needed someone who could deal with the likes of Benton without causing a fuss.

Her first husband, whom she'd divorced years ago for tom-catting around? They'd become good friends in recent years, but . . . no, he was out of town at the moment. Think again, Bea.

Ah. She knew the very man. She used her mobile phone to contact CJ Cambridge, the grey mandarin who was a behind-the-scenes figure in some unspecified but powerful government department. She'd come to know him quite well in recent years. True, he had several times hinted he'd like to know her even better, but she could deal with that.

'CJ? I'm in trouble. Are you free tonight?'

*   *   *

CJ climbed into Bea's taxi. 'So, where's the fire? Brief me.'

She did.

He nodded. 'Ah. When it comes to finance, perhaps Max is not as clever as he thinks he is. Would you like me to play the part of an old friend who rather disapproves of your working when you could be at home soothing my brow and cooking me delicious meals?'

'In your dreams.' She looked at her watch. 'Shall we make a move? We're half an hour late. Not too bad.' She paid off her cab with a good tip and allowed CJ to take her arm as they walked round the corner and into the foyer of the restaurant.

Max and Benton were there, both looking at their watches. Max bounded to his feet. 'Mother, you're late!'

'So sorry, dear,' said Bea, offering her cheek for an air kiss. 'I'd half promised to go out with CJ tonight and, when he reminded me, well, it seemed a good idea to invite him to join us, instead. So, how are you, and how is my beautiful daughter-in-law and my darling grandson?'

Max was frowning even while he tried to smile a welcome. 'Fine, they're both fine. They'll be joining me in a few days' time. Good to see you again, Mr Cambridge. Do you know Benton, managing director of one of our most successful private companies? Just what the government ordered, right?'

Benton was on his toes, looking from one of the party to the other, not sure what to make of this development. He thrust his hand out to Bea. 'I can't tell you how much I've been looking forward to this.' He brayed his infamous laugh.

Bea instructed herself not to wince.

Benton turned to CJ. 'An old family friend? What a pleasant surprise.' Making it clear he wasn't pleased at CJ's presence. Clearly, he'd planned an evening with Bea cast as Piggy in the Middle.

'Somewhat.' CJ was giving nothing away.

The maître d' was hovering. 'A table for four, sir?'

Bea said, 'I thought this place might be named after "A capella" for unaccompanied singing, but I don't think so, do you?'

The decor was white, black and red, with geometric shapes on the walls and a low level of lighting. She'd often wondered if low lighting was intended to hide poor cooking, but the tables seemed pretty full so perhaps it would be all right. The music was another matter: wailing pipes of some sort, not easy to identify. But at least the sound level was not ear-battering.

'Specialities on the board,' said the maître d', seating them near the door to the kitchens and indicating a large blackboard on the wall, just too far away to read. 'The menus . . . and the wine list.' He handed a menu to each of them, but laid the wine list on the table before CJ, which amused Bea. There were times when CJ could be as unassuming as a dormouse, but tonight he exuded effortless authority. The waiter had got it right.

Benton laid not one but two iPhones on the table and rubbed his hands. 'Cold night. Brrr. Mrs Abbot, my better half tells me you're not fond of lobster. Is that right?'

'Indeed. It doesn't agree with me.' Bea was surprised that he'd remembered.

'And you, Mr . . . er, Cambridge, is it? I was at Oxford myself.' Benton treated them to another of his laughs.

CJ's left eyebrow rose one millimetre. It was clear to Bea, if not to Max, that CJ didn't believe Benton had been at any of the more prestigious of the Oxford colleges. Possibly Oxford Brookes, the former Polytechnic? Not, Bea told herself, that there was anything wrong with Oxford Brookes. What was wrong was that Benton had tried to pass himself as a graduate of a top university and, failing to convince, had reinforced Bea's poor opinion of him.

Max laid his own iPhone on the table and attempted to take the wine list from CJ.

CJ might be softly spoken but it would take a braver man than Max to wrench a wine list from his grasp. 'A white wine to start with? It will be fish for you, Bea, won't it? Not smothered in sauce. I see they do a sole meunière. I'll have that, too.'

'What, no starters?' said Benton. 'I'm hungry.'

'Something light, perhaps?' said CJ. 'Bea?'

'Splendid,' said Bea, squinting at the specialities board and failing to decipher the menu on it. 'So long as it isn't shellfish.'

Max leaned back in his chair, almost toppling it over in an effort to read the menu on the board. 'I fancy a steak. How about you, Benton?'

'I'll join you.' Benton was eyeing CJ, trying to work out whether his inclusion in the party was going to work for or against him. 'So, Mr Cambridge; what do you do for a living?'

CJ's nose twitched. In a cool voice, he said, 'I suppose you could say I'm an . . . adviser.'

'Hah! To one of the big companies, I trust. Much moolah, eh?' He rubbed his thumb across his fingers, grinning.

CJ allowed an expression of distaste to cross his face. He turned to Max. 'I hear you're being appointed to—'

Max looked alarmed. 'It's all officially hush-hush at the moment.' He shot a glance Bea couldn't read at Benton.

'Of course,' murmured CJ, who didn't make that sort of mistake by accident. Information of all sorts drifted CJ's way. Bea wondered what he had heard. Whatever it was, it seemed to be something Max hadn't seen fit to pass on to Benton. Max seemed annoyed that it had even been hinted at.

Benton frowned. He was bright enough to know something was going on that he didn't understand, but not bright enough to alter his plan of campaign. 'Max and I have something to celebrate tonight. Mrs Abbot, I am so delighted you could join us. It will be in all the trade papers, of course, but you should know in advance that Max is being voted on to our board of directors. Where's that wine waiter? We need some champagne!'

Bea stilled. So this was what Sybil had been hinting at? She said, 'My dear Max. I can't keep up with all your little triumphs. Congratulations.' Her tone was dismissive, and she saw his face fall. Now she came to see him up close, despite the poor lighting she couldn't help notice that he looked somewhat strained.

He was in trouble. Her stomach twisted. He was her one and only chick, and though she sometimes thought he lacked common sense – well, quite often she thought he could have done with sending to his room until he'd learned that all that glitters is not gold – he was still her son and whatever touched him also touched her.

'Brilliant news!' Benton glistened with triumph. His teeth looked expensive.

CJ gave a tiny cough. 'I bet that set you back a few quid, Max.'

Max moved uneasily in his chair. 'Well, what are mortgages for?'

Bea felt faint. She knew perfectly well how much of a mortgage Max still had on his flat near the river. She knew, because she'd helped him to buy it. Along with his parents-in-law. Her mouth was dry. 'A second mortgage, I suppose?'

'It will be a sound investment.' But there was sweat on his brow. He wasn't as happy about it as he pretended.

Benton jumped in. 'Why keep capital locked up in bricks and mortar when it could be set to work for you in the marketplace?'

Bea tried to hide her unease. She looked around for the waiter. 'I must admit I'm hungry. I was working late, there were interruptions, and I seem to have missed lunch. But no champagne for me, please. It doesn't agree with me.'

Benton treated her to a smile which looked sour. 'So many things disagree with you, Mrs Abbot, don't they? How unfortunate.'

And that, my dears, is a threat.

CJ put his hand over Bea's, warning her not to reply. He said, 'Well, what a happy occasion this has turned out to be. Don't let's talk business any more. We're here to enjoy ourselves, aren't we? Waiter!'

Benton launched into a dissertation of how excellent his firm was, how there was nothing to compare with it on the market, how all their employees were as happy as sandboys and how soon they would be receiving medals from a certain ministry . . . at which Max tried not to look shifty.

Did Benton also add that Mr Holland was about to be knighted by the Queen for services to industry? If so, Bea missed it, but she heard enough to make her heartily sorry she'd accepted Max's invitation.

The food was tolerable. The wine was overpriced. The music was turned up in volume as the evening wore on, so that eventually Bea received the impression that Benton was opening and shutting his mouth soundlessly, like a goldfish.

She made an excuse to leave as soon as their coffee had been served. Max helped her on with her coat, saying in her ear that he'd be round to see her in the morning.

Quite. She'd seen that one coming.

Going home in the taxi, Bea said, 'I think Max must have re-mortgaged his flat. I wonder if he's also mortgaged the house his parents-in-law bought him in his constituency.'

'Wouldn't his wife have something to say about that?'

'You're right. Oh, that's a relief! The deeds are in their joint names, because her parents helped them to buy. So she must have agreed to the mortgage, which means her parents won't let him go to the wall. I can't say I like it, but I suppose you'll now say he's a grown man and should be allowed to go to the dogs if he wishes. Unfortunately, I can't agree. I'm his mother. However foolish he's been, my instinct is to rescue him from his folly.'

'Benton assures us that Holland and Butcher is an old, established firm with a good reputation.'

'And a rubbish management. They're doing all they can to create a merger with the Abbot Agency, so that I can wade in and sort them out.'

'I don't think Benton would want you to take over. He'd want to be top dog.'

'So he would. Can you see me acting as his junior partner? Over my dead body.'

He twitched a smile. No comment.

She said, 'In my book he's a bully who's terrorized his wife and upset his workforce. Oh, and I understand the balance sheet doesn't look too good.'

'Now, how did you come by that information?'

'Never you mind. But I'd bet my life on it being accurate.' She smiled and laid her own hand on his. 'You are a good friend, CJ. Thanks for coming with me tonight. I'd have shamed Max by losing my temper and walking out if you hadn't been there to keep me calm. Every instinct I have tells me that Benton's a bad lot. He substituted zircon for a diamond in his wife's engagement ring and told her he did it to pay off a debt to a previous girlfriend. And then, hello! Surprise! She died. Run over in the street.'

'Ah. He reminds me of a man I knew once. Part Albanian, part Lithuanian. A toxic mixture.'

'A con man? What happened to him?'

'A life sentence. He was a murderer.'

THREE

Bea couldn't go straight to bed – which is what she was longing to do – because as she put her key into the lock she could tell that all was not well within.

For one thing, the alarm didn't ping as she entered. She'd set it when she'd gone out, because there'd been no one else in the house. Maggie, her ugly-duckling-turned-swan of a protégée, must have returned from her evening out and turned the alarm off. Fine. But she ought to have reset it.

Also, when Maggie got in the first thing she did was to turn on the television and the radio. Maggie seemingly couldn't exist without noise, but there wasn't a sound to be heard.

There were no lights on in the living room but there was one in the kitchen, so that's where Maggie must be. Only, without radio or TV?

Bea called out, 'I'm home!' as she double-locked the front door and re-set the alarm.

A muffled sound came from the kitchen. Bea braced herself. Maggie, in tears? A problem with her difficult, demanding mother? No, that couldn't be it. Her mother had gone off on an expensive cruise to the West Indies.

Was Maggie having trouble with her boyfriend, a delightful young man of mixed race? He had a good job and loved Maggie to distraction. What could have gone wrong there?

Bea found Maggie in a huddle on a stool in the kitchen, her arms overflowing with Winston, their heavyweight cat. And yes, Maggie had been crying.

Bea thought it best to ignore the tears. 'Fancy a goodnight cuppa?'

Another strangled sound. Maggie turned her head away from Bea.

Bea forced herself to be cheerful. 'Horrid night out, but at least the meal was tolerable. Tea, coffee or cocoa?'

'Nothing.' Maggie slid off the stool, dumped Winston on the floor and slipped past Bea. Usually, she took the stairs up to the top floor two at a time, thundering up them with no respect for other people's need for peace and quiet. Peace and quiet didn't often occupy the same world as Maggie.

This time, nothing. Nada. Silence.

A door closed quietly on the top floor.

Maggie must be seriously upset to start behaving like an adult.

Bea asked Winston, 'Well, what was all that about?'

The cat twined around her ankles. At least Bea knew what he wanted. She fed him, made herself a hot drink and went up to bed. She'd had enough for one day. Let tomorrow look after itself.

Thursday morning

Bea didn't sleep well, but was up bright and early next morning. She couldn't afford to lie in when there was work to be done, and she remembered all too clearly that Max had announced his intention of calling on her that day. She dressed with care and took trouble over her make-up, giving special attention to what her late husband had called her 'eagle' eyes. Bea believed that if she looked as if she were in control of a situation she was three-quarters there. She also believed that if she went down to the agency rooms looking like a slob, dressed in a tatty dressing-gown, down at heel bedroom slippers, with her hair all over the place, and wearing no make-up, then her staff would treat her accordingly.

The house was too quiet. Judging by the dirty dishes left on the table – and not put into the dishwasher as usual – Maggie had got up at her usual early hour, had breakfast and left. All without turning the TV or the radio on?

This was serious.

The girl had left a note on the kitchen table to say that there was a crisis over a new kitchen being installed up in Hampstead, and that she wouldn't be back till late.

Bea fed Winston before she remembered Maggie had probably already done just that. No wonder he was putting on weight, getting two breakfasts for the asking. And what, pray, was wrong with Maggie? No doubt she'd come clean in due course.

A nice, quiet breakfast with the daily papers, without any necessity to make small talk or even listen to the radio. Winston, that enormous furry brute, purred loudly as he ate, and some blackbirds squabbled over the nuts Maggie had hung in the laburnum tree in the back garden. Otherwise, it was blissfully quiet . . .

Except that the toaster had gone on the blink. Bea fiddled with the controls and out shot the toast, making her jump. Oh well. Perhaps that useful but not essential piece of equipment was due for early retirement? Put it on the shopping list.

She developed a slight tension headache.

Downstairs she went to greet the members of the staff as they trickled in. The day's password was given out. Computers were booted up. Telephones began to ring. Queries were handed to Bea. The youngest member of the staff prepared to make the first cup of coffee of the day.

Max arrived.

Bea didn't think he looked as if he'd slept well, either. 'Coffee? It'll be up in a minute.'

He declined, leading the way into her office. 'I thought you were a bit off last night, Mother. You didn't make Benton feel very welcome.'

Bea acknowledged that Max had made a good start. The best defence is always attack.

'Really, dear? Perhaps because I didn't know he was going to be there. I'm wondering if I should have my hearing tested. The music was a bit loud. But it was lovely of you to invite us out. I know CJ appreciated it, being on his own so much.'

Max hadn't come to talk about CJ. 'The fact is . . .' He didn't know how to proceed.

Bea helped him. 'You're going to be put on some important government committee or other? Something to do with British industry, encouraging small companies to show what they can do? With grants to give out to deserving cases?'

He reddened. 'CJ told you?'

'I guessed. I'm a clever clogs, you know. I also know that Benton is giving you a directorship in his company, in exchange for funds. How much is he asking for, and is it worth it?'

'It's not like that.' Almost, he squirmed. 'I need directorships in different companies to give me the background, the experience necessary to assist the government in its aim to search out and reward, to encourage those firms which are exhibiting the best of British . . .'

She booted up her own computer and watched the emails pile in. One was from Leon, saying he'd booked a table for them at the Ivy. Was that all right?

She emailed back: '*I regret. I have other plans.*' And deleted his email.

Forcing her mind back to Max, she tried to be soothing. 'Of course I understand. You scratch my back, and I scratch yours. I suppose it's all right, if the price is not too steep. Forgive me for checking my emails. There's rather a lot going on.'

'That's what I wanted to see you about. Holland and Butcher are—'

One of the office girls came in with a cup of coffee for Bea.

'Thank you, dear,' said Bea. 'Are you sure you won't have a cup, Max?'

'Quite sure.' He waited till the girl had left and took a seat, leaning forward, forearms on thighs, the picture of earnestness. 'The thing is—'

'No.'

'You haven't heard what—'

'I can read the subtext. Benton has somehow or other persuaded you into thinking it would further your career if you had a director-ship in his company. Personally, I wouldn't think it would do you much good, but I'm not going to argue. I suppose you want the directorship to prove to your lords and masters that you'd be an asset on this government project of yours.'

'Yes, but—'

'Only, I don't think Benton's been entirely honest with you. Holland and Butcher is not doing as well as it should.'

'That's not true.'

'Have you had a look at their books?'

'Have you?'

'I've heard that they've cut their dividends to the bone. I know that at least one of the other directors is unhappy about this, and I've heard that Benton hasn't been handling their workforce as tact-fully as he might.'

He gaped.

'Close your mouth, dear. You look like a goldfish.'

Another email from Leon pinged on to the screen. *'Simpsons in the Strand?'*

Almost, she smiled. Should she go? No, no. *'Sorry. Busy.'* Delete.

Max rubbed his forehead. He was getting quite worked up. 'Now, Mother, you—'

'Benton has talked you into remortgaging your flat and giving them the money, to get them out of a financial black hole?'

'No, not exactly. The thing is, we've got both our names on the deeds of the flat here and our house in the constituency. Nicole's parents insisted, and of course I didn't think there'd be any trouble – her consenting, I mean. But she can't see how releasing capital now would—'

'She refused to remortgage.' Bea's shoulders relaxed. 'Well, I must say, that's an enormous relief. I could see you losing both your homes.'

'I wouldn't be losing anything.' He was nothing if not obstinate.

She drank her coffee. Aah. That was better. She would feel almost human again soon.

He cracked his knuckles, an annoying habit he fell into when

worried about something. 'The thing is,' he said, giving full
weight to every word, 'that Benton suggested, and I thought it an
excellent idea since we're all going to be working so closely together,
that you take out a mortgage on this house and invest in the company.
To seal our pact, as it were.'

She snapped, 'Don't be ridiculous!'

He persisted. 'I thought you'd understand how much this means
to me, and that you'd be happy to help me out.'

She hadn't got through to him. Nothing she'd said had caused
him even a flicker of doubt. There was a sheen of perspiration on
his forehead. He was being driven by ambition, or fear, or . . . what?
She didn't understand why he was so fixated. What hadn't she been
told? Was a piece of the jigsaw missing?

A third email came in from Leon. She didn't open it. She laid
her hands in her lap and concentrated on her son. 'Listen, Max.
This house is worth a lot of money but it is not only my home, but
also a home for my two lodgers: for Maggie, and for Oliver when
he's at home. It provides me and my staff with a living. Our agency
is not large but it has an exclusive clientele and that is partly due
to our position in this area. We employ a considerable number of
people so that we can give personal service to each of our clients.
I enjoy work and I intend to keep on working as long as I can.'

'But—'

'I haven't finished. These houses need regular maintenance, and
I need to pay into a pension pot. I can only do that while I work.
You want me to jeopardize all that by throwing it into a firm that's
rapidly going to the dogs?'

'Of course not. As a director of H & B, you'll get a good return
on your investment.'

'Not all the directors would agree with you.'

'That's because things have been allowed to slip. Benton needs
you to work with him—'

'Nonsense, Max. He wouldn't want to work *with* me. He'd like
to boss me about, yes. But not to work *with*. I don't think he has
a high opinion of women.'

Max flinched. Ah, somewhere she'd touched a sore spot.

She said, 'He doesn't consider that women are equal to men.
He's a bully, Max. Oh, not with men who'll stand up to him, but
with women in general and with his wife in particular.'

He made an impatient gesture. 'She's out of it, or will be shortly.

A great disappointment, that marriage. He thought he could make something of her, but—'

'She was fresh out of school when he got her pregnant—'

'She's a real drag on him. No help to him at all, and a slut around the house. Not exactly bright, you know. He's put up with her for years, but he's decided to cut his losses and go for a divorce. He'll get custody of the boys, of course.'

Bea took one deep breath, let it out. 'What he hasn't told you is that he got her pregnant so that she'd marry him and to earn the approval of her father. She told me he got her to make over her shares in the business to him. He substituted a zircon for the diamond in her engagement ring to pay off an old flame . . . and now he's going to tip her out on to the rubbish heap and go after someone else?'

He flushed. 'He's outgrown her. What's wrong with that?'

What was wrong with that? Was this really Max talking? Her only son, who'd been brought up to respect marriage and . . . ah! This was the new Max, who'd fallen under the spell of a fast-talking New Man.

She said, 'What does Nicole think of this?' Max's skinny, whiny wife had been born with a silver spoon in her mouth, had never needed to work and was never satisfied with anything. Her parents were well-to-do and proud of a son-in-law in the House of Commons. Bea had never liked the girl but had done her best to keep the marriage going, not least because Nicole had produced a satisfactory grandson.

Max blustered, 'What do you mean, "What does Nicole think of this?"'

Bea closed her eyes momentarily. 'Nicole has refused to back you in getting a second mortgage. She wants . . . Ah, I think I see what's been happening. She wants you to climb the ladder. You're a good member of parliament, painstaking and reliable. You look after your constituents' interests admirably. But, you didn't go to Oxford or Cambridge, you don't move in the top echelons of society, you haven't a Double First and you are not a television pundit. You are excellent backbencher material but you are not brilliant in debate.'

He winced.

Bea nodded. 'Most women would be thrilled to call you their husband, but Nicole wants more. Is that it?'

He clenched his hands between his thighs. 'She has every right to expect—'

'A good return on her money?'

'She would like me to make a better showing—'

'To climb the ladder faster? She wants you to get into this government initiative, but to do that you have to show you can pull in some directorships of various firms. Sensibly, she won't jeopardize her home to help you. And neither will I.'

Silence. Almost, he seemed to groan. 'If necessary I can take out a big enough loan to cover what I need, provided you guarantee it.'

She felt sick. 'No.'

'I'm desperate. If I can't get this sorted, Nicole will leave me.' He looked at her with the puppy-dog eyes of a small boy wanting to be told there really wasn't a nasty red dragon under the bed.

And she knew, just like that, from one breath to the other, exactly what had been going on.

Benton had been cultivating Max for some time. Months.

Benton had met Nicole.

Nicole had been listening to Benton and comparing him to Max.

Benton was planning to chuck his wife and go for a bigger prize.

Nicole was planning to chuck Max and marry Benton because he was a showy, fast-talking braggart who might be expected, in due course and with her parents' help, to succeed Max as their local member of parliament and climb the glittering ladder of fame.

Bea could see it all, and she hadn't a clue how to stop it. She stared at her computer screen and opened Leon's last email. '*Eel pie and mash in the East End?*'

It was a flattering offer. Not the eel pie – which she didn't think she'd like much – but it was a consolation that Leon wanted her company enough to keep chasing her. She would think about that, later.

Meanwhile, back to Max. She attempted to buy time. 'Max, every instinct tells me to run as fast as I can away from Benton and his schemes, but I am aware that this is not a businesslike attitude. Perhaps, when I've looked into the matter further, I might be persuaded that the prospect of a good return on my money is not just a figment of your imagination. First, I need facts and figures. I need a business plan from Benton. I need him to suggest how we might work together. I need to consult my accountant and Maggie and Oliver.'

A flare of hope. Was she really going to help him out? Followed by a frown. 'You don't need to consult anyone else about it, surely?'

'Yes, Max. I do. My accountant can pick up anything I miss on the balance sheet. As for Maggie and Oliver, this is their home, and if I'm going to take out a loan on it, then they have the right to be consulted.'

A dismissive gesture. 'A student who's away at university, and a girl who's always been a misfit!'

'Oliver has a brilliant brain, Maggie's heart is as large as London, and I am very fond of them. Those are my terms; take it or leave it.'

'Oh, I'll take it, of course. I'm sure, once you get to know Benton, you'll realize he's going places; he's just the man to drag the Abbot Agency into the present.' He stopped, noting Bea's icy stare. 'Not that I mean you aren't doing the best you can, under the circumstances.' He tried on an uneasy laugh. 'You've been wonderful, really splendid, taking over the agency and making it pay—'

'Max, if you say, that I've done well "for a woman"—'

'Oh, well.' Another uneasy laugh. 'Just joking. Everyone says you're a marvel, got the place running on an even keel, everything hunky-dory and getting along tickety-boo as they say. After all, I know how much effort it takes to run this place, having been there and done that.'

Yes, he'd taken the agency on for a short while but had not done well. Perhaps it would be unkind to remind him of that.

'And then, eventually . . . Not that we want it to happen straight away, but it will all come to me in due course.'

She started. Was he implying that after her death . . .?

'I suppose –' an artificial laugh, though he was not joking – 'I could twist your arm and say I have every right to ask you to consider the future from my point of view.'

'I'm not that decrepit.'

'No, of course not.' Now he was the one to soothe. 'You're absolutely wonderful for your age. But we never know what's round the next corner, do we? A car crash, a fall down the stairs . . . And where would we be then, eh? You have made a will, haven't you?'

She stared at him and through him. She'd made a new will immediately after her dear Hamilton had died during an extended holiday far from home. The travel agent had suggested it was a wise precaution to take before she made the long journey back to London by plane and, stunned as she'd been in her bereavement, she'd dutifully made a will in which she'd left everything to Max.

Since then she'd taken in two youngsters who were as dear to her – if not more so – than Max, and had learned that even though her son had many sterling qualities, he was not the best of businessmen. If she were to die tomorrow, she could see Benton taking control of the agency through Max, and she could also see that he would turn Maggie and Oliver out. Of course he would. Max had never liked her having lodgers, and he'd love to live in this nice big house himself. Nicole would like it, too. They'd hinted as much in the past. More than hinted.

Bea had forgotten all that. She'd buried it under layers of pretending that everything in the world was absolutely fine.

Another thought struck her; it might be best to leave Max with the impression that she had not made a will since Hamilton died. She was horrified at herself, but a nasty little worm at the back of her head was jumping up and down and shrieking that it would be wise . . . even safer . . . to keep him in suspense.

'A will?' she said, frowning. 'Yes, I really must. Otherwise there might be all sorts of complications; tax, and Hamilton's relatives having to be taken into consideration—'

'What?' Had he gone pale? 'You mean, someone might contest the will?'

She shook her head at herself. 'You're right. I must get that sorted, soon as. I'm glad you reminded me. It's the sort of thing which can so easily get overlooked. One doesn't like to think one's not immortal.'

'No, of course not.' He was thoughtful. 'You need to get on to it, though. I'll get my solicitor to ring you, make an appointment. I suppose you might want to leave a few thousand to your grandson, and a couple of hundred each to your lodgers, something like that?'

Despising herself, she went into a Little Woman act. 'I think I have to use Hamilton's solicitors. He'll have the original will, won't he? And, if I'm right, he also holds the deeds of the house.'

'Ah yes. You'll need those if we take out a mortgage.' He rubbed his hands. 'Well, well. Glad that's settled. A good morning's work. I'll get Benton to fax through some paperwork for you; I'm sure he can lay any qualms you might have to rest. He knows the business inside out, after all.'

Bea nodded and saw him leave. He looked a lot less worried than he had. And she felt wretched.

Back at her desk she opened Leon's last email.

'The Ritz for lunch?'

She typed back: '*I'm busy. Bring in some sandwiches for us both and I'll take a break for half an hour. I'll supply the coffee.*' She hesitated. Was this the right thing to do?

Yes, because Leon did not seem to have been drawn into Benton's plans but he might – just might – have some helpful information about how to thwart him. Well, he *might*.

She pressed 'send' and picked up the telephone. Max was right. She ought not to have let the making of a new will slip out of her mind. She made an appointment for the morrow and turned back to her computer.

FOUR

Thursday at noon

A commotion in the big office. Bea could hear the girls laughing.

Bea opened the door to find that Leon had arrived and was distributing sandwiches for everyone from a cool box which also contained bottles of fruit drinks. 'Sparkling apple juice? Blackcurrant drink? I thought I'd better not bring alcohol in . . . or not on my first attempt at storming the citadel, anyway. Sorry, they wouldn't let me have proper glasses. Hope you can manage with these plastic ones.'

'What on earth!' Bea found herself laughing.

He spread his hands wide. 'Why shouldn't we treat ourselves now and then?' He carried the cool box into her office. 'Sandwiches. Smoked salmon and cream cheese, beef and horseradish, egg and cress. Hope there's something you like. Apple or blackcurrant?

Apple?' He pulled up a chair and poured the bubbly liquid into a
glass for her.

She felt herself relax. Smile. 'You're after something.'

'Pleasant company to while away an hour in an otherwise aimless
life.'

'Charm will get you nowhere.'

'It usually does, you know.' He actually had a dimple when he
grinned.

She grinned back. 'Cheers. And thank you. It was a grim morning
till you arrived.'

'Thought it might be. I've been listening to my brother. He really
believed that the archangel Gabriel in the form of Benton the
Adventurer had been sent down from heaven to ensure that his latter
years flowed with milk and honey . . . or steak and brandy, to be
more accurate.'

'Until he discovered his idol had feet of clay?' Now why
had she said that? As she dipped into the cool box, she noted he'd
stopped eating for a moment. So she was right and something major
had disturbed Mr Holland's faith in his protégé. She said, 'Yum.
Are you sure you don't have any shares in Holland and Butcher?
No axe to grid at all?'

'None. I was going to keep well out of it but, despite myself, I
feel some concern for my niece.'

'What do you think is going on there?'

'I'm not sure. Only just arrived. I expected a routine family visit.
You know? How are you, lovely weather we're having, can I treat
you to lunch sometime? I imagined I'd pay, pat the children on the
head and leave. I could still do just that. I tell myself.'

Bea treated him to an old-fashioned look. 'So why don't you
want to get involved in the firm? Surely you're the best person to
sort them out?'

'Let me explain. I was an inconvenient afterthought for my
parents, looked after by an au pair till I was old enough to be
dumped in boarding schools, not good at games, not particularly
clever, too scruffy to be of use in the training college. I got out as
soon as I could. Do you blame me?'

'Not at all.' The sandwiches were delicious. Not from the local
corner shop.

'A schoolfriend's father had a dry-cleaning business which he
wanted to offload on to his son. Son refused to touch it, as he was

set on going to university. My family didn't think it would be worthwhile supporting me after I'd turned eighteen . . .'

Bea narrowed her eyes. In her book he was more than bright enough.

'So I needed to earn a living. I was offered a job and a room above the dry-cleaning shop and took it. I like smoothing out the creases in life for people. Spreading a little happiness. Returning clean clothes for soiled. I reorganized and repainted, I advertised, I made a success of that first shop, borrowed money to buy it, found another, got a loan to buy up the second shop's lease and did the same thing . . . and so it went on. I didn't tell my family that I was doing all right for myself, thank you, because they'd written me off as a dropout. In the early years I used to turn up for funerals but decided life was too short to spend time with people who kept referring to me as the Black Sheep of the family.

'I wasn't invited to my niece's wedding. I gather it was a hurriedly arranged affair. The only Holland who's ever tried to keep in touch with me is my sister Sybil. She has a strong sense of family duty, which I lack. Despite her age, she is pretty spry and keeps up with the modern world. Better, in my opinion, than my brother does. She used to email me several times a year with news of the family. She says – and I think she's probably right – that my brother ought to have retired some years ago. He has some vascular problem, walks with difficulty, hardly ever leaves the house. Over the years he's expanded into different areas: car hire, laundromats, employment agencies, that sort of thing, which he runs under the umbrella of Holland Holdings. He and Sybil are the main shareholders in each of the companies, though a few friends and some of the senior staff have been given shares now and then. He employs a small staff at head-quarters to manage the finances and the PR, and he appoints general managers to run each company. Recently he has, I believe, relied too much on a favourite few to run his organ-ization . . . but there, he tells me he keeps them on their toes by swapping the managers around from one branch of the organ-ization to another.'

'Gracious!' Bea's mind went into free-fall, thinking of the manager of a hire-car firm suddenly being asked to run . . . 'Ah. Is that what happened to Holland and Butcher?'

'Correct. He relies on that particular firm for servants to keep his household running smoothly. For years he had a general manager who was reasonably competent and kept the house going. When that man retired, my brother appointed a man named Butcher, who turned out to be a poor choice.'

Bea grimaced. 'Indeed. He's currently languishing in prison. And this man Benton came from where? Don't tell me! The hire-car firm?'

'Exactly. My brother appears to promote people who promise him the earth, so long as he himself doesn't have to make any effort. His companies have done well enough for him in the past but they've all taken a dip in the recession, and this has affected the dividends upon which my sister lives. Holland and Butcher's results have been spectacularly bad. Sybil contacted me when she found that her dividend there had been cut to the bone. She wanted me to do something about it. I declined. She announced she was coming over from the States to sort things out. She ordered me to meet her to discuss it.'

'So you did.'

He refilled her glass and his. 'Cheers. Yes, that was a mistake, wasn't it? But I was at a loose end. I'd had a good offer for the dry-cleaning chain and was trying to decide whether or not to sell. I've always worked. What would I do with my time if I sold out? I'd almost decided to carry on when . . .' He looked into his drink.

'Everything changed, overnight. I'd had a twenty-five-year relationship with a businesswoman who refused to marry me, didn't know how to cook and didn't care to try, but was a wonderful companion and great in bed. She had an aneurysm. Nothing could have been done. No one knew anything about it. The day after the funeral I signed the papers to get rid of the dry-cleaner's and put the house we'd shared on to the market. I took a short lease out on a service flat and moved into it, but didn't unpack. I thought I might take a long holiday. I thought it was probably stupid of me to look up the family, but when my sister actually phoned me – something she'd never done in all those years – I decided to look them up.

'I rang my brother, said I was thinking of spending a few days in London. True to form, he said immediately that he didn't have any room for me – despite living in a country mansion – since our sister was going to be moving in with him for the duration of her visit. I didn't tell him that I'd fully intended to book myself into Claridge's or the Ritz and treat myself for once, because he seemed to think I'd need a bed and breakfast somewhere cheap. He said that his right-hand man, Benton, would make arrangements for me to stay somewhere suitable.

'Benton duly rang and asked me to have lunch with him. A steak house. Medium rare, as you might say. Not first rate but middling. It was clear he'd been making enquiries about me, knew I'd sold my company. He went on about how H & B was in great shape but needed capital to take over a domestic agency. He said it was divine providence that I would be able to join the board of directors and invest in the family business at this point in time. I knew rather more about the poor balance sheet than he imagined and I'd taken a dislike to him so, in a moment of divine inspiration, I informed him that I was head over ears in hock to the Inland Revenue. That I was, in fact, an undischarged bankrupt. You should have seen his face!'

Bea felt her mouth curve into a smile. 'His research hadn't been as thorough as yours?'

'He's an idiot. I thought he'd brush me off and that would be the end of it, but no. After another brandy he said I must be finding life very uncomfortable, and he invited me to stay with him and Dilys. I must admit I'd envisaged a large detached house with a double garage, and guest bedrooms en suite. I thought my niece would be serving up home-cooked food and hanging on my every word. I'd never even met her children. I had nothing better to do, so I thought, why not? Just for a few days. Take them all out for a meal or something by way of payment. What he didn't tell me was that the house is tiny, shabby, cold and uncomfortable, that the two boys are badly behaved little hooligans, and that my great niece had been moved out of her tiny bedroom to make way for me. Oh, and there's only one bathroom for six people, though I believe there is a shower in the master bedroom.'

His tragic expression made Bea laugh. 'So why haven't you moved out?'

'I ask myself that a dozen times a day. I tell myself that I am not of a sentimental disposition. I do not turn soft when confronted with stray kittens and homeless waifs. I am a hard-headed businessman who has got along very well all these years without needing any contact with my family.'

'You're concerned about Dilys?'

He threw up his hands. 'The air in that house is full of cross-currents. Stinging retorts whistle past my back, morphing into smiles when I turn around. The two boys despise and taunt their mother and sister. They don't go so far as to hit them yet. I hope. But they jostle and push them around. All this originates with Benton, of course. He tweaks the little girl's hair. Both she and Dilys flinch when he gets close. He apologized to me for them, saying how stupid they are.

'I tell myself this has nothing to do with me, that Dilys wouldn't thank me for trying to rescue her, that you can't help people who are born to be victims. When Sybil dragged us along to meet you, it did occur to me that *you* could save them if you wished, though I could see that you didn't want to. Naturally, I applauded you for that. Sensible, very.'

'But . . .?'

'Well, I fancy you something rotten, as you must realize. You remind me so much of my ex.'

Bea was amused and even flattered. She told herself to be wary of a man who used the best butter so lavishly, and who had just admitted to telling a thumping lie to Benton. She repeated, 'But . . .?'

'My niece was first down this morning. She switched on the toaster and got a nasty shock. It might have killed her.'

Silence. Bea froze in mid-chew. What was it with toasters? Might she have given herself a shock when she'd fiddled with hers that morning?

He took the last sandwich and bit into it. Poured them both out some more of the bubbly apple drink.

Bea finished off her mouthful. 'You think he engineered it?' She tried to sound incredulous, and failed.

A shrug. 'She had to sit down. She was shaking. He was not sympathetic. He let fly with a tirade about how stupid she was with anything practical. He said he's had to restrain her from poking into the toaster with a metal knife before now. She dissolved into tears, tried to hide them. He made her repeat after him that she was a silly little thing who ought not to be allowed out by herself. The boys almost choked with laughter. The little girl went so pale, I thought she'd vomit all over the kitchen table. Her name is Bernice, and she appears to be reasonably intelligent. Neither she nor her mother could eat any breakfast. My niece may be a silly little chit, but she doesn't deserve what's happening to her.'

Bea remembered what Max had said about Benton getting rid of Dilys. Bea had jumped to the conclusion that Benton planned to divorce his wife. She hadn't thought of murder. 'Do you think that he planned to have you staying in the house as an impartial witness when an "accident" kills her?'

A level gaze from eyes which were more hazel than brown. 'What do *you* think?'

She did not want to get involved. 'I have no idea. There is always gossip, of course.' She brushed a crumb off her lap. 'Supposition. Rumour. Slander.'

'Who is your rumour-monger? You have proof?'

She shook her head. 'A loose wire may be no more than a loose wire. Loose talk costs money.'

One of the office girls came in with a cafetière of coffee and some cups on a tray. She said to Leon, 'We want to thank you, all of us. It was a lovely thought.'

'My pleasure.' Another charming smile. The girl left, also smiling.

Bea poured coffee.

He said, 'Oops. I've forgotten the after-dinner mints.'

'It's lunchtime.'

'We'll have to make sure we have some after dinner tonight, then.'

'Not tonight. Soon, perhaps.' She sat back in her chair and tried to think. Max was in trouble, needed her to rescue him . . . and if she didn't, if she did nothing, then he'd take out a loan at prohibitive interest rates, knowing him . . . and lose his money, because Benton was not the man to rescue the fortunes of H & B, was he?

She said, 'Why don't you accept their offer, take charge of the firm and get rid of Benton?'

'Throwing good money after bad? I know nothing about that sort of business. It would be a disaster. Besides, why should I?'

She grimaced. 'You want me to pull your chestnuts out of the fire for you instead?'

He grinned. 'It's worth a try, isn't it? You have all the skills needed, you dislike Benton and you don't like the thought of Dilys being hounded to her death. Plus, you're already involved through Max.'

Bea looked at the clock. 'I have a three o'clock appointment. Someone's references haven't checked out and I'm not going to find the woman a job until I know what's happened. I don't take anyone on without references, you see.'

'From me, you mean?' He produced a couple of cards and laid them on her desk. 'You can check out the sale of my business and my house, if you wish. I believe that sort of information can be accessed through the Internet. Of course, I could be deep in debt and these sales might be keeping me from a debtor's court. Now, how do you check that?'

'Have we a mutual friend or acquaintance?'

'How about my member of parliament? I'm an active and generous supporter of the Liberal party, so he'll remember me. What else? Do you need a reference as to my character? I promise you I have contracted no particular disease; I am a member of a gym, swim several times a week but don't do press-ups or weightlifting.'

Bea tried not to laugh. 'What about your morals?'

He raised his hands in mock indignation. 'No grubbier than most. I am told I was baptized, I know I was confirmed, but I can't say I go to church on Sundays, except at Christmas and Easter. I sleep soundly, I enjoy my meals and a glass or two of beer in the evenings. I like the Beatles but not the Rolling Stones. I adore Gilbert and Sullivan but abhor Wagner. I read James Patterson, but not Dostoevsky. Will that do?'

Now she did laugh. 'I will check, you know.'

'So you should.' There was a tap on the door, and he stood. 'Your appointment, I assume. May I call for you at eight this evening?'

She nodded, forgetting she'd intended to keep him at arm's length for a while. Well, why not? 'Nothing elaborate. A steak house, perhaps? Oh, and about Dilys. My experience is that you can't rescue those who are in thrall to their abuser.'

'So you get at it another way, by eliminating the abuser.'

How on earth did he think that could be done?

She dealt with her visitor – no references, no job, sorry – and turned back to her computer to check Leon out. Yes, and yes. The dry cleaning business had existed, he'd been the sole proprietor, it had sold . . . yes . . . and for a nice sum, too. The house was still on the market but it had been priced at over two million, so . . . Difficult to check on debts, though.

She hesitated about ringing Max, but did eventually do so. 'Dear Max, I'm trying to check up on one of the Holland clan. Do you happen to be acquainted with the member of parliament for . . . I have the name here somewhere. One of the Exeter constituencies. He's a Liberal Democrat, so you may not—?'

'Which Holland? The one who's just crawled out from under a stone? Benton says he's no good to us. He hasn't been in touch with you, has he? The nerve of the man!'

'He's been to see me, yes. He's staying with Benton, it seems, and—'

'Benton took pity on him. More than I would have done. Mother, don't let him fool you. He's an undischarged bankrupt looking for a handout. He hasn't asked you for a loan yet, has he?'

'Nothing like that. He's invited me out for a meal this evening.'

'Mother! What are you like! You'll be landed with the bill.'

She was silent. She didn't think she would be landed with the bill. She didn't think Leon was an undischarged bankrupt. Only a tiny wriggle of common sense insisted that she check him out before she saw him again. But perhaps Max wasn't the best person to ask?

She said, 'I'll remember to take my cards with me, in case he defaults.'

'Whatever will you do next!' He cut the connection.

Bea made a childish face at the phone, dialled the House of Commons and asked to speak to the Liberal Democrat member for Exeter. The West Country was a Lib Dem stronghold and there were three who might fit the bill. She quoted the address of his house and was passed to a secretary who was regretfully unable to give out any information about . . . But if she liked to write in . . .? No, sir was not available at the moment.

Bea wondered what else she had expected.

So she rang the man who knew everything and was discreet about it. 'CJ, a small problem. I am trying to keep out of the Holland and Butcher fiasco, but there's been a development which may lead to the involvement of the police. I've been contacted by a man called Leon Holland, long estranged from the main branch of the family, who is concerned about the health and safety of Benton's wife. He may be right to worry, but he's an odd customer and I can't say that I trust him altogether.

'I've tried to check up on him as far as I can. He's just sold his

business and put his house on the market and that all seems above
board, but I need a character reference before I decide whether or
not to take him seriously. He says he's a Lib Dem supporter for a
certain constituency in Exeter, and his member of parliament will
vouch for him. Unfortunately, said member's secretary won't give
me the time of day.'

'A man can give money to a political party and yet not be someone
you'd wish to leave alone in a room with the family silver. You
don't trust him?'

'He's an interesting personality, not easy to read. I'm not sure
what I feel about him.'

'You are attracted to him?'

She tried on a laugh for size. 'I wouldn't go as far as that.'

A pause. Bea could hear him tapping . . . on his desk? He had
long fingers, very clean nails, always manicured. She made a note
to book herself in for a manicure tomorrow. He said, 'Leave it with
me.'

So she did.

Thursday evening

Bea hoped that Maggie would return before Leon came to collect
her for the evening, but there was no sign of the girl by the time
the office closed for the evening.

Oh well. Time for a shower and to decide what she should wear.
Nothing too flashy, something warm but of good quality.

Bea took care with her make-up, reminding herself yet again
to make another appointment with her manicurist. She decided
that a fawn and white cashmere sweater with a cowl neck would
be warm enough for a casual winter date, teamed with her favourite
caramel skirt, which was long enough to cover the tops of her
boots.

Bea loved boots. She had a collection of them, long, medium
and short. These particular boots were new and in suede, soft as
silk. She zipped them up to the knee and checked that her skirt
hung correctly. She hesitated about whether to wear jewellery or
not. She always wore the wedding ring Hamilton had given her,
and during work hours she wore costume jewellery: a stickpin on
a collar and a string of beads, or a modern pendant to match whatever it was she was wearing. Now she pinned on an antique gold
brooch in the shape of a flower and, not without hesitation, pushed

her diamond engagement ring on to her finger. She was aware that she was sending various messages to Leon by wearing her engagement ring. She was reminding him that she still thought of her deceased husband, and she was also reminding him that Dilys's ring was not all that it ought to be.

As she left her bedroom, she thought she heard a door close overhead. She hadn't heard Maggie come in. Surely the girl wouldn't have crept up past Bea's door without popping in to say she was back?

Bea hesitated. The front doorbell rang. Leon was on time, and it would be rude to keep him waiting. Bea decided to deal with Maggie later and went to open the door.

There was a good steakhouse not far away, on the main road. A trifle on the noisy side because the wood floor had been left polished and waxed, without carpet or rugs. But, the service was good, and Bea was hungry. As was Leon.

He asked, 'Wine or beer?'

She remembered that he liked beer. She hadn't had beer for a long time. So why not? 'Beer would be fine.'

They both declined starters and ordered steaks.

'Well,' he said, 'have you had time to check up on me?'

'Some. More to come.'

His eyebrows quirked. 'Confess: you wouldn't have bothered if I hadn't made that stupid joke about being an undischarged bankrupt.'

She smiled. He was right, of course. 'No comment.'

'I'm an idiot. I've been trying to work out why I lied to Benton and, well, I'm not liking myself very much. I thought I had got over it, but the rejection by my family seems to have gone deeper than I thought. I invented the first lie I could think of in order to avoid being dragged into their machinations. I'm *conflicted*. Is that the right term?'

'You mean that, despite yourself, you share some of your sister's feeling for the family?'

He pulled a face. 'Duty. Such a dull word.'

'How about reinventing yourself as a white knight, riding to the rescue?'

'Like Don Quixote, you mean? Tilting at windmills?'

She had to laugh, thinking he was excellent company. He held her gaze. His eyes were definitely hazel, with pronounced crow's feet around them. She half-smiled, feeling the pull of attraction . . . and then lowered her eyes to break the spell.

Her pulse was a little too fast. She had put all that side of herself to sleep when Hamilton had become ill and died. Her first husband, Piers – who was still around and who flitted in and out of her life now and again – had tried to reawaken her recently, but she'd resisted. It was uncomfortable to be reminded of sex. At her age, too!

He cleared his throat. 'Benton tells me you're in the habit of taking in waifs and strays.'

Now how had he come by that information? Ah, Max had talked to Benton, and Benton had talked to Leon. The information corridor between the conspirators – if that is what they were – was well established, and anything she said might go back the same way.

She said, 'Waifs and strays? In a way, I suppose. Maggie was wished upon me by her mother, who didn't want the girl hanging around at home after she'd been sucked into a disastrous marriage and then dumped. She's an ugly duckling who's turning into a swan. She housekeeps for me part-time, but has a successful career as a project manager. Oliver is at university, studying something in the realm of Higher Maths, don't ask me what. Way beyond my brain power. I would have supported him through university but he's won a bursary here and a prize there and is almost paying his own way. He helps me out at the agency in vacation time. They're both great. They call me Mother Hen.'

'Mother Hen?' His eyelids crinkled. He liked that. 'So they're both off your hands, really?'

'Monetarily, yes. But they're great company and I think of them as my second family.' Except that Maggie was in trouble . . .

The steaks came, and they didn't talk much as they ate. The food was good and not overpriced. Satisfactory.

'Afters?' he said.

She leaned back in her chair, replete. 'Coffee. Decaffeinated.'

He ordered. He had the same knack as CJ of being able to summon waiters when required. 'Have you thought any more about Dilys and what can be done to save her?'

'Some, yes.'

'If – and I'm just toying with the subject, you understand – Benton invited me to stay in order to have a witness when Dilys has an "accident", then the next "accident" might prove fatal. Do you agree?'

'I do and I don't. She's your brother's only daughter. Doesn't he have some fondness for her? Wouldn't her disappearance rebound on Benton?'

'Not from what my sister says. Like me, Dilys was an afterthought, born when my brother was well into his fifties, and her mother went off into the blue when the child was old enough to go to a boarding school. Just like mine. The Hollands don't have a good track record in raising children. Dilys is no great brain, apparently. The family never expected her to be anything but a passenger till she married. I suppose they thought she might bring a suitable man into the business, but they don't seem to have made any effort to introduce her to suitable men. I don't think my brother cares tuppence for anyone or anything but his own comfort.'

Bea wondered if Leon himself would ever have a child, and how he would treat her if he did. He was now, presumably, at about the age that his brother had been when he sired Dilys. Had Leon ever wanted a child? Had he been too busy? Had his partner refused to have one?

She said, 'Is the house in Dilys's name, or in his?'

He rubbed his chin. 'I'm not sure. I assume it was a wedding present. Benton tells me he handles all the finances because she can't be trusted to pay the utility bills on time. I know she's signed over her shares in H & B to him, and I suspect he's also had her make a will in his favour. She's a sitting duck. So tell me, Mrs A., how to get rid of him.'

She shook her head. 'Kind sir, you do me too much honour.'

'Nonsense.' The lines of his face hardened and for the first time she caught a glimpse of an acute businessman behind the carefree exterior. 'You've studied the man, as I have. He's a braggart, a con man. He's taken over Holland and Butcher by convincing my brother he's the bee's knees but, either because of previous bad management, or his own inability to keep the ship sailing merrily along, he's heading for the chop unless, perhaps, he can manage to refinance H & B. Excuse mixed metaphors. So, what will he do next?'

Bea responded with caution. 'If he's stripped her of all she has, he might be on the lookout for another meal ticket?'

His eyes narrowed. 'You've heard something?'

'No, no.' Crossing fingers and toes.

He thought about it. 'Is there nothing we can do to stop him? I shall probably regret saying so tomorrow, but I'd like to take a hand in the game. Only, I can't make bricks without straw. Give me something to go on, Mrs Abbot.'

She thought through what she'd learned about Benton. 'I'm told he had a previous entanglement which might be worth following up. Dilys says he sold her diamond to pay off his previous girlfriend, who subsequently met with a fatal road accident.'

'Bless you, my dear,' he said, laying a platinum card on the bill. 'I knew you'd come up trumps. I'll get the details from Dilys tomorrow. Now, are you going to invite me back for a brandy?'

FIVE

Thursday evening

Back at the house, Leon lingered on the front doorstep, clearly hoping that Bea would change her mind. 'Are you sure you won't invite me in for a nightcap?'

'No, Leon. You knew I wouldn't. I paid for my supper with information and, as a working woman, I don't invite strange men into my house for a nightcap or for any other purpose.'

He raised his hands in the air. 'You can't blame me for trying.'

Without giving it much thought, she said, 'It's too soon, too raw, for you to be thinking of replacing your partner.'

In the light of the street lamp, his face turned into a mask.

She put her hand on his arm for a moment and pressed it. For comfort. Then she let herself into the house and closed the door in his face. Once inside, she dealt with the alarm and reset it. Then stood, trying to work out whether Maggie was in or not.

Yes, the girl had left a pair of boots under the hall table. There were no lights on in the kitchen. Winston the cat appeared, to do some stretching exercises and inform Bea that he hadn't eaten for a week and would perish if she didn't feed him immediately. A lie, of course.

Bea fed the cat and turned off all the lights downstairs. Maggie and Oliver had a two-bedroom flat upstairs, complete with living room, kitchen and bathroom. There was no reason why Maggie should not have eaten upstairs by herself. She was not obliged to wait up for Bea, or to maintain constant contact.

The fact that she usually did was neither here nor there. Wasn't it?

Bea climbed the stairs, with Winston at her heels. He would sometimes condescend to sleep on her bed. Sometimes he'd go up to sleep with Maggie. It depended on his mood.

The house lay quiet around her, but there was a leak of light from the top floor. No music. There was definitely something wrong if Maggie were at home but sitting in silence.

Bea tapped on the door to Maggie's living room and waited for permission to enter. There was a scramble of sound and Maggie called out, 'Come.'

The girl was sitting hunched up on the settee, with her arms around her knees. Had she been crying? Possibly. The television was on, but the sound had been muted. Maggie was a good house-keeper and normally kept her rooms tidy. Today there was a certain disarrangement of newspapers and empty coffee cups which hinted at distress.

Maggie was not a beauty in conventional terms. Her hair could be sprayed any colour from magenta to strawberry blonde according to the way she felt when she woke up in the morning. Her clothes were sometimes outrageous and always colourful. Maggie dressed to reassure herself that she existed.

Today her hair seemed to have resumed its normal mouse colour and she was dressed in black.

This was bad. Handle with care.

Bea said, 'I haven't seen you for a couple of days. Missed you. Want to share a late-night cuppa?'

Maggie shook her head, not taking her eyes off the muted television. 'I'm all right. Just a bit . . . Work, you know. January blues.'

Unasked, Bea took a seat. 'I usually buy a bunch of daffodils when the dark days get me down.'

'Good idea.' A dull tone of voice.

Bea was seriously concerned. 'What's wrong, Maggie?'

A shrug. 'Nothing for you to worry about. Honest. I must have picked up some sort of bug. I'll be all right soon.'

'If it's that bad, I'll make an appointment for you to see the doctor in the morning.'

'Don't do that.' A sharper tone. Maggie reached for the remote and clicked the television off. 'If you must know, I had a row with Zander, and we've broken up.'

This was serious. Zander – short for Alexander – was a serious young man with a good job, who'd been Maggie's loving and understanding boyfriend for some time now. Bea didn't know whether the relationship had moved on from boy/girl, to man/woman, but she rather thought not. Zander was old-fashioned. He believed in respecting and loving his woman. He believed in commitment. He'd been very patient with Maggie, waiting for her to . . . to grow up? To realize that she was worthy of love?

'I'm sorry,' said Bea, trying to pick the right words. 'I thought he was right for you.'

Another shrug. 'He assumed I was his for the taking.'

'Nonsense!'

Maggie uncurled. 'He wants to own me.'

Bea rolled her eyes. 'Come off it, Maggie. Zander wouldn't.'

'He . . . I said, why didn't he move in here with me? There's plenty of room, and it would save him the rent of his place. He acted like I'd insulted him.'

'So you had. Maggie, this is ridiculous. What really happened? Did he ask you to marry him?'

Maggie raised both fists in the air. 'Why shouldn't he move in with me? You wouldn't object, would you?'

'He wants you to make a commitment to him?'

Maggie spun herself off the settee and switched on the main lights. She turned on the radio and began to dance to it. 'Boom, tiddle tiddle . . . Boom!'

Bea reached over to switch the radio off. 'Maggie, take five! Ask him for time to consider. Don't—'

'Don't panic, Mr Mainwaring!' she said, quoting a well-known oldie of a television show. 'Don't panic!' She twirled round and round, putting on an act. Then, just as suddenly, collapsed back on to the settee. 'So, yes. I panicked. Told him to get lost. Said I was never going to . . .' She caught her breath. Sobbed. 'I told him I didn't want to see him again.'

'Silly girl,' said Bea. She moved over to the settee and put her arm around the girl. 'You know you love him to distraction. He's a gem of the first water and you don't want to lose him. Why don't you phone him, say you were taken by surprise—'

'I wasn't. I've seen it coming for weeks.'

'Ask him to forgive what you said because you need to think things through.'

'I asked him to move in with me, and he said he wouldn't. He said that if I respected him—' Again she broke off with a sob.

Bea picked Maggie's mobile from the mess on the table and handed it to her. 'Ring him. If you don't, I will.'

Maggie struck the mobile out of Bea's hand. 'It's too late for that. I'm not going to let him get me down. He didn't love me enough, and it's good that I realized it before I wasted any more time on him.'

'Maggie!'

Maggie sprang up and made for the kitchen. Then froze. 'That's your phone ringing downstairs.'

There is something about a phone ringing late in the evening which tells you that this is not a sales call. This is urgent.

Bea had an extension of the phone in her bedroom. She had turned the voicemail on, hadn't she? Yes, she had. The voice clicked in as she was halfway down the stairs. She could hear her own voice asking the caller to leave a message and then . . . Leon's voice, almost shouting, 'Bea, for God's sake!'

She picked up the phone. 'Yes?'

'Thank God. Can you come? Dilys was in the bath, unconscious. I'm doing CPR. I've called the ambulance, but the boys . . . and I've no idea where Benton is!'

'Address?' Bea reached for something to write on. Her Bible flyleaf would do. She took the address down and tore out the page. 'I'll be right there.'

Maggie was at her side, her own problems forgotten. 'Trouble? Can I help?'

'Desperate. Do you know where this terrace is?'

Maggie had an encyclopedic knowledge of this part of town. 'Not far. Near Earls Court Road. Will we take a cab, or the car?' Parking in this area was limited, very. Bea's car was nearby but it was unlikely they'd find a parking space at the other end.

Bea dialled. 'I'll get a cab. You get your coat. It's cold outside.'

* * *

They got there in record time. Traffic lights turned to amber and green as they approached, and there seemed to be fewer cars on the road than usual.

Benton and Dilys lived in a pretty little street not more than a mile away. Late-Victorian villas. Ironwork balconies and bay trees in the forecourt. No garden. Three bedrooms unless a loft conversion had been done, which, in this case, it hadn't. Two receptions, kitchen and bathroom. Lights on downstairs.

Bea paid the taxi off while Maggie rang the doorbell. Insistently.

A commotion in the curtains of the bay window. A boy looked out, made a rude gesture and vanished. Sound thumped. They had the television on with the volume turned up high?

A wisp of a child opened the door, reaching the catch with some difficulty. She was wearing soaking wet pyjamas and had nothing on her feet.

Bernice?

Her eyes were huge but she was controlling herself. Just. She pointed upstairs and led the way, stumbling over the bottom step then scampering up on all fours.

Maggie followed Bea into a nightmare. A small, old-fashioned bathroom, the floor awash with discoloured water slopping over on to the landing. An unpleasant smell.

Leon, still in his overcoat, dripping water, on his knees, working on a man-sized doll.

Not a doll.

He said, 'Am I doing this right? Do you know how to . . .?'

He didn't stop pumping.

Maggie said, 'Let me.' She knelt at Dilys's other side and took over.

Leon sank back on his heels and closed his eyes.

Bea's eyes were drawn to the mirror over the washbasin, on which someone had scrawled the word 'Sorry'. In lipstick?

Was this another attempt to murder Dilys? Or was it attempted suicide?

Bea delved into her handbag for her mobile phone and began to take pictures. The message on the mirror, the large, claw-footed old bath still half full of water, the wine glass on the side . . . Leon wet to his armpits, the front of his coat stained, his trousers dark with water. His shoes . . . Oh dear.

Dilys lying on the floor.

Maggie working on her.

Bernice hovering, in silent anxiety.

Water scurried around Bea's boots. Water with something nasty in it. Vomit?

Leon tried to help himself up by pulling on the washbasin. Failed. Sank back down again. 'The paramedics say there's been a multiple car crash out near the hospital. They're diverting, soon be here.'

Bea looked at a medicine cabinet on the wall, marked with a red cross and with a child lock on it – a broken child lock. Might there be something in there to explain why Dilys had let herself slip under the water? True, it was a very large, high-sided bath, and she was not a big woman, but . . .?

Bernice knelt in the water by her mother's head, not touching her, but very close.

Maggie didn't stop working on Dilys but said to the child, 'What's your name?'

'Bernice.' A thread of a voice.

'I'm Maggie. Do you know how to feel for a pulse? Put your fingers on your mother's neck, half way round. Can you feel anything?'

The child did as she was told. Shook her head.

Bea pulled a large towel from the rail and draped it over Dilys's naked body. It was cold in the bathroom. No sense the girl getting hypothermia on top of everything else.

Leon's arms hung at his side. 'Bernice was in the hall when I got back. She'd found her mother asleep in the bath. Under water. Couldn't lift her out. She told the boys she had to use the landline to call for help. They laughed at her, wouldn't let her in. Playing some video game or other. Her mother's mobile is in her bag in the living room. Also out of reach. Bernice is a star.'

Bernice looked up at him. A trustful look.

Maggie worked on.

Bea moved round the room, opened the medicine cabinet, took a snap of the contents. Well-stocked for minor ailments. Nothing untoward.

Leon managed to get himself off the floor and on to the bathroom stool. 'I got her out of the bath. No pulse. I tried to get her to sick up, and she did, but . . .' He made a defeated gesture. He looked older than his years. He pointed to a wine glass on the edge of the bath. 'Whisky, do you think? Sleeping pills? Someone needs to look at that.'

Bea took the rest of the towels off the rail and began to mop up around Dilys.

Leon said, 'I got Bernice to take my phone out of my pocket, told her what numbers to press and when she got through she held it up to me so that I could speak to the medics. I tried Benton. Not answering. Then my sister. The same. One of the boys came up, wanted the loo, I told him to get lost.'

Was Leon actually crying?

Bea decided not to notice. She bent over Dilys, whose hair was all over her face. Poor kid. Poor, desperate child.

Maggie worked on, encouraging Bernice to keep her fingers at her mother's throat. 'You're doing great, lovey. As good as any medic.'

Leon said, 'I thought I could go to the hospital with her but didn't know what to do about the children. I don't know where Benton is. Then I thought of you.'

Bernice gave a little jump. She looked up at Maggie with a startled expression.

Maggie smiled at the child. 'You can feel a pulse now?'

Bernice nodded.

Maggie sat back on her heels.

Yes, there was a slight movement in Dilys's chest.

Very, very slight.

Was it enough?

They concentrated.

Dilys sighed, coughed. A stream of discoloured water shot out of her mouth. Neither Maggie nor Bernice drew back.

'Excellent!' said Maggie. 'Well done, Bernice.'

'A star indeed,' said Leon. 'Excellent, Bernice.'

Bernice managed a brief smile.

Dilys murmured something. Her eyelids flickered. But she did not regain consciousness.

Bea investigated the cupboard under the basin. Bathroom cleaners, toilet cleaners, toilet rolls, a large pack of paper towels in a clean plastic bag. She emptied out the bag and put the wine glass it, stowing it in her handbag.

She looked down. Her boots were ruined. Her coat and skirt would have to be cleaned before she wore them again.

The others were in a worse state.

Everything that Maggie had on ought to be dumped. And as for Leon!

Bernice ought to be put under the shower and soused down, then dressed in clean clothing.

Bernice was shivering. 'Why doesn't Mummy wake up?'

Maggie answered: 'She needs to go to hospital and be properly nursed.'

She needed her stomach pumped out, if Bea were any judge of the matter.

The doorbell rang.

One of the boys shouted up the stairs. 'Someone's at the door!'

'I'll go,' said Bernice, trying and failing to stand up.

'No, you won't,' said Bea. 'I'll go.' She went down the stairs, holding on to the banister, and opened the front door to the paramedics. 'Upstairs. Found in the bath. Possibly taken an overdose though I haven't found any pills yet. CPR administered, breathing on her own, but far from well. Not conscious.'

The paramedics nodded and tramped up the stairs.

One of the boys poked his head out of the downstairs room. 'What are you doing? Daddy says not to let anyone in when he's not at home.'

'Do you know where he is?'

'Nah! Pooh! You smell! And who are you, anyway?'

Bea leaned against the wall. 'A friend of your mother's. She's very ill.'

A shrug. 'Oh, Silly Dilly's always whining about something.' He disappeared back into the room before Bea could box his ears.

One of the paramedics thundered down the stairs and went out to the ambulance, which was double-parked in the middle of the road. Gone to fetch a stretcher?

A phone was ringing somewhere. Not hers. She checked. No, it was the house landline in the sitting room. No one bothered to answer it.

Following her usual practice, Bea sent the photos she'd just taken to her computer back at the office. She'd had someone try to destroy evidence on her phone before now and wasn't going to risk it happening again.

The paramedic pounded up the stairs with a stretcher.

A car tooted outside. The ambulance was blocking the traffic.

Voices were raised in the street.

Bea thought of going out and explaining what had happened to the impatient drivers but didn't. They could work it out for themselves.

She went on leaning against the wall. It had been a long day.

Car doors slammed. More raised voices. 'What the . . .?'

Was that Benton?

Yes. Storming in, face of fury. 'What's going on?'

The two boys erupted into the hall, in a babel of explanation. 'Silly Mummy's been stupid again, we left her alone like you said, honest, but that stupid Bernice, and then the man came, the one that didn't bring us any presents, I hate him, and then she came –' pointing at Bea – 'and another woman, and they say Mummy's gone and done something extra stupid this time, and we can't get to the toilet, which isn't fair . . .'

'What!' Benton was furious. He turned on Bea. 'What the . . .!'

'Leon found her in the bath, unconscious. He kept her alive till we got here and now the paramedics have taken over. Bernice was a star.'

'Was she, by Jove!' He didn't look pleased at that, either. 'I don't see why you're here. Why didn't he ring me?'

'He tried. He rang me because he needed someone to look after the children if Dilys needed to go to hospital.'

He gnawed his lip, his eyes switching from left to right.

'Daddy!' One of the boys tugged at his arm. 'I need to go to the toilet.'

'He shouldn't go upstairs,' said Bea.

'What?' For the first time he glanced up the stairs. 'Oh. Really? You mean she's . . . Where is she?'

'In the bathroom. On the floor.'

'Oh.' He hadn't got his head round this, had he? He said to the boy, 'Use the one in our bedroom.'

'But you said we were never to—'

'Well, for once I say you can.'

'Me, too!' His brother was not to be outdone. Both of them rushed upstairs, fighting for precedence.

Benton didn't seem to know what to do next. He asked Bea, 'Is she going to be all right?'

Bea wasn't sure what answer he wanted to that question. 'I hope so. If they can get her to the hospital in time.'

His eyes switched to the open door. 'The traffic's backed up to the main road.'

The paramedics came slowly down the stairs, carrying Dilys, strapped into a stretcher, between them.

Benton watched them pass him.

'Aren't you going with her?' said Bea, noting that he didn't seem anxious to do so.

'What? I . . . Oh, yes.' He went after the paramedics saying, 'I'm her husband. I've just got back from a meeting. How is she?'

'The sooner we get her to the hospital . . .' Their voices faded as they took Dilys out to the ambulance.

Without a backward glance at his children, Benton got into the ambulance, too.

'Where's he going? Who's going to look after us?' The elder boy, appearing on the landing. For the first time he seemed to realize that here was a problem which might affect his well-being.

Leon came out on to the landing. He looked exhausted. 'Don't worry. I'll stay here with you.'

Maggie followed him out, carrying Bernice, who had her arms around Maggie's neck. 'Bernice needs looking after. I'll give us both a wash down and find some clean clothes for her. I'll stay, too. I can sleep on the floor in her room tonight.'

'Clean clothes?' said Leon. 'Good idea. There's a shower in the master bedroom at the front. I'll use it after you. The boys are in the back bedroom, and I'm in the small room at the front. I think that was hers before I came. I've no idea where she's been sleeping.'

The elder boy reappeared, adjusting his trousers. 'She's supposed to sleep with us on a lilo, but we don't like that, so she waits till everyone's asleep and then goes downstairs and sleeps on the settee.'

Leon looked even grimmer than before. 'Tonight she sleeps in her own room, and I'll take the settee downstairs. Boys, it's late. Suppose you get ready for bed. Use your parents' bathroom, just this once.'

'We want to use ours. We've got our toothbrushes in there.'

The other boy put his head into their bathroom. 'Hey, it stinks! What a mess! I'm not going in there till it's been cleaned up.'

Bea left them arguing. The television was still blaring in the sitting room. She went in and turned it off.

Peace and quiet.

She looked around and said, 'Wow!' to herself.

What had originally been a sitting and a dining room had been thrown into one. The wall between the living room and the kitchen had also been removed, making an L-shaped space. A gigantic TV and all the other pieces of electronic kit which seemed to be obligatory in today's modern homes were prominently displayed, but the room had been wrecked by the boys playing some sort of Wii game. Chairs had been overturned, cushions thrown around, newspapers, articles of clothing and what might be the boys' worksheets for homework had been tossed here and there.

In the kitchen area, someone had washed up after supper, set the saucepans on the side to dry, and started the dishwasher. The boys had been rampaging in there, too. The door of the fridge hung open, and there was a trail of crisps on the carpet through the living room.

After a moment's thought, Bea took photos of the state of the kitchen and living room. She investigated cupboards, shut the fridge door, checked that the back door was locked, and roughly tidied the main room so that Leon could at least reach the settee. She left one side light on and returned upstairs clutching a roll of black plastic bags.

'Bless you,' said Leon, taking the black bags off her. He had divested himself of his overcoat, had opened the bathroom window, pulled the plug out of the bath and was trying to clean the floor. He was making a good job of it.

The boys were running in and out of their bedroom at the back of the house, complaining. 'Daddy said we could use his bathroom, so why is that woman in there with Silly Sister?'

'I want to go to the loo again.'

Leon said, 'Shut up, both of you. Be thankful you're clean and dry, which is more than your sister is. You can use this bathroom in a minute.'

The elder boy pointed at Bea. 'What's *she* doing, taking pictures?'

Leon clapped his hands. 'Bed! Now!'

The boys' bedroom door banged shut.

Bea said, 'Drop the dirty towels into this black plastic bag, and let me have your clothes to wash.'

'My shoes, my overcoat . . .' He grimaced.

'Perhaps Benton will replace them?'

He was surprised into laughter. 'I doubt it. I'll get some clean clothes out of my suitcase. The rest can go to the dry-cleaner's tomorrow.'

Bea went to see how Maggie was getting on.

A tiny shower room and loo had been carved out of a corner of the main bedroom. Bea tapped on the glass door, and Maggie put her head out. 'Bea, this is awful. The child's arms and legs are covered with bruises. Is this her father's doing? She won't say. Can you find her a hot drink? She's shivering.'

'Ask her if I may take photos of her bruises.'

Maggie's head disappeared. She returned in a minute, shaking her head. 'She says she'd rather not. They're supposed to be a secret. What can we do?'

'Nothing for the moment, I suppose. I'll find something for her to wear. How about you?'

'Dilys's dressing gown is behind the door. I'll wear that. I'll put my clothes in the washing machine downstairs and then hang them up to dry. Or maybe there's a drier? They'll be all right by morning.'

'Give me your things, and Bernice's. I'll see to them.'

Down she went with the soiled clothing, used a clean saucepan to make a hot drink for Bernice, checked the washing instructions and put the clothes into the washing machine on a low temperature programme. Went back upstairs.

Explored the cupboards in the small bedroom at the front of the house. Two good-looking suitcases were stacked at the end of the bed. They must be Leon's. In one of the cupboards she found a small stack of unisex children's clothes, jeans and T-shirts and some trainers. None of them new. Hand-me-downs from the boys?

There was also a pair of wellington boots with pink flowers on them. Bea remembered Dilys saying that her daughter had loved her wellies with the pink flowers on them, and how she'd yearned for an umbrella with ladybirds on. Bea had imagined brand-new wellies and umbrella. The actuality was somewhat different. These wellies were well worn, in fact somewhat scuffed, and had probably come from a charity shop. And there was no pretty umbrella in sight.

Bea took out a selection of clothing and handed it to Maggie, who was tenderly towelling the little girl down.

For a moment Bea allowed herself to stand still, doing nothing.

Then she realized that if she stopped doing something, she'd realize
how tired she was. She refused to give in to fatigue. There was
something else she had to do before she left.

There'd been a second 'Sorry!' message on the mirror in the
master bedroom, also in bright-red lipstick. She must have a photograph of that before she called it a day.

SIX

Friday morning

Bea woke at her usual time, felt unusually weary, stretched,
wondered why the house had an empty feel to it, and remembered what had happened. Said something uncomplimentary
about Benton, reached for her Bible to read a few verses, was startled
by the alarm going off, and forced herself out of bed.

She'd a feeling this was going to be another difficult day.

She dressed in haste, made a couple of magic passes at her
face with the minimum of make-up and tottered down to the
kitchen. Winston was already there, pacing the floor, impatient for
what would be his first breakfast of the day, since Maggie was at
Benton's.

And Dilys?

Her landline trilled. Leon. 'How are you?'

'Up. Just about. Any news?'

'Benton's back from the hospital. Dilys survived the night, but
it's still touch and go. He's in a foul mood. Tried to take it out on
your Maggie, who treated him to a mouthful in return. I like that
girl.'

Bea smiled. 'She's a great lass. Is Bernice . . .?'

'Woke screaming with a nightmare. One of the boys slept
through it, the other woke up and was furious with her. They
were neither of them at all concerned about their mother till they
realized she wasn't going to be able to cook them their favourite
breakfasts and organize getting them off to school. Bernice is a
different matter. Maggie can't move for the girl clinging to her
leg. I don't think she should go to school, but I'm packing the
boys off there with a note to their teacher. Benton's gone to bed

to catch up on his sleep, defying anyone to so much as whisper in his vicinity. I've told him he's on his own with the boys from now on but that I'll stick around till he's up and about again, when I'll go to a hotel.

'Maggie says she'll be with you in half an hour to collect her worksheets for the day, and that she's bringing Bernice with her. Says the girl can follow her around. I suppose it's better than letting her stay here in the house by herself. Her father certainly won't trouble himself to look after her. I'll see if Sybil will take the girl in for a few days.'

'You've got everything organized. Brilliant.'

'And you? What were you up to with your little phone last night?'

'Recording evidence. Did you know that Bernice's arms and legs are a mass of bruises?'

'What! You mean he's attacked his own daughter?'

'Looks like it. I don't see Dilys doing it, do you?'

A painful silence. Eventually he said, 'What do you propose to do with the evidence you've collected?'

'I suppose it depends whether Dilys lives or dies.'

'Yes.' Heavily. He disconnected.

Well, that was a good point. What did she intend to do with the photos she'd taken?

Breakfast. Good coffee to wake her up. The toaster had developed a mind of its own. It had put itself on Fast Forward and ejected bread at high speed when it was done. Bother!

Fridays were always busy, but she had a good staff and could leave the usual flood of enquiries to them. She checked what food she had in the freezer, found and dialled the mobile number of Detective Inspector Durrell. He answered with a grunt. Not in a good mood.

'Bea Abbot here. Do you fancy a home-cooked lunch?'

'I'm up to my eyes in—'

'Home-made soup; courgette and Stilton. Spaghetti Bolognese. An almond croissant and good coffee.'

'Bribery and corruption.'

'Twelve noon? You've got to eat at some point.'

'You have an ulterior motive, of course. I'm in the middle of—'

'Olives stuffed with garlic to start with.'

He sighed deeply and cut the connection. She retrieved the

ingredients for the promised lunch from the freezer and cupboard, put them where Winston couldn't get at them, and took her first cup of coffee downstairs to get a start on the day's work. First job: to print off the photos she'd taken the previous night.

She was soon immersed in her work.

Maggie arrived and called out, 'Hello!' Bernice was holding on to Maggie's sweater as if it were a lifebelt, which was probably what it felt like. Maggie whisked into her office, collected some paperwork and removed herself and Bernice.

Bea reflected that no harm would come to the child in Maggie's care, and it would take the older girl's mind off her upset with Zander.

Friday noon
'Half an hour, that's all I can spare.' He meant it, too. Of medium height and mixed race, Detective Inspector Durrell was devoted to his family, and he was a good friend to those he respected, which included Bea.

'You eat, I'll talk,' said Bea, putting olives and a bowl of hot soup in front of him.

'I'm not wasting your time. I know the police usually can't interfere until a crime has actually been committed. In this case I'd like you to be forearmed.'

'Crime?'

'Murder. She's still alive as of ten minutes ago when I checked at the hospital, but the prognosis is not good and the evidence I gathered last night will have been washed away by now.'

He grunted. Reached for some bread to go with the soup, while keeping an eye on the spaghetti she was popping in to some boiling water. 'As you say, until a crime is committed—'

'I know. Let me fill you in on the background.'

He ate, she talked. When he pushed his empty spaghetti plate away, she brought out her photographs. 'This is the bathroom. When we arrived, Leon was working on the girl. Then Maggie took over, helped by Dilys's daughter. Here is the message on the mirror. Note the bright colour.'

'Her writing?'

'Block capitals?' She shrugged. 'Perhaps. Here is the photo of the wine glass which we found on the edge of the bath, empty. I put it in a clean bag and brought it away with me.'

'You said "murder". I don't investigate suicides.'

'Bear with me. This is the picture I took of a similar message on the mirror in the master bedroom. The same bright red.'

'So, what's wrong with that? A suicide note, as plain as a pikestaff.'

'Dilys was a mouse, but she kept her house clean and tidy. She wouldn't scrawl on mirrors if she were thinking of suicide. She'd write a neat little note, put it in an envelope and address it to her husband, because she wouldn't want the children to see it.'

'So?' He reached for the almond croissant, keeping his eye on Bea the while.

'And she didn't have a bright-red lipstick.'

'What?' He nearly dropped the pastry.

'Here is a photograph of the dressing table. From my own observation of her, she wore very little make-up: a dab of crème powder, a trace of eyeshadow, badly applied, and a pale-pink lipstick. Her skin was slightly greasy, and she would never have bought an oily lipstick which would write so easily on a mirror. Here is a second photo, taken of the only lipstick on show – you see the make and name? It is, believe me, neither cherry red nor scarlet, but a pale-rose colour. Not terribly becoming, but that's by the way.'

He looked at the photos. Got out a magnifying glass and scrutinized the evidence. 'The red lipstick wasn't something she'd bought and discarded? Perhaps in a drawer?'

'After using it for a suicide message? I looked. No other lipstick. Lipsalve, yes. Colourless. She wouldn't have been seen dead in a lipstick of that colour. I'm sure she thinks it would brand her as a loose woman.'

He took a deep breath. Scowled at her. 'I really don't have the time to—'

'There's more. I took the liberty of opening their clothes closet. They've got a big, built-in one across one wall. It looks a bit odd in a Victorian villa, but that's not my affair. This is a picture of the contents. As you can see, his expensive clothes take up two thirds of the space. Her stuff is . . . Well, the term "charity shop" leaps to mind. When I first met her, she was wearing a black silk dress which she probably thought made her look sophisticated and in fact didn't suit her at all. That was there, and it was the only evening wear she possesses.'

'Which doesn't mean—'

'It means he spends money on himself, but not on her. Oh, and this is a photo of her jewellery, which she keeps in an old chocolate box in her top drawer. The "diamond" in her engagement ring is a zircon. There's a couple of dated pieces of costume jewellery which probably belonged to her mother, and a thin string of cultured pearls. Benton is reputed to be tired of her; he's got her to sign over her shares in the company to him. He's failed as a businessman and is about to lose his position in the firm unless he can bring in fresh capital. I suppose he could mortgage the house, but she'd have to agree to it.'

'Why wouldn't she agree?'

'She might. Or maybe he's mortgaged it already, in which case . . . I'm told he's looking to be rid of her. I know, I know! That's just gossip, but this isn't the first time she's had a near miss with death. She had a nasty accident with a defective toaster the other day.'

'You think he planned that as well?' He was not amused. 'What would he do with his children, if he got rid of her?'

A gesture of frustration. 'I don't honestly know. He does seem to value the boys, but the girl's arms and legs are a mass of bruises. She wouldn't let me photograph them because she said they were a secret. You could at least get someone to look into that.'

He was the doting father of a young family. 'Yes, I can alert the Child Protection Services. But that's about it. You don't really think he staged his wife's suicide attempt, do you? How, when he wasn't even in the house at the time?'

'I've been thinking about that. We don't know when he left the house but I don't think she was long under water or Leon wouldn't have been able to rescue her. Benton could have poured her out a drink with a sedative in it and told her to freshen up and take a bath because he was going out and the boys were playing games downstairs. She'd have done whatever he told her to do, got in the bath, drunk whatever it was he'd given her. He wrote on the mirrors and left the house, while she was still alive but sleepy. If it weren't for the lipstick being the wrong colour, I'd not be bothering you with this.'

He shook his head. 'You're overreacting. She might have wanted to make sure he'd see the message so went out and bought a bright lipstick especially for that purpose. No, no. It must have been an accident. For a start, she might well have gone to sleep in the bath but not slipped down into the water.'

'Agreed. Maybe he isn't aiming to kill her, but to stage a number of such incidents to give everyone the idea that she's unstable. Perhaps he's just gathering evidence for a divorce.'

'Come on! Without her, he'd have to pay someone to housekeep and look after the children. He'd be far worse off financially.'

'I know. I've been going round and round in my head, trying to work out what he stands to gain by all this, and why he invited Leon to stay when it's obviously not a suitable house for guests. I thought it was so that he'd have an impartial witness to his wife's mental frailty, but if so, that's backfired, since Leon saved her life.'

'Or perhaps –' a grin – 'allowing myself the liberty of using my imagination for once, perhaps he was setting Leon up for the role of murderer?'

'Oh, you.' She aimed a blow at him and missed. Laughing. Then she sobered. 'Do you really think that Benton might . . .? Oh, nonsense.'

He prepared to go. 'I can't act on what you've given me.'

'I know that. But if Dilys does die, then you will look into it, won't you? And chase up Social Services to do something about the child? Meanwhile, just in case, could you get someone to look up Benton's past? There's a rumour of a girlfriend whom he paid off with the diamond from his wife's engagement ring. They were married – let me see – in the summer, ten years ago. Apparently, the girlfriend was killed that October, in a hit and run accident in a quiet cul de sac, and no one's been prosecuted for it. I could bear to know more about that, couldn't you?'

'You're mad, you know that? Completely and utterly mad.'

'Yes, but you'll do it, won't you?'

He gathered all the photo printouts together, tapped them into a neat pile, and stowed them away in an inner pocket. 'I'll do something about the child, but women in these situations never turn on their abuser. You know very well that if she survives, she'll refuse to press charges against her husband.'

'And if she doesn't survive?'

He tapped his pocket. 'Then I'll take another look at the evidence. And you'd better hand over that wine glass while I'm here. What's the betting it contained whisky?'

'I'm not a betting woman. Oh, I did check by the way. There were no sleeping pills in the cabinet, but I didn't go through the rubbish to see if he'd discarded an empty packet somewhere.'

'You are a marvellous cook, Mrs Abbot, but you've given me indigestion.'

Once he'd gone Bea cleared away the remains of the lunch, thinking hard. So far Benton had been making all the running. What would his next step be, and how should she counteract it? She looked at her watch. She had an appointment with her solicitor at four. Should she cancel it?

Her mobile trilled. Leon.

'I stayed till Benton was up and about, but I'm off in a minute, checking into the Kensington Park Hotel. This call is by nature of a storm warning. He's seeking whom he can devour. There's talk of pictures illicitly taken and children being kidnapped. He's been on the phone for a while, don't know who to, but he looked pleased afterwards which gave me a bad feeling. He says he's got something to sort out and then he's coming over to visit you, with Max in tow. I told him that my sister had agreed to take Bernice in for a while. He couldn't have cared less. I've been told to deliver the child to Sybil in time for tea. I'll pick her up from you later, shall I?'

'Is Sybil staying at the same hotel as you?'

'No, she's out at the family mansion near Gerrards Cross. Posh place. Got its own guest wing, and a resident housekeeper who'll probably give notice when Sybil starts interfering with the domestic arrangements, which she is sure to do. As for Benton's boys – wait for it – he might well have been planning an "accident" with his wife, because his sister arrived half an hour ago and is moving in to look after him and them. He told me to give her my keys to the house. She's going to sleep in Bernice's room, apparently.'

'What about Bernice?'

'Surplus to requirements? Demoted to the lilo again?'

'Ugh. What's the sister like?'

'Very blonde. A man trap. She makes me shiver.'

'Dilys is not dead yet.'

'I don't think it matters. As far as he's concerned, Dilys is yesterday's news. "She's let him down," he says. In sorrow, blowing his nose. He says he's in deep grief for her but he has to think what's best for the boys. About Dilys, have you checked recently? I was going to go to the hospital, but this development—'

'I'll check in a minute.'

'You did take some pictures, didn't you? What did you do with them?'

'They're in a safe place.'

He disconnected.

Well, Benton had got everything planned, hadn't he? Moving his sister in to look after the boys. Well, that answered one of the questions that had been worrying Bea. And he was on his way to see her? So, what should she do now?

First thing: ring Maggie. 'How are you both doing?'

'We're fine. Bernice has been a great help to me this morning, haven't you, love? Holding the end of the tape, helping me measure up for a new kitchen at this kind lady's house. We're going to have some hot chocolate in a minute, and then we're going to go for a little walk in the park and decide where to have lunch. We'll be with you about two, I suppose. Is that all right?'

'Splendid. Leon's arranged for Sybil to look after Bernice for a while.'

Next. Ring the hospital. 'I'm enquiring after a woman who was brought in yesterday evening suffering from an accident in a bath. She's called Dilys . . .'

Transferred to another office.

Click, click. 'Who did you say you were asking for?'

Bea repeated the details.

A lilting, Asian voice, disapproving. 'She discharged herself against medical advice about an hour ago.'

'What? Did her husband . . .? No, wait a minute, he can't have . . .'

'Someone brought some clothes for her and took her away. She told us it had been arranged for her to receive treatment in a private clinic.' The phone disconnected.

Bea didn't know what to think. Had Benton's phone call, the one which Leon hadn't been able to overhear, been arranging for his wife to be whipped away so that she couldn't give her side of the story? 'Treatment in a private clinic?' That sounded ominous.

Another question. If Benton was short of money, how was he going to pay the bills at a private clinic? Had he been planning to send her somewhere for 'treatment' all along? Would Dilys emerge in one piece?

The phone rang. Sybil. A harsh voice, accustomed to being obeyed. 'Are you there, Mrs Abbot? Have you the slightest idea what's going on? I've just rung the hospital and they say my niece discharged herself even though they said she was still very poorly. I rang that skunk Benton and he denied all knowledge, but he would, wouldn't he? So I tried Leon but he's not answering his phone, probably realizing it's me. Do you know anything about this?'

'No, I don't. I find it very worrying.'

'So do I.' A pause. 'You think Benton's stashed her some-where?'

'It would seem so.'

'Would the police act if we reported—?'

'No, they wouldn't. She discharged herself.'

'She's a nitwit.'

'Agreed. But she's over eighteen, and we don't have any grounds for—'

'And you're no better.' Disconnect.

Ouch. Well, perhaps Sybil was right. Bea didn't think she'd handled things too well with Benton and Max so far.

It was time to take Carrie, her office manageress, into her confidence.

Friday afternoon
A long peal on the agency doorbell.

Bea's office door was thrown open, and violence entered the room.

Bea and Carrie looked up from the papers spread out on her desk. Bea's main computer had been removed for the time being but her laptop sat on a table nearby, showing a screen saver.

'Yes?' said Bea, taking off her reading glasses.

'You!' Benton advanced on her, pointing his finger at her. 'I'll have your guts for garters.'

'Could you keep your voice down, please?' said Bea. 'The child's worn out.' She indicated the settee, where Bernice was sleeping, covered by one of Bea's pashminas, thumb in mouth, fingers curled around nose, free hand clutching a tiny teddy bear.

Benton hoisted the manageress out of her chair with a hand under her elbow. 'You. Out.'

'Oh, really!' said Bea, managing to sound amused. 'Well, Carrie; as the gentleman's in such a hurry, perhaps we can finish this later. But, hold on a moment . . .' She picked up a file and handed it over. 'I must admit I'm concerned about this lad here, who's had hardly any work experience. Could you check for me? And you'll see that that package goes off? Good. And oh, I almost forgot, if the embassy calls back—'

Benton's colour rose. An unpleasant sight. 'Get the hell out before I—'

'Temper, temper,' said Bea. 'Please, keep your voice down.'

Carrie quirked an eyebrow at Bea and went out, shutting the door softly behind her.

Max hovered, making ineffectual calming movements with his hands. He said, 'Mother, this is serious! If what he says is true, you broke into his house last night—'

'No, dear. I was invited in by Leon Holland to try to save Dilys's life, which Benton hasn't yet thanked me for, though I suppose he will remember his manners at some point. Do sit down, Max. You're making the place look untidy.'

Max sat on the edge of a chair. 'You were caught illicitly taking photographs—'

'I thought it was important to retain the evidence of Dilys's state of mind. I've never seen a suicide note written on a mirror before.'

'What have you done with it?' Benton picked up the piles of paper on her desk – looking for what? Her mobile phone?

Bea frowned. 'Please don't disturb my papers, Benton. They're all in order at the moment.'

He swept the lot off the desk, snarling. 'Ah!' He pounced on her handbag, emptied the contents on her desk, picked out her mobile phone and threw it against the wall.

Bea recoiled. 'What are you doing! How dare you! You can't just force your way into people's offices and destroy their belongings.'

'There!' He stamped on the phone, once . . . twice . . . three times.

He wouldn't want to destroy the phone unless the evidence was incriminating. His sister's told him he got the lipstick wrong, and he wants to make sure I can't produce any evidence.

She half rose from her chair. 'Please, leave now! Or I'll call the police.'

He thrust his face at her, crowding her back in her chair towards the wall. 'Max says you transfer pictures from your phone to your computer. This it?' He hauled the laptop back on to her desk. 'Show me where you keep your pictures, woman! Now!'

'I'll do nothing of the kind. What on earth makes you think you can act like—'

'This does!' He thrust his fist into her jaw, once, twice. Lightly, but making sure she rocked in her chair each time.

Max shot out of his seat, twisting his hands together. 'No, Benton. You can't. You mustn't. Look, if it's so important, I'll find them for you . . .' In a fever, he pounced on Bea's laptop and set to work on it. 'Yes, here's her photo gallery . . . but . . .' He looked up at Benton. 'There's nothing recent.'

'What! Show me!' Benton swung the laptop round, to check. And straightened up. Slowly. 'She's put them somewhere else. Bitch! What have you done with them? Answer me!'

Bea stood up, slowly, trying not to shake. 'I told you to leave.'

'I said, "Answer me!"' He picked up the laptop and smashed it down on the corner of her desk.

Bernice yelped in her sleep and curled herself into an even smaller ball.

Bea said, 'I wish now that I *had* transferred all my recent pictures from my phone to the laptop. Pictures of my grandson and our last big party . . .' She allowed her eyes to fill with tears. 'I thought there was plenty of time and now . . . I'm sending you a bill for my phone and laptop, and I shall expect a cheque by return.'

He seized her wrist and drew her close. 'If I thought you were lying, I would . . .'

'Steady on!' Max was alarmed but not going to interfere.

Bea said, 'How dare you!'

He laughed in her face, released her with such violence that she fell back into her chair. He walked around the room, looked out on to the patio garden, adjusted his tie. Considered what he'd learned, decided he was not finished yet. He yanked the chair by the desk out and seated himself. 'Now let's get one or two things straight. You have no option but to play ball with me. Ask Max. He'll tell you. Holland and Butcher are going to take over your agency. Max is about to made a director, and so are you. You will take over my duties at the firm, and your office staff will run both companies. You and I are going to work so closely together in future that we will speak with one voice. All dealings with the press will be handled by me, or by Max. You will back Max's application for a loan, offering this house as collateral. Do you understand?'

'You must be mad!'

He grinned, revealing white, too white teeth. 'You've run out of time. Max has been too clever for you. He's let me have your client list and the contact details of several disgruntled employees and employers who will be only too glad to tell their stories to the press – unless you cooperate.'

'What?'

He ticked them off on his fingers. 'Two men allege sexual discrimination. I imagine they are gay, but that makes an even better story, doesn't it? Then there's the woman who says you refused to pay her for work done, and another who claims you supplied a cook who stole from her . . . Just imagine what that will do to your saintly image!'

'What?' she said again. She laughed in his face. 'Oh, really! Benton, those cases go back fifteen years, maybe more. And they concerned unreliable characters whom you could never produce in court.'

'If we circulate their details to your client list—'

'I'd sue the pants off you. Publish and be damned.'

He straightened up. Smiling. 'I'll leave Max to show you the error of your ways. But, before I go, I'm going to give you something to remember me by.'

He's going to hit me!

I could duck, but . . .

Max will surely not stand for—

He hit her, hard. First on one side of her jaw . . . she rocked back in her chair . . . and then the other.

He wiped his hands off, one against the other. 'Now we know where we stand, don't we? Max, you've let your mother go her own way too long. You need to teach her some of the basic facts of life.'

The door swung to behind him.

SEVEN

Bea put her hands to her face. Tenderly. Her cheeks were swelling.

Blood. A trickle down her cheek.

He'd been wearing a signet ring, had cut her.

Max hovered: panic, alarm and guilt fought for precedence. 'Mother, you should have listened to . . . Let me . . .'

He offered her a tissue from the box on the table. She struck his hand aside.

No one has ever hit me before.

Max said, 'Shall I get you some water?'

In a moment anger will replace Max's concern.

The child on the settee made a mewing noise. Bernice was awake. Had she witnessed the attack her father had made on Bea? He'd walked out and left her like a piece of unwanted luggage. Though perhaps it was just as well that he hadn't taken her with him, considering the treatment the child had received at his hand.

Bea hauled herself to her feet and made it to the settee. 'All right, little one? A bad dream, was it?'

The child looked terrified. She whispered something.

Bea bent closer.

'I've wet myself. Don't hit me!' She ducked her head under her arms.

Of course she'd wet herself, poor scrap.

Just as she'd anticipated, Max was moving into angry mode. 'Mother, we've got to talk, to straighten this out . . .'

Bea pulled the child into her arms. 'It's all right, my love. Maggie brought your suitcase with her, and we've got a change of clothes for you. And then—'

'Mother!'

'Get lost, Max.' She lifted the child up off the settee. Her cheeks were stiffening up. Blood was running down her neck.

His voice rose to a shout. 'You're not listening! I was only showing Benton how much I could help when he takes over the agency. It never occurred to me in a million years that he would raise a hand to you. He's out of his mind with worry, you see, and—'

'Max, this child needs first aid, and so do I. I would like you to leave before I say something I might regret.' She took a step towards the door, realized she wasn't going to make it while carrying the child, and fell back on to the settee. 'Bernice, do you think you could manage to walk by yourself? We've got a nice toilet here, and we can clean one another up. How does that sound?'

The child slid on to the floor. One hand still grasped the teddy bear. It looked new. Maybe Maggie had bought it for her? Bernice held out her hand to Bea, who took it.

Carrie appeared in the doorway. 'Is everything all right? Oh!' Seeing the devastation.

'Carrie, will you see Max out?'

'Mrs Abbot, your face!'

'It will heal. Come along, Bernice. Clean-up time. Did Maggie tell you that you're going to stay with your Auntie Sybil? She looks ancient but she really cares about you and your mummy.'

A bad idea to mention the child's mother.

'Mummy?' Again that look of dreadful anxiety.

'She's being properly looked after. I'm sure you can see her soon.' Crossing fingers and toes.

Max said, 'Mother, you're making a terrible mistake. I can't let you—'

'You have a choice to make, Max . . . between me and everything I represent, and Benton and what he represents. Until you've decided, I don't want to see you. Please leave your keys on my desk and go.'

She was in shock. Time expanded so that she saw Max leaving her in slow motion . . . and then it shot forward as she helped Bernice to her feet and rushed her towards the toilet, passing Carrie who was looking distressed and saying something Bea didn't catch.

The girl stripped off her wet clothes. Oh, the bruises on her thin arms and legs!

A rush of anger. Bea was shaking. She held on to the washbasin. Was she going to be sick?

Control yourself, Bea. She looked into the mirror and saw that there was a drying trickle of blood down her cheek and on to her neck. She hurt in various places. Were her own arms bruised where Benton had grasped them? She fought for control.

She put her head out of the door. 'Carrie?'

'I'm here. Do you need a stitch in your face?'

'A picture or two.'

Carrie kept her head. She produced Bea's smartphone, the one she'd hidden when expecting Benton, the one which had recorded what had happened to Dilys. Snap, snap. The damage to Bea's face was added to the rest of the evidence against Benton.

Bea knelt beside the child. 'I'm afraid your daddy's been hurting you, too. Will you let me take a photo of your bruises now?'

Bernice nodded.

Carrie muttered threats against Benton, more or less under her breath, as she took more photos.

Bea said, 'Don't worry, Carrie. He's not going to get away with it.' Brave words.

Bernice wept throughout, trying to stifle her tears, trying not to make a sound which might bring further punishment down upon her. Hanging on to her teddy bear.

Bea helped the child into clean, warm clothes. Not very nice clothes. T-shirt and jeans. Possibly her brother's hand-me-downs? They were all marginally too small for her.

Carrie took charge. 'Now you go and sit down in your office and let me attend to you, Mrs Abbot.' Bea went. Bernice climbed on to her lap and hid her face in Bea's shoulder as Carrie attended to their various cuts and bruises.

Two shadows entered the room. Bea's pulse went into overdrive.

Ah, not Benton. Thank God.

Her pulse slowed.

Leon, horrified. 'Bea, your face!'

Bea tried to laugh, pressing her hand to her wounded cheek. 'Well, Leon. You've just missed all the fun and games. And Sybil? Nice to see you again. Bernice, this is your Great Aunt Sybil.'

Bernice, terrified, clinging to Bea, wouldn't even look up.

Sybil held out her arms. 'Let me see you, child.'

Slowly, Bernice turned her head. One eye enquired who this stranger might be. Bea gently urged Bernice to turn round. 'It's all right, love. It's your great aunt.'

To her credit, Sybil didn't try to force the pace. 'Why, Bernice! You're the spitting image of what I was like as a child.'

Bernice was, almost, interested. Still clinging to Bea, she turned her head fully to inspect Sybil. Eye met eye. Exactly the same shape and colour of eyes. Interesting. Would Bernice develop into someone like Sybil if she had the good fortune to escape from her father's orbit?

'Auntie Sybil?' A mere whisper. Bernice was still hanging on to her little teddy bear, reluctant to leave the safety of Bea's lap.

'What a little poppet you are,' said Sybil. 'You're coming to stay with me and your great-uncle for a bit, till things calm down. But I can't take you home looking like Orphan Annie. Haven't you anything better to wear?'

Bea indicated the child's open suitcase. 'That's all she's got. You might like to inspect her bruises as well. Upper arms and legs. He was careful not to hit her where it might show.'

'What!' Sybil looked at Leon. 'I thought Benton was supposed to be fond of his children.'

Bea was grim. 'Of his boys, yes. But he says women have to be taught their place.'

She imagined Benton trying it on with Sybil. Now that would be interesting to watch.

Sybil blinked. She looked lost for a second or two, then made up her mind which way to jump. 'I've never had chick nor child. I never wanted them when I could have had them, but it looks as though I've been given a second chance. I suppose I might enjoy buying Bernice some new clothes.'

The child whispered, 'Mummy?'

'Your mummy's quite safe for the moment. We'll be able to visit her soon. Come.' Sybil tried to take child off Bea. For a moment, Bernice resisted, not sure who to trust.

Bea kissed Bernice and helped her to stand on her own two feet. 'It's all right, love. You'll be safe with your great aunt, and staying with her will be a great adventure. Here, take one of my cards. Give me a ring in the morning to let me know how you're getting on. Hold on a mo. I'll put Maggie's mobile number on as well. Oh, but I suppose . . . Have you got a mobile phone?'

The child shook her head.

Sybil said, 'Give me your card, Mrs Abbot. I'll make sure the child rings you in the morning.'

'And Maggie?' said Bernice.

'If you must.' Sybil led the child off, still clutching her teddy.

Bea tried to stand. Didn't make it.

Leon said, 'Put your feet up. Is someone getting you a cup of tea?'

Carrie said it was all organized and set about clearing up the mess, with many a tut-tut. One of the juniors brought Bea a cup of tea, strong, laced with sugar. She sipped. Her lip hurt. Her face hurt. Her arms hurt. She was in shock and not enjoying it.

'What happened?' said Leon. 'Surely Benton wasn't stupid enough to attack you? Couldn't you have stopped him?'

Bea closed her eyes. 'Benton was playing with a marked deck of cards. He thought he held the joker because he's got Max so twisted he doesn't know which way is up. Benton didn't realize I was playing with a marked deck, too.'

Carrie grinned. 'We arranged everything before he arrived. I took Mrs Abbot's smartphone and kept it in my drawer, and put an old mobile in its place in her handbag. Just in case. And he went for it. Then he thought she might have transferred her pictures to her computer and—'

'The pictures you took last night? Are they so damning?'

'Yes,' said Bea. 'They show the "suicide" was staged. Dilys doesn't own a bright-red lipstick, and my pictures prove it.'

Carrie produced a bowl of ice cubes and a clean tea towel. She put some cubes into the tea towel and handed it to Bea to put on her face.

'But . . .' Leon was bewildered. 'Whose lipstick was it?'

Bea gave him an old-fashioned look.

'Ah. You think his sister helped him to stage the "accident"? She has turned up at an opportune moment, hasn't she? Which means . . . I rather think I'm out of my depth here.'

'Ditto,' said Bea, holding the compress to her face. 'Ouch. Carrie and I rather thought he might try to get rid of any evidence I collected so not only did we swap the mobile phones but, just to be on the safe side, we also swapped my computer for a laptop we no longer use.'

'So the pictures are safe?'

'Of course,' said Carrie. She shot an enquiring glance at Bea, who closed her eyes. Bea didn't think there was any necessity to tell Leon about *all* the precautions she'd taken that afternoon. She trusted him to a certain extent, but not enough to tell him everything.

She didn't tell him, for instance, that not only had she given a set to the police, but she had also printed off a second set which had been posted off to her solicitor's that afternoon.

Carrie asked Leon to help her restore Bea's computer to its original position. He did so, casting concerned glances at Bea every now and then.

The junior came in with some aspirin. Nice girl. Practical. Bea couldn't remember her name for the moment, which was odd because she really did know it. 'Thank you.'

She began to shiver.

Reaction, of course.

Leon said, 'You need to rest.'

'I've an appointment I must keep at my solicitors.'

'Taking out an injunction against Benton?'

'That would be too good for him,' said Bea.

'And then have supper with me?'

Bea shook her head. 'Despite my brave words, I feel rather shaken. I think I'd better rest – and have a good think.'

Anger was good. It kept me going. Now I've stopped being angry and know fear. Benton knows all about fear, doesn't he? Once a woman's been hit and not reciprocated, when he approaches her again she remembers the pain and cringes. He only has to lift his hand, and she'll wilt.

As I am cringing at the thought of being hit again.

I am ashamed of my fear.

If I'd hit back, if I'd somehow managed to prevent his attack, I'd feel better now . . . or would I? He was so strong!

He thinks he's broken me, and maybe he's right.

He hasn't broken me through Max – though the damage he's done there is bad enough and I shall have to deal with that at some point – but through pain.

Only, I can't . . . No, I won't do as he asks.

Dear Lord above, help!

She closed her eyes for a moment, wanting to blank out the past hour.

Leon touched her hand. Concerned for her. 'Are you all right, Bea?'

She opened her eyes. 'Did I doze off?'

Benton may think he's boxed me into a corner, but there's a couple of escape routes he doesn't know about.

She got to her feet with an effort. 'Could you bear to drive me to my solicitor's? It's not far. I can get a cab back.'

'I'll get you a taxi. I didn't bring my car into London.'

'No, of course you didn't. It's terrible for parking. Carrie, can you lock up and see to everything?'

'Of course. Please, Mrs Abbot, look after yourself for a change.'

'And that special package did go off?'

'Of course it did. There,' said Carrie, looking around at the straightened office, 'all shipshape again. And I'll prepare an invoice for the damage Mr Benton has done.'

Two hours later

As Bea drew up in the taxi, she noticed that there were lights on in her living room though nobody had drawn the curtains. Downstairs, the agency rooms were dark, closed for the night.

Perhaps Maggie was back and preparing something nice for supper? No. Maggie liked to work in the kitchen and rarely bothered to put the lights on in the living room. And if she did, she would have drawn the curtains. Not Maggie, then.

Bea pulled herself up the steps to the front door. Let herself in. The alarm had been turned off. Through a half-open door she could hear voices in the living room. Music poured out of the kitchen. Maggie might be in the kitchen, yes. So who was in the living room? Ah. Two overcoats had been thrown across the chest in the hall. One was Max's navy blue, and the other was a cream-coloured cashmere and wool affair that could only be Leon's.

Only then did she spot a large backpack which had been dumped by the stairs. Brilliant. With any luck that might be the cavalry arriving.

As she slipped off her coat, she could hear Max talking, being persuasive, laughing, high on excitement. Telling the others that his future was bright, that the moon was made of green cheese and that he was just the man to import it into the UK and make a fortune.

Maggie appeared in the doorway to the kitchen, fidgeting, anxious. Music swelled out from behind her. She looked as if she were going to cry. 'Carrie told me; are you all right? And Bernice, the poor little sausage?'

'I'll be fine after a good night's sleep. Bernice is in her great aunt's care. She'll be safe there. She's going to give you a ring tomorrow.'

Maggie gulped. 'She was so brave, helping me all morning, loved the hot chocolate we were given at the client's place, then we had soup and sandwiches in the cafe near the park, and when I bought her that little teddy bear she nearly cried . . .' Sniff. 'Then all of a sudden she drooped, she was so tired, so much has happened, and she was so worried about her mother. Is her great aunt going to be good to her?'

'It might be the making of both of them. Provided Benton will let her go.'

'Him!' Maggie's teeth snapped as if she were taking a bite out of the man.

'Quite. Now I'd better deal with . . .'

Maggie said, 'Call me if you need me.'

Bea walked into the sitting room to see Leon sitting by himself on the settee, watching Max with narrowed eyes. Max was standing in front of the fireplace, gesticulating, in full flow. High as a kite. *On excitement, we trust, and not on alcohol.*

A third man, young, slender and darker-skinned, rose from his chair to put his arms around Bea, holding her with care but allowing her to see how distressed he was and how much he cared for her. Her protégée and sometime lodger; Oliver, the clever university student.

The cavalry had indeed arrived.

'Dear Oliver,' said Bea. 'What a lovely surprise. Home for the weekend?' She whispered in his ear, 'Did CJ ask you to come back?'

He said aloud, 'Yes, of course. I could do with a break.'

So Mr Cambridge, that grey mandarin, had alerted Oliver to the fact that Bea was in trouble, and summoned him home. Well, good.

She kissed Oliver's cheek and then, holding him away from her, said, 'Isn't that splendid! But Oliver, dear, I'm supposed to be having supper with CJ. Do you think you could ring and make my excuses? Ask him to come here for a potluck supper instead. Eight o'clock?'

Without a flicker of surprise, he went to do her bidding.

Max now held out his arms to her, too. 'And one more? Me, too? Now that everything's been sorted, and the future looks rosy. Phew!

I thought for a moment this afternoon that you were going to dig
in your toes and make life difficult for everyone, but now I know
you've been to the solicitors, well, all I can say is, "Let's
celebrate!"'

Bea smiled faintly. Did he really imagine she'd have left Oliver
and Maggie a pittance? Well, best keep quiet about dividing everything
equally between the three of them – for the time being, at any rate.

Leon uncrossed his legs, frowned as if he would speak, but
desisted.

*What game is Leon playing? I wish I knew. He sits on the
sidelines and yet . . . and yet he stirred himself to save Dilys's
life.*

She said, 'Who let you in, Max?'

'Why, Oliver did, of course. And then Leon came, wanting to
know if you were all right, which, as I told him, of course you are.'
He put his arm around her, hugged her tightly, pulling her off
balance. For a moment there she was off her feet. 'Silly Billy
Mummy!'

He'd never treated her so roughly before. But then, he hadn't
seen anyone manhandle her before, either. The taboo of not harming
a woman had been broken, and now he believed he could treat her
the same way.

Anger and shame coursed through her. Anger gave her energy.
Shame, that her son should treat her so . . .

She must be careful. She mustn't give the game away yet. *Dilys
is still alive, so far as we know, so the police won't act against
Benton. The Child Protection Agency might swing into action soon
on Bernice's account – or not.* All Bea had done was to buy time
to think about what to do next. However, she was not going to let
him get away with knocking her about, because next time he'd go
one step further, and then another. No way.

'A word.' She led Max out to the hall. Shut the door behind her.
Reached up and took his ear lobe in her fingers and twisted. 'I
thought I'd taught you to treat women with respect.'

Eyes watering, he tried to twist out of her grip. 'Ouch! Mother,
what . . .!'

She gave his ear one more twist and released him. 'Try to
imagine what Nicole would have done to you, if you'd treated her
that way.'

She opened the front door, picked up his overcoat and considered throwing it out on to the steps. It would give her great satisfaction to do so, but perhaps it was a somewhat childish way of getting her own back? She handed it to him with a smile. 'Take care. It's raining hard.'

'I'm seriously worried about you, Mother. If you can't take a joke!'

'Your pulling me around like that was no joke.'

'Oh, well. As long as you've been to the solicitor's.' He tried to retrieve his jaunty air. 'I must spread the good news.' He took out his smartphone and went down the steps, trying to maintain his dignity while struggling into his overcoat. 'Taxi!'

The first taxi that came along was occupied and went on by. Max waved at another, which was also occupied.

Bea continued to hold the door open, waiting for Leon, who had taken the hint and was donning his overcoat. He put his arm around her from behind. 'Are you all right? Can I help?'

'Keep your great niece safe.'

'Is that all? Am I not invited to join your council of war this evening?'

So he'd worked out that her impromptu supper party had a serious agenda? She shook her head. She didn't trust him enough.

'I'll ring you tomorrow.' He produced a large umbrella, unfurled it and walked out into the street to snag yet another taxi without waiting for Max . . . who was left damply gazing after him. Bea shut the door on the night to find Maggie and Oliver waiting for her.

'Bless you, my children,' she said, and let them take care of her.

Friday evening

Bea rested while Maggie threw something together for supper. They ate round the central unit in the kitchen, as soon as their guest arrived. Then, with coffee provided, they gathered in the living room to hear Bea's tale of woe.

CJ Cambridge took the high-backed chair, as of right. The grey man sat with immobile face and fingertips touching. A judge in mufti.

Oliver had his elbows on knees, his dark good looks a contrast to Maggie's pallor. The girl was still wearing an all black outfit, but had wound a bright-red bandanna around her short-cropped hair.

There were pink shadows under her eyes, but she was making an effort to put her own troubles behind her for the moment.

Bea gave them chapter and verse, emphasizing the difficult position she was in. 'So,' she said, winding up the tale, 'the police won't act because Dilys hasn't died – yet. Oh, I wish I knew where he'd put her! My imagination is working overtime, thinking she may be in some hell-hole of a private clinic, perhaps sectioned "for her own good".'

Maggie said, 'Well, she could do with a rest from that monster.'

'True. And I'm sure that, even if he's paying through the nose for her treatment, a reputable doctor would soon realize where the real trouble lies. Then the police may or may not take Bernice's bruises seriously. I hope they do, but it may take a while for them to act. In the meantime, Benton has turned his attention to me, supported by Max.'

Oliver was in shock. 'Max stood by and let that man hit you? I can hardly believe it.'

Bea produced a tired smile. Her face hurt and she felt worn out, but this had to be done, and done tonight. 'Let me tell you how I see things with Max. He's in a cleft stick. If he doesn't work his way into directorships in various private companies, he's not going to get invited on to the quango which handles such matters, and will remain a backbencher pure and simple. That might be enough for some. But Nicole doesn't want to remain the wife of a backbencher. She wants him to climb the ladder and take her with him. If he doesn't, I believe that she will discard him for a better prospect. If Nicole discards him, he loses not only his wife and child, but also the backing of his in-laws and therefore his safe seat in parliament. His political future and his marriage are in jeopardy and—'

CJ raised his hands to stop Bea. 'I know you've never liked your daughter-in-law but—'

'I've tried to like her,' said Bea. 'I've never said a word against her to Max. I've supported her in all sorts of ways, and of course I'm delighted that she's given me a grandson. But I've studied her over the years to find out what makes her tick. It's ambition, not for herself – as she is at least aware that she's no great brain – but for her place in the world. Her parents have money and have used it to further Max's career because that's what she wanted. If Max fails her, then I don't think she'd hesitate to look out for someone who would boost her further up the ladder, perhaps eventually acquire a title. She's a shallow, self-centred, grasping little—'

CJ said, 'She may be all of that, and I don't entirely disagree with you, but . . . evidence, Bea?'

'Oh. Well, no. Perhaps I did get carried away there, but . . . Look, I'm sure I'm right about this. Benton has been cultivating Max for months. He's been in and out of that household all the time, and I'm sorry to say that he's exactly the sort of man who'd appeal to Nicole.'

She lifted her hands in defeat, seeing the doubt on their faces. 'All right! I agree that's just supposition. I'll go to see her as soon as I can. She should be bringing little Pippin back down to London any day now that Parliament's sitting again.'

CJ said, in a mild tone, 'Guesses apart, you've heard Max say that he's worried about his future, and that Benton offers him a way out. I'll accept that as a working premise.'

Oliver still wasn't happy. 'But for him to let someone strike you!'

'He didn't like it,' said Bea. 'I could see he was stifling doubts about the course he'd chosen, but he couldn't see any alternative. Where Benton leads he's going to follow in the hope that it will work out all right. I understand where he's at, and I can't altogether condemn him for it.'

Oliver shook his head. 'That doesn't excuse his behaviour.'

'Oliver, if you were asked to do something a bit dicey but not illegal and told that if you didn't you'd lose whatever it is that makes life worth living for you, wouldn't you do it?'

He had to think about that. 'Ah. Well. Doesn't everyone have something they wouldn't want to lose? I don't like to think I'd cave in if I were threatened with being thrown out of university, but I might. I hope I wouldn't, but I might.'

CJ moved uneasily in his chair. 'I dare say we all have a private nightmare . . . There is no need to specify, but . . .' He raised his hands in a gesture of surrender. 'You are right, of course, Bea.'

Maggie started up out of her seat. 'I'm not sure I'd be able to cope with being beaten, time and again. I saw Bernice's bruises; some were yellow and some black. That child's been abused over a long period of time. If a man attacked me I hope I'd have enough courage to fight back, but . . . would I? Especially if he waited a while, and then came at me again. Consider his record. I've seen for myself that he's been hitting women. His wife, his daughter, and now Bea. He thinks it's the quickest way to getting what he wants. Oh, call me a coward if you like, but I've seen it happen to a school friend of mine. She was the outgoing sort, sporty but not academic, you know? I was one of her bridesmaids when she got married, great galumphing creature that I am, but she didn't mind. Then she stopped being a happy bunny. A few months after she got married she started walking into doors and tripping over steps. Or so she said.

'It was ages before I understood that he was beating her up whenever he got drunk. She said it was all her own fault for being clumsy. Then he said I was a bad influence on her and that she didn't want to see me any more. She committed suicide a week later. I've always blamed myself for not interfering, though what I could have done, I don't know. But I do know that a man can destroy a woman by using her as a punchbag, and so I have to be frank with you. I'm not sure I could stand up to being assaulted like that.'

Bea's voice cracked. 'Maggie, I think you are the bravest of us all, because you've had actual experience of what can happen in such a case. If you'd asked me this morning, I'd never have guessed how it would make me feel. At first I was angry, but now I have moments when I think of him threatening me and I want to give in and do whatever he asks, even though I know I'd despise myself if I did. I have to find a way to defeat the man, and for that I need you, all of you, to help me.'

Oliver put his arm round Maggie and gave her a hug. '"Imagination makes cowards of us all." That's Shakespeare. Real courage comes from outfacing the danger. I don't know how I'd react if I were being beaten up every day, either.'

CJ did not care for frivolity, and somehow his stillness got through to them and they all turned to him. 'So, Bea; you are in trouble. I might not have appreciated how much until Maggie explained exactly how Benton's assaults can work. No one here thinks either of you are cowards, and we realize you are in very real danger. What you haven't pointed out is that if you cave in, Maggie and Oliver will lose their home, and I, I must admit, would find this life less tolerable without your presence. But, before we go any further, may

I ask whether you consider the man Leon to be a potential ally or an enemy in this situation?'

EIGHT

Bea played for time. 'You were going to make some enquiries about him for me.'

A dismissive gesture. 'I could find nothing which would draw him to the attention of the police. He is a self-made man, who seems to have had a crisis when his partner died.' Clearly, CJ didn't approve of men who gave way to grief and indulged in crises. 'He was on a shortlist for consideration to stand for Parliament as a Liberal Democrat, but his move away from the south-west has probably put paid to that.'

Was CJ jealous of Leon? Well, now: there's a thought.

Bea said, 'No debts?'

'A blameless citizen, apparently.' CJ cracked his knuckles. 'What do *you* make of him, Bea?'

'Frankly, I don't know. From what he's told me of his background, I think he's long been estranged from his family and is taking a certain amount of pleasure – no, that's not the right word. Not pleasure exactly, but . . . satisfaction? – in watching his family's business disintegrate. He says he's refusing to help the family firm out of their difficulties, even though he seems to me to be more than capable of doing just that.'

She hesitated. 'This is just an impression . . . There's something going on at Holland Holdings which I don't understand. I can't think that Sybil would have flown over just because her dividend at H & B has been cut. There must be more to it than that. I'm wondering if they think Benton is involved in some big scam, something that would affect the whole organization and not just H & B. I can't see why Leon should have accepted an invitation to stay with the man, unless it was to study him.

'He's a man of lazy charm, and a liar. On the one hand he told me he has money in the bank from selling his business and his old home, that he's renting a service flat somewhere and is considering buying a flat in the Barbican for weekend use . . . but on the other hand, his house is still on the market and he told Benton he was an undischarged bankrupt. He didn't interfere when I was threatened, but he did save Dilys's life and he seems concerned about Bernice. Oh, I really don't know.'

'You don't trust him?'

'I'd trust him in some matters, perhaps. But not in others.'

Oliver recognized his cue. 'Let me find out what paper trails he's left in life.'

'Before you start,' said CJ, 'what evidence do we have that any crime has been committed? I don't mean hearsay. I mean evidence that will stand up in court.'

Bea said, 'I have some, though probably not enough. I have the photos I took on my smartphone, which I transferred to my computer, and printed out. I gave one set to my friend the detective inspector and sent another set through the post to my solicitor. I can print out another set for you whenever you wish. I believe these show that Dilys's "suicide" was nothing of the kind.

'Benton believes he's destroyed both my phone and my computer. He's mistaken. Come to think of it, I must look at the small print in my insurance details; perhaps I can recover the cost of both that way. I'm not going to hold my breath waiting for Benton to cough up for them. Oh, and another little precaution Carrie and I took before Benton's visit. We set up my little tape recorder and left it running throughout the interview.'

Oliver nodded. 'Satisfactory. So you've got evidence that he threatened and hit you?'

'Sort of. There's the sound of the slaps, but maybe that's not enough. He doesn't actually say, "I'm going to hit you!" Which is what we'd need if this came to court. And if it did, would Max back me up? To tell the truth, there was a moment when I could have ducked, or kicked him, deflected him in some way. A split second. The thought crossed my mind that if he did hit me, Max would see what Benton was really like. But it didn't work.'

Oliver was holding back anger. 'Max didn't intervene?'

'I don't think he likes himself very much at the moment, but no; he didn't intervene. I had hoped he would, but I have to come to terms with the fact that he didn't. It's distressing, but I can't just cut him out of my life. He's my son, and he's in trouble. I must try to save him from himself if I can.'

CJ's fingers twitched. A sign of impatience with lesser mortals.

'What precautions have you taken to safeguard your position, and what do you want us to do about it?'

Bea said, 'Nothing much. Just sign a few pieces of paper for me. Oh, and I'm a bit short of cash, so do you think you could turn out your pockets and see what you can lend me?'

Saturday morning

A restless night and a painful awakening. Her face felt raw, and she could hardly open one eye. She decided there was no point in trying to slap on make-up to disguise what had happened to her. It might even be possible to turn her bruises to her advantage?

She felt sluggish and unwilling to face the day, but she knew – or thought she knew – that there would be more pressure put upon her that morning and she must prepare herself to meet it. She picked up her Bible, found her reading glasses had dropped to the floor, couldn't be bothered to pick them up, hoped God would understand if she didn't spend time with him that morning and forced herself out of bed and into the shower.

Downstairs, she fed Winston, made a cafetière of coffee and poured some out for herself. She drank it black. Shuddered. Put in some sugar. Decided not to tussle with the toaster, but managed to deal with a bowl of cereal. It was a dark morning, cloudy but not cold. She could hear movement in the office below. The agency was doing so well that they now had to staff it on Saturdays, too. Bea wondered if she should go down there and help. Decided against it. Dawdled.

Maggie came downstairs, talking on her smartphone, dressed all in black but with a purple and yellow scarf wound around her throat. The purple matched her eyeshadow. It didn't look as if she'd slept well, either. Bea wondered whether or not to mention Maggie's problem with her faithful boyfriend and decided that this was not the moment to do so. Maggie was being bright enough as she talked to . . . whoever.

'But that's terrific. I can't wait to see them. Hold on a mo. Here's Mrs Abbot, who would like a word.' She mimed the name 'Bernice' and handed the phone over to Bea.

'Mrs Abbot?' A small voice, not at all sure that it was welcome.

Bea said, 'Bernice, my dear? How lovely to hear from you. How are you getting on?'

'Very well, thank you.' A well-brought-up poppet. 'I've just had breakfast in a huge kitchen and Maria said I could have whatever I like to eat but she offered me so many things it was difficult to choose so she chose Weetabix and scrambled eggs and toast for me. I'm going out with Aunt Sybil in a minute. She said she couldn't have me going around in my brothers' old clothes so she bought me a coat with a hood lined with soft fur and a skirt, which feels very odd because I've never worn a skirt before, and a top which is all fluffy and striped leggings to match. And I've got my own big room with a rocking horse in it that used to belong to my mummy, and Aunt Sybil says we can go to see her soon.'

'Ah,' said Bea, hoping that wasn't all wishful thinking.

'I must go now,' said the polite little voice. 'Aunt Sybil says I must wash my hands and brush my teeth and be ready to go out with her in five minutes, and she doesn't want me to keep her waiting.' Click. Off went the phone.

Bea handed Maggie back her mobile. 'How do you think she's doing?'

'She's a little soldier. She says it seems very quiet because the boys aren't around. I would have thought it would be a relief to her to be away from them for a while but I think she's a born worrier. She said a nice lady called Maria brought her up some hot milk when she went to bed and showed her how to work her very own telly, and read a book to her before she went to sleep last night. She says she's supposed to be seeing her mummy soon.'

'Yes, she told me that, too.'

They both frowned. Then Maggie gave a great sigh. She turned Bea towards the light and, without changing her tone, said, 'Your face looks awful. Does it hurt much? Have you tried arnica?'

'No, but I do have some somewhere. I've heard it helps. So, there's no real news of Dilys? I can't bear to think of her in a locked ward somewhere.'

Maggie poured herself a mug of coffee and drank it, standing. 'How about we kidnap Benton and threaten him with a hot iron to make him tell us where he's taken her?'

'Don't tempt me. You're working today?'

'I have a couple of appointments which I can cancel if you think I'd be of any use to you here.'

'No. You go. Max hasn't any keys to get in now, so I'll only receive visitors downstairs and can call on the staff for help if things get awkward.'

Maggie pinched in her lips. Bea had got hurt yesterday even though her staff had been within call. 'Well, you've got Oliver now. He was up till the small hours on his computer. Still asleep now, I think. Shall I hoick him out of bed for you?'

'No need.' Oliver appeared in an ancient T-shirt and jeans, bare-foot, yawning, his hair all over the place. 'Is there some coffee?' He dumped a sheaf of papers on the table. 'This is as far as I've got. Maggie, are you cooking breakfast?'

Maggie thumped him one. 'Cook your own. I'm off. Give me a ring if you need me.' She went out, slamming the front door behind her.

There was a lot of other noise going on somewhere. People shouting? Downstairs in the agency rooms? Oliver turned his head, listening.

Bea got out the frying pan. 'I must find my reading glasses. Do you want full English breakfast?'

'Brain food needed, definitely. What's going on downstairs? Can the girls cope?'

'Expect so.' Bea investigated the contents of the fridge. Did she fancy a cooked breakfast herself? No. Her tummy was too uncertain, fearing what would happen next.

She had recognized at least one of the voices. Max, arguing with Carrie.

Bea had had a stout door with a good lock installed across the bottom of the stairs leading from the agency rooms to the ground floor of the main house. Someone was pounding on that. Max?

Oliver said, 'Carrie has keys to that door?'

'She won't use them without phoning me first. What did you find out about Benton?' She started to fry some sausages.

Oliver poured himself a large glass of orange juice. 'I didn't get far with him before I got caught up with investigating the Holland dynasty.' He shoved the papers towards her. 'Prepare to be amazed. Old Man Holland is a multi-billionaire who likes to keep out of the limelight but has fingers in pies from India to Indianapolis. Once I'd worked out that Holland and Butcher was just one small company in a consortium, I had access to a lot more information through trade papers. So, the head office is in the country mansion, but . . . wait for it . . . his registered offices are in the Cayman Islands, which cuts his tax bill to almost nothing. You've never met him, have you?'

'I understood that he was a decrepit old man who couldn't be bothered with the detail of running his business any more and had installed a series of general managers to do it for him. I've only had contact with Mr Butcher – he was the managing director before Benton – and what a nasty piece of work he was! And then with Benton.'

'Mr Holland is a spider, running his various operations from his home. He's chair or president of each of his companies, here and overseas, but installs managers to do the nitty gritty and rarely appears in public. As far as I can see, he inherited the training college from an uncle, diversified first into a window-cleaning business, and then into the service industries. Finally, he made the move into information technology – that's where the Indian end of the business comes in – and after he started that, the world was his oyster. Holland Holdings are all over the globe, and his shares stand high in the marketplace.'

'Phew,' said Bea, adding bacon and tomatoes to the sausages. 'Why does he still bother with a piddling little organization like Holland and Butcher?'

'I suppose the business rates are less in the sticks than they would be in the city.'

'No, let me think. I'm sure there's another reason. Leon told me that his sister had moved in with her brother, who had a big house with a guest wing, out in the country. Sybil took Bernice there. Bernice told me she's now sleeping in a room which once belonged to her mother. What if this mansion were the original Holland family house? And, if it's that big, it might also be where they train the Holland and Butcher domestic staff?'

'Well, it is his main residence, apparently. Unlike most billionaires, he doesn't seem to have acquired houses in other parts of the globe. Having a school to train staff on the premises must be a convenient way to keep a big house going these days. I'll check.'

There was more banging from below and more raised voices.

Oliver said, 'Aren't you going to let Max in?'

'He can wait.'

The landline phone rang. Oliver picked it up. A furious babel of sound. Eventually, Oliver said, 'Calm down, please. If you want to see Mrs Abbot, well, I'm afraid she's not down yet. She had a bad night. We were in two minds about taking her to hospital but—'

More sound and fury.

Bea cut some tomatoes in half and added them to the bacon and sausages.

Oliver said, 'No, I'm not going to get her out of bed just when she's managed to fall asleep. Why don't you come back tomorrow when—'

Bea inhaled. The smell of bacon cooking was delicious. Perhaps she'd be able to manage a few bites herself. Now what about a tin of baked beans? And weren't there some mushrooms somewhere?

'No, Max!' said Oliver, with some force. 'I am not going to let you in. If you're so desperate to make amends for what your friend did to your mother yesterday, then I suggest you go out and buy her a bottle of champagne and some flowers, and bring them round in an hour or so's time. Oh, and some fruit. She's not able to eat properly, may have to go on slops for a few days, and we're rather worried about one of her teeth which is loose and that means a trip to the dentist and we're not sure—'

Max cut the call.

Bea cracked some eggs and added them to the mix. 'You do lie well.'

'Practice. Is all of that for me?'

Bea touched her swollen face. 'Most of it, I suppose.'

'He's got someone with him. Not Benton.'

'A loan shark, I expect. Could you do with some more coffee?'

'Why not? I'll get working on Benton's records afterwards.'

'I must phone my daughter-in-law. It's about time we had a heart to heart.'

Saturday, 11 a.m.

'Mother. You're feeling all right now, I trust?' Max laid a bunch of flowers on her desk. Not an impressive bunch, but one plucked from a bucket in the nearest newsagent's. He looked like a puppy who knows he's misbehaved but is hoping not to be punished for it. 'Benton is a bit of a joker, isn't he? Of course, he was kidding when he said he'd tell your customers about those little mishaps from the

past. I told him he should apologize, and I'm sure he will. That
makes you feel better, eh?'

She had decided not to sit at her desk this morning, but had
laid down on the settee with a pashmina over her legs. A small
table beside her held bottles of aspirin, arnica and a glass of water.
Also, her reading glasses. 'He went too far. As you can imagine,
I didn't sleep well.'

'I must say, you don't look too bad, do you? Er. This is Mr
Green, who has kindly . . . I mean, we came before but you . . .
Anyway, we went away and had a coffee and now we're back.'

Evidently.

Bea nodded to Mr Green. Jewish? Probably. Fattish, definitely.
Pleased with himself, yes. A toughie? Oh yes. 'Now, I am not
exactly one hundred per cent today, but as you've been so insistent
. . . to what do I owe the pleasure?'

Max looked at his watch. 'Fact is, bit of a rush. It will only
take a minute and I'll be out of your hair. It's all a question of
maximizing our opportunities, to take advantage of—'

Bea put her hand to her bruised cheek. 'I don't think I'm up
to discussing business today, Max. Perhaps some other time?'

'No, it has to be done now.'

'Why?'

'Well, because Benton won't wait, and if I let this opportunity
slip—'

'He's a nasty piece of work, Max. Don't have anything to do
with him.'

Silence. Max looked at Mr Green. 'You talk to her.'

Mr Green produced a thin smile. 'Mothers always want to do
their best for their children, don't they? Max tells me you have
always been so supportive. This is a wonderful opportunity
that will never come again, and I know you wouldn't wish him
to miss it.'

'Mother.' Max leaned over to speak in her ear. 'For God's sake,
sign. Otherwise I don't know what Benton might do next.'

Bea replied in her normal tones. 'Do you think he'll go as far
as trying to murder me? That wouldn't get him anywhere, Max.
Remember, I need to sign my new will before you benefit to any
extent.'

Max flushed. Mr Green looked thoughtful. Then he looked at
his watch and produced some papers from his briefcase. 'I fear

this delay . . . Running late. Mrs Abbot, I believe you are the sole owner of this desirable property, which is clear of mortgages or other—'

'Well, no. Not exactly.'

Max exploded. 'What? What do you mean? There's no mortgage on this property. You own it outright.'

'Well, yes. That's true. But houses like this need a lot of maintenance, and we've had to take on more staff which means the wages bill creeps up, and the insurance has almost doubled, so that although I'm sure I'll be able to meet the terms of the repayment, things are not exactly easy at the moment. So when one of my friends suggested that I take out a loan privately—'

Mr Green rapped out, 'What sort of loan?'

'Just to tide me over. I'm afraid the interest rate is rather high, but—'

Max was furious. 'You went to a loan shark? Mother, I can't believe this is happening.'

'What sort of loan?'

Bea tried to look guilty. 'I have to repay that before I can borrow any more money. I must say it was a boon at the time, but—'

Mr Green swept his papers back into his briefcase and stood. He made Bea a small bow, treated Max to a chilly stare and left the room.

Max put his head in his hands. 'Oh, Mother. What have you done?'

Bea wanted to put her arm around him and confess that the loan amounted to all the cash that CJ, Oliver and Maggie had had about them the previous evening, totalling fifty-two pounds and ninety-seven pence. Oliver had had to subsidize Maggie who had left her bag upstairs. And then they'd all signed a piece of paper which confirmed the loan to Bea, and that she'd have to repay it before taking on any other loans. Oliver had made photocopies for them all.

Her stomach twisted. Her baby boy was in trouble, and it was in her power to wave a magic wand and rescue him. She sighed. She couldn't afford to let him off the hook yet.

She said, 'Are you going to ask Benton to come round and put more pressure on me to help you out? Do you think he'll try to beat me up till I sell my jewellery or something?'

'No, no. Of course not. I didn't want him to . . . I never thought he'd actually . . .'

'He beats his wife and his little daughter. I've seen the bruises.'

'That's ridiculous. Of course he doesn't. You'll be making out he killed his first wife, too.'

What first wife?

Max flushed. 'Forget I said that. He wasn't married before. It was just a liaison. He told me all about it. She went crazy when he broke it off and threw herself under a bus or something.'

'Just as Dilys went crazy, took an overdose and tried to drown herself in the bath?'

'Exactly. Or, well, you know what I mean.'

'He's unlucky with his women. Do you know which clinic he's taken Dilys to?'

'What?' A blank stare. 'She's still in hospital, isn't she?'

So he didn't know.

She said, 'There's a word for men like him, Max. And it isn't a nice one. Forget him.'

'I can't. You don't realize—'

'You have a choice. The straight and narrow or the primrose path – though this particular primrose path seems to have been salted with personnel mines, so much so that I fear you're going to get badly hurt – or the straight and narrow, which means breaking with Benton.'

'You're a fine one to talk, taking out loans at an extortionate rate of interest? I'd thought better of you, I really had. And if that's all you're going to say, I'm off. There's more ways than one to get what I need.'

He banged out of her office, and she was left to reflect that it might have been better to give him the loan he wanted, rather than let him flounder around in loan-shark-infested waters. Had she done the right thing?

Her head ached. She took some more arnica and a painkiller, and then dozed for a while. She came fully awake, realizing there was something important that she had to do, that very moment, no messing about. So, what was it?

She groaned. Visiting her daughter-in-law was never a pleasure and could be a real drag. But it had to be done.

She didn't bother to put on a lot of make-up, but seized a winter coat, checked she had her smartphone in her handbag, called in at the local shops for some essential purchases, and hailed a taxi to take her down to a prestigious block of flats down by the Thames.

'Home' was not the word Bea would have applied to this chilly, ultra-modern flat, where the heating was never adequate and little Pippin was rarely allowed to play in the living room. Nicole liked to present herself as a doting mother, but that front was for the cameras. Bea had long suspected that in reality Nicole believed children should be seen and not heard.

Today a distracted Nicole answered the door with her fair hair rather messily loose around her shoulders. She looked as thin and elegant as usual, but also somewhat harassed. On seeing Bea, she said, 'Oh, it's you!' And, in a different tone, 'Pippin, I said NO!'

'Welcome back,' said Bea, ignoring the cold tone. 'I brought you some flowers to brighten the place up on your return. It must be so difficult living for half the year in London and half in the North.' She'd brought flowers which had already been arranged in a special container which included water. They were expensive. 'And a bottle of champagne to celebrate your return. Also –' bending down to receive a hug from the toddler who'd hurtled across the hall to clasp her legs when he heard her voice – 'a little something for my adorable grandson.'

'Oh. Yes. Kind of you. Do come in. I'm afraid Pippin's being very naughty at the moment, refusing to go down for his rest, and we're all at sixes and sevens, only returned last night, I haven't really unpacked yet and I can never find anything . . .'

'Can I help?' Bea picked Pippin up and cuddled him. He was warm and loving, so like his father at that age.

'And I found a long auburn hair on Max's jacket, so I know he's been playing away.'

Oh dear. Bea forced a smile. 'You know Max. A magnet for the babes, isn't he! Now you're back, you can protect him from them.'

Nicole took Bea's coat, hung it up, and caught sight of her mother-in-law's bruises for the first time. 'Whatever have you done to yourself?' A look of consciousness came over her face. Bea understood that Nicole had already been told what Benton had done to her.

'I walked into a door,' said Bea, carrying Pippin into the living room and seating herself with him on her lap. 'Yes, Pippin; this is for you.' She handed him a tissue-wrapped ball, which he proceeded to unpack with a crow of pleasure. Bea looked up at Nicole. 'Not a door, of course. Someone's fist. A man who thinks women ought to be taught their place. He hasn't tried it on you yet, has he?'

'What?' Nicole's eyes flickered this way and that. She was a bad liar. 'How dreadful. Who was it?'

Bea didn't reply.

Nicole coloured up. Yes, she'd known all right. 'Max said something about . . . But I said it was nonsense, of course. I mean, people don't go around hitting people unless . . .' She tried out a laugh. 'Did you trip and fall, or something?'

'No trip. No fall. He hit me, twice. He believes women need to understand that men always know best. Unfortunately, I didn't agree with him.' She softened her tone to talk to Pippin, who had managed to find his way through the paper to a colourful ball with a tinkling bell inside. 'There, now. If you roll it along the carpet, you can make music.'

Pippin squeaked with pleasure, clambered down to the floor and set the ball rolling. He scrambled after it, propelling it across the room. There was a bell of some sort inside. An irritating sound.

Bea said, 'Sorry about the noise, Nicole. It's going to drive you crazy.'

Nicole took an elasticated band from her wrist and tied her hair back. 'You must have said something appalling, done something to provoke him. I'm sure he must have been very sorry afterwards. That he'd hit you, I mean. I understand you refused to see sense.'

'I don't think he's at all sorry that he hit me. I rather think he'd like to do it again. He certainly hasn't made me any apology. Did he tell you what it is he wants me to do?'

'Well, yes. In general terms.' Nicole fidgeted. 'A merger is obviously in everybody's best interests. I really don't understand why you're being so obstinate.'

'Because I don't think I could work *with* him, never mind work *for* him. That's the beginning, middle and end of it, Nicole. I said "no" and he thinks he can beat me into submission.'

Tinkle, tinkle went the bell in the ball.

Nicole flushed. 'Now you're being ridiculous.'

Pippin retrieved the ball from under a chair and sat with it on his lap, rocking it to and fro and gurgling with pleasure. He loved his present. Bea winced. 'I really am sorry about that bell, Nicole. Perhaps you can put it out of action in some way?'

'He has lots of musical toys. I let him play with them as much as he likes, in his own room. It's time for his rest, anyway.' She scooped her son up. He roared with indignation but she carried him off to his bedroom, dumped him there, and shut the door on him. He beat on the door, once, twice . . . and then was quiet.

Nicole said, 'I don't see why you can't take his advice.'

'After being beaten up for the crime of disagreeing with him?'

'But if he knows best . . . I'm sure that was a momentary loss of control, and it will never happen again.'

'I suppose I should be glad that he hasn't started on you, yet. He's a serial abuser, you know. You should see his wife's bruises, and his little daughter's, too.'

'Nonsense.' But her eyes shifted to and fro.

'Did he tell you his wife had to be hospitalized a couple of days ago?'

'Yes, of course. She's mental, you know.'

'You don't know where he's put her now, do you?'

A blank look. Nicole didn't know.

Bea tried one last ploy. 'His sister appeared on the scene pretty promptly. I wonder how she's going to cope with his two boys. Have you met them yet?'

'He says they're both very advanced for their age and will do well in private schools.'

'They could certainly do with being taught some manners. Yes, a private school might well be the answer to that problem, but who's going to pay for it, I wonder? His wife has to clothe herself from the charity shop and the house could do with some money being spent on it. Granted, it's a pretty little place, but it's only got three bedrooms and there's no loft conversion.'

Nicole looked thoughtful. Worried, even. Was she imagining herself trying to fit into that household? Bea couldn't see Nicole settling for a small house with two galumphing boys. Bea got to her feet. 'You haven't had the pleasure of meeting the boys yet? I expect that'll happen soon.'

Nicole produced an artificial smile. 'Oh, really? Do you think so?' Playing for time.

'Lovely to have you back in London. You must let me know when I can have Pippin for the afternoon.'

They air-kissed. Bea left.

NINE

Bea got back to find Oliver working in *her* office, at *her* computer. Her first thought was to tell him to find himself a desk somewhere else, but she managed not to do so. After all, she'd asked him to help her, hadn't she?

By now the agency had closed down for the weekend, with all emergency phone calls diverted to a member of the staff. It was a dark January afternoon and Oliver had switched on the lights but not pulled the curtains across the window. He was surrounded by the remains of a takeaway meal and half-drunk cups of coffee. Why was it that some people couldn't clear up after themselves? Bea shed her coat, closed the curtains, cleared away cups, disposed of the remains of the meal.

Oliver didn't look up from the screen. 'What did you say Benton's last name was?'

She lowered herself on to the settee, easing off her shoes. She considered getting herself a hot drink, decided against it. 'Benton is his last name. His first name is Ben. Short for Benjamin, I assume.'

'Ben Benton. It has a certain ring to it. Right, here he is. I'm into Holland Holdings' website, sloppy work, they haven't deleted past newsflashes. The first mention of him is . . . yes . . . ten, no, eleven years ago in which he features as Salesman of the Year for the Holland car-hire firm with the slogan, "Contact me for all your needs on that special day." He's got handsome teeth, I must say. Next, he's given a shove up the ladder and appears as second-in-command at Holland and Butcher . . . they call it a "training college" and not a "school" by the way . . . followed almost immediately with an update featuring his extravagant wedding to Dilys. Marquee in the grounds, cast of a thousand, three bridesmaids in black, bride looking puffy-faced in white—'

'Is the training college in the same building as Mr Holland's mansion?'

He pressed keys. 'There's an aerial photograph of the site

here.' He turned the computer round so that she could see the impressive spread. The original house was mid-Victorian, an enormous white elephant of a place with extensive grounds running down in terraces to a lawn on which the first occupants had probably played croquet in the dim and distant. The lawn was sheltered by huge cypresses. Beyond that lay a shrubbery, and to one side was a walled kitchen garden complete with greenhouses.

'Extensive,' said Bea. 'How much do you think it costs to keep it going?'

'I suspect there's some kind of tax dodge going on here. Can you see that at the back of the house there's a courtyard? It presumably started off life as stables and housing for carriages and was later turned into garages for cars. Access to the courtyard from the outside world is through an electronic gate with a guard on duty, and beyond that there's a car park which contains . . . let's do a rough count . . . about forty places. I imagine the buildings in the courtyard are now offices and we're looking at the nerve centre of Holland Holdings. He is probably setting off the costs of the estate by claiming his house and grounds are all part of the offices.'

'Including the Holland and Butcher training college?'

'I think . . . No, that's in another building, some way off.' He moved the computerized picture around the site and enlarged it. They were now looking at a not particularly attractive thirty-year-old concrete and glass building, some four storeys high.

Oliver enlarged the picture again and roamed the site. 'Ah. Got it. If you come in by the main entrance, the road splits in two. The right-hand lane directs visitors to the Holland and Butcher Training College . . . see the sign for it? . . . while the left-hand lane leads visitors around the back of the main house to the courtyard and the offices of Holland Holdings. There's a serious alarm system on both buildings. The old man is well protected.'

Bea mused: 'I'm trying to think what it must have been like for a young girl like Dilys, fresh out of school, living in that isolated house. She may not have had much self-confidence to start with . . . No, scrap that. That's just surmise. She told me she used to help in the office at Holland and Butcher in the holidays. She didn't mention her father's larger organization. Perhaps the family didn't think her bright enough to go to university? Leon says they didn't think it worthwhile in his case. In the old days I suppose Dilys would have been sent off to take a shorthand and typing course, or to train as a nurse. She wouldn't have had enough brains to teach. But nowadays . . . what do they do with young girls nowadays? Turn them into receptionists and personal assistants? Anyway, the family found her a sort of non-job at Holland and Butcher. What did she do there? Filing? Taking phone calls? Running errands?'

Oliver chimed in. 'And there was the handsome, whitely smiling Benton—'

'Salesman of the Year, promoted to Assistant Manager. Taking notice of little Dilys—'

'Seizing the chance to make up to the boss's daughter—'

'Her father would not have been best pleased for her to make what in his eyes must have been a poor choice, even though he'd promoted Benton himself. Leon said the wedding was hurriedly arranged. I think Benton set out to get her pregnant. He's a chancer, and this was too good a chance to miss. The marriage was celebrated publicly, paid for by her father because he'd have hated it to be known that his daughter had been banged up by the first man who came along. The happy couple were bought a pretty little house in a prestigious area in Kensington, she was given shares in Holland and Butcher and a directorship. If she'd been a stronger character, this might have been the making of her as a businesswoman, but Benton kept her pregnant and sapped her confidence until she had no will left of her own.'

'So he got the job of manager because he'd married the boss's daughter?'

'Well, there was a bit of a hiatus. At one point I heard the firm had collapsed and a new buyer was in talks with Mr Holland, but what I think really happened is that he rescued the firm himself because it's so convenient for him to have his big house and gardens staffed by people trained in one of his own companies. So it wasn't only the fact that Dilys had married one of their own which caused him to appoint Benton as his new managing director. It must have seemed an obvious solution to his problems.'

'Benton has proved to be a disappointment?'

'He might have been the best salesman in the world, but he's no manager. He's been promoted beyond his capabilities. Not good with the staff. And, the dividends have been cut to the bone. Now, let's see if we can work out a timescale. Neither Mr Holland nor his sister would have approved any of his ventures running at a loss, so even though Benton was his blue-eyed boy, pressure must have been put on Benton to improve the trading figures . . . upon which Benton resuscitated the idea of a merger with the Abbot Agency, intending that I'd manage the college under his orders. Unfortunately for him, I took a look at their proposition and decided against it. Benton panicked. He couldn't afford to take "no" for an answer from me as his balance sheet was looking increasingly unhealthy and the old man was breathing down his neck. So Benton contacted Max and sold him the idea of a long and happy relationship with lots of money on the side. And Max bit.'

'But Bea didn't and doesn't.'

'And gets slapped for her pains. The question is: what will Benton do next? I'm surprised he hasn't been in touch today with another offer I can't refuse.'

'He sent Max, didn't he?'

'And I told him no dice. I'm worried about Max; he might do something stupid in an effort to satisfy Benton.'

Oliver turned back to the computer. 'How old is Benton?'

'Thirty-five-ish?'

'Mm.' Oliver worked the keys. 'I think I've got him, Basil Benton—'

'Basil?' Bea laughed. 'Really, Basil? No, it can't be him. His name is Benjamin.'

'There's no other Benton born in that year . . .' He scrolled up and down. 'Or in any other year around that time. Perhaps it's not him. According to this, he was born in October 1978, father a shipping clerk, mother a machinist. Humble beginnings in a tower block in the East End. Might that be him? The next census would . . . Yes, Basil appears again, same father and mother, still in the tower block, but . . . no sister. It can't be him.'

'I could understand why he might want to change his name from Basil. If it *is* him.'

Oliver grunted. 'Where's his little sister, then? I'll try the next

census. Yes, there's Basil. Still no sister. We're barking up the
wrong tree. Back to the beginning. Where are you, Benjamin
Benton?'

Bea reached for the phone. 'Hang on a minute while I make
a phone call. I'm concerned about Dilys, and I'm going to ask
Benton what he's done with her.'

'You don't really think he'd let you visit her, do you?'

'He might. But I'm thinking he might be getting just a wee
bit panicky about the way his plans have failed to work out, first
with me and then with Max. Perhaps a little push from me might
get him to make a mistake. Hello? Hello? . . . That's not Benton.
Ah, am I speaking to his sister?'

'Ginevra Benton, yes. Who is this?' A warm, breathy voice,
in a hurry. Noises off. Angry shouts from children in the background. The boys at play?

'Mrs Abbot speaking. Where can I contact him?'

'He's not here.' And then, half covering the receiver, she
shouted, 'Shut up, shut up, you little horrors!' to the boys.

'I'll try his mobile.'

The woman's voice sharpened. She sounded angry. With the
boys? Well, Bea wouldn't have liked to have been left in charge
of them, either. Ginevra said, 'You won't reach him that way.
He's left his mobile here by mistake.'

'Perhaps he's visiting his wife in hospital?'

'Just a minute . . .' The woman half covered the receiver with
her hand. Bea could hear her shouting to the boys at the other
end. Something about breaking their limbs if they didn't shut
up? Which didn't seem to be having the desired effect.

Bea raised her voice. 'Hello? Hello?'

A breathy: 'Yes. I'm here.'

'You probably don't know this, but I took some photographs
at the house on the night we found Dilys in the bath. The photos
show that Dilys did not try to commit suicide. Your brother tried
to destroy that evidence and failed.'

'What!' Alarmed. 'I don't know what you mean!'

'I tricked him into thinking he'd destroyed the evidence, but
he hadn't. If he doesn't produce Dilys alive and well by this
time tomorrow, I'll take what I've got to the police. Will you
please tell him that?'

'You wouldn't dare!'

'Try me.'

The phone went dead.

Oliver leaned back in his chair. Bea's office chair. Amused. 'There's nothing like putting your head in the tiger's mouth, is there?'

'Mm. I can't see him waylaying me with a knife, can you? But it's odd. That woman gave her name as "Ginevra Benton", as if "Benton" were her surname. You say the census doesn't show Basil as having a sister so, much as it would amuse me to think he was christened Basil, I do think we're on the wrong track there.'

Oliver worked the keys. He scrolled down and up, playing with the different sites, while Bea continued to frown at the phone.

At length Oliver leaned back and slapped the desk. 'I do not believe this. Benton as a family name crops up all over the place. There's quite a few of them. But I can't find a boy with the surname of Benton who has a sister named Ginevra. Are you sure she exists?'

'She's real enough. Leon met her, and I've just spoken to her on the phone. She's living in his house, using his landline phone in the living room, trying to keep the boys quiet. Where, oh where, has their fond papa gone?'

'He's at work, I suppose.' Oliver glared at the screen. 'Where are you, Ginevra Benton? Why can't I find your birth certificate? Are you older or younger than your brother? And if Benton's not the Basil from the tower block, why can't I find him, either?'

Bea got to her feet, moving stiffly. Yesterday's bruises were making a nuisance of themselves, and she needed to put her feet up and have a rest before she did anything else.

Besides which, she could hear Maggie coming down the stairs. A subdued Maggie, but one who was doing her best to sound bright and cheerful. 'Hello, oldies! How goes it?'

Oliver said, 'Enough, already. I'm switching off for the day. You don't object, do you, Mother Hen? Maggie and I are going out on the town, hitting all the high spots between here and Piccadilly—'

'Stupid!' Maggie aimed a blow at him and missed. 'A meal and a pint in a pub, that's all.'

Bea wondered if Oliver might have more luck pleading the case of Maggie's patient boyfriend than she had done herself.

Oliver vacated his chair. 'What about you, Mother Hen? Why don't you come with us?'

'Tell the truth, I could do with a spot of peace and quiet. A snack and early to bed for me.'

'You'll take care not to open the door to strangers?' Oliver was only half-joking.

'Teach your grandmother!'

'If you're not coming, may we borrow the car? Then we could go out to a quiet pub I know in the Denham area.'

'With my blessing, children.'

They tramped off up the stairs. Bea switched off the lights in her office and followed them, remembering to lock the door from the basement level as she did so. She heard the front door close behind the youngsters as she went into the kitchen to feed Winston and prepare a snack for herself. She was oh so tired.

The phone rang. Max, in a state. 'Mother, you are in? Good. I must see you. I'll be round in five minutes.'

'No, you don't. I'm going to bed early, not receiving tonight.'

'How can you joke when the sky's about to fall in on me?'

'Calm down. Tell me, in words of one syllable, what's so urgent—'

'Benton's threatening to . . . He's given me till tomorrow morning. You wouldn't understand, but—'

Panic crawled up and down her spine. 'You haven't been dallying with yet another blonde, have you? No, this time it's a redhead, isn't it? Take it from me, Nicole already knows.'

'What do you mean?' Blustering. Unconvincing. 'There was nothing in it, I swear, a couple of drinks . . . But Benton said that if Nicole had the evidence . . . She's been so difficult recently, you've no idea. I really don't understand why you can't do the right thing and help me out with—'

She crashed the phone down. She hadn't intended to. Her hand had acted without direction from her brain.

She was breathing hard. She wouldn't ring him back and apologize. Anyway, there was nothing to apologize for, was there? There was no way she was going to mortgage her future and the future of all those who depended upon her, by getting into debt for a man who was so stupid that he couldn't keep his trousers zipped up in the wrong company.

She. Would. Not. Do. It.

With shaking hands, she put some soup to heat up in the microwave and laid out the ingredients for a ham sandwich. And then the phone rang again. If it was Max . . .

It wasn't.

It was a high, breathy girlish voice that came and went. Bea had some difficulty in making out what she was saying. 'Oh, Mrs Abbot, it is you, isn't it? I've managed to get away, but I'm so afraid, and I don't know who to—'

'Dilys?'

'I thought, if I could only get to a phone box, and I did, but—'

'Where are you?'

'I'm not sure, because I ran and ran, and I got lost, but—'

'If you're in a phone box, there should be a place name on it somewhere.'

'Oh. Oh, yes; there is, but . . . I can't stay here, in the light, he might find me, but if I hide nearby, at the back of the pub, that would be all right, wouldn't it?'

'What's the name of the pub?'

'The Red something. I can't quite . . . It's on the corner but I can't . . . A bus passed me a moment ago, a double-decker. I would have got on it but I haven't any money.'

'What number bus?'

'It's gone round the corner.'

'Did you see where it was heading?'

'Bayswater Road, I think. Oh, I know I'm being stupid, but it's so bright in here, I feel as if I'm in a spotlight. You will come, won't you?'

The phone went dead. If only Bea hadn't let Oliver have the car! Well, it couldn't be helped. She ordered a taxi. No time to waste. She made sure the grilles over the downstairs windows were locked, the curtains drawn and the alarm set. She snatched up her coat and bag and ran down the steps into the street. As she went she entered the clues she'd been given on to her smartphone . . . A pub called Red something. A bus going down the Bayswater Road.

'Where to, missus?' A drizzly rain. A black cab with a black driver.

'Bayswater Road for a start. A friend of mine's in trouble, has run away from her abusive husband, wants me to fetch her, but hasn't given me much to go on.'

'Bayswater Road? Traffic's heavy tonight. Might take a while.'

'My friend said she's in a phone box opposite a pub called the Red something, not far from a double-decker bus route which goes down the Bayswater Road. Any ideas?'

'The Red Rum pub, named after a famous racehorse. You never go to the races? Hold on tight.' He made a U-turn in the road.

'Not really my scene.' She held on tightly, willing him to make good time. Unfortunately there was, as he'd warned her, a lot of traffic about. They moved a foot at time. Then two cars' worth. And then idled.

'Not a nice area, that,' he said. 'You sure about going there?'

She grimaced. 'Needs must. She sounded dead scared. Wouldn't wait in the phone box.'

'Lucky to find one that hasn't been vandalized.'

She nodded. They inched forward. She started to pray. *Dear Lord, keep her safe. Don't let him find her before I do. Let the traffic ease up . . .*

The traffic eased, and he shot along. Stopped at the next set of lights. The driver was doing his best. *Dear Lord, keep her safe.*

Across the Bayswater Road they went and turned off it, going north. A less prosperous area. Traffic lights winked red. Cars drew up in a queue.

He said, 'The road's blocked ahead. I know a back way.' The taxi twisted and turned through side streets. They said a London taxicab could turn on a sixpence. They probably could in the old days. Perhaps not now. But still, this man knew how to drive all right.

They moved into a quieter, darker area where the streets were not as wide. No trees in these streets. Multiple occupancy houses? The odd corner-shop and pub.

A flare of light as a pub came into view. Red Rum, named after the racehorse.

The driver drew in to the kerb. 'Not a good area for her to be waiting around in. You sure this is it?'

'There's the phone box.'

'No one in it.'

'She said she'd hide round the back of the pub.'

'Don't get out.' Click. He'd locked the doors so she couldn't get out even if she'd wanted to. He drove slowly round the block, looking for a woman who might be hiding in a doorway, or even behind a wheelie bin. No sign of Dilys. They ended up where they'd started, facing the pub.

'Perhaps she's moved down the street into a better hiding place?' said Bea.

'What I don't like,' he said, 'is those two big blokes on a motorbike behind us. Take a butcher's. All in black, with their visors down. A dark night like this, you can hardly see them. They was sitting right there when we first arrived, and they haven't moved. Your friend wouldn't be wearing that gear, would she?'

Bea took 'a butcher's', rhyming slang for taking a look. 'Butcher's hook' equals 'look'. Two large men on a powerful motorbike, anonymous heads turned towards them. Watching? Waiting?

She said, 'Dilys is a little bit of a thing. Those two are probably waiting for someone to come out of the pub.'

'By the pricking of me thumbs, something wicked this way comes. My old Mum used to say that. She also said it helps to have a good nose for trouble, and I reckon I'm smelling something rotten at this very moment. Don't you get out, missus.'

Bea hadn't the slightest intention of getting out. The presence of those two men was giving her a bad feeling, too. 'Do you think they've come after Dilys, too?'

'We'll go round the block again once more to be sure, shall we?'

He drove off slowly, and this time the motorbike also moved off, keeping a little way behind them. Turn left. Straight on. Another left turn. Another. And . . . back to the pub.

The bike idled its way to a stop in exactly the same place as before, about a car's length behind them.

No Dilys.

Bea's mouth was dry. 'You think they're waiting for me to get out of the cab?'

'That's a nice handbag you're carrying. A good watch and earrings, too.'

She clasped and unclasped her handbag. 'You really think they're only out to rob a passer-by?'

'No, I think you've upset someone, missus. This Dilys's husband, perhaps?'

'You don't think she's here, do you?'

He shrugged. 'We looked, didn't we?'

'You think this was a trap. I was to be lured here and . . . what? Beaten up?'

'The man on the back of the bike is holding something. Want to take a chance on it being a stick of Blackpool Rock?'

'Dilys really has gone missing though. Do you think we could go round the block just once more? Then if we see her, I could whip her into the cab before they could catch me.'

He set off again.

The motorbike followed, this time closing the gap between them.

Turn left.

The bike moved out and turned left, too. But now the two blank visored heads were turned towards the cab. The bike kept pace with the taxi.

Bea shrank back into her seat. She was annoyed to find that she was shaking.

Dear Lord, what do I do now?

Turn left again . . . and the cab driver put his foot down, leaving the bike far behind . . . for a short fifty yards.

The traffic lights ahead turned red.

The cab driver swore. 'Get their licence number, right?'

Bea peered at the bike. 'It's too dark to see it properly. I can't make it out.'

Had the licence plate been dirtied deliberately? If so, it meant that this attack had been planned.

Two helmeted head drew abreast of the cab. Idling.

Waiting.

One of the men shouted her name. 'Mrs Abbot!'

So they knew who was in the cab. It *had* been a trap.

The cab driver said, 'Your name Mrs Abbot?'

She nodded. 'Yes.'

A gauntleted fist struck the window at her side, but it did not break. She drew in her breath sharply.

A fist or a stick went *rat-a-tat-tat* on the cab roof.

The cab driver said, 'What the . . .!'

Bea's breath caught in her throat. 'Look, you can't risk your cab—!'

The lights changed, and they shot forward.

The bike kept pace with them. Every now and then the driver veered close, and the passenger banged on the window or the roof.

'Hang on, missus!'

He hung a left turn, and then a right. They made up a few seconds of time.

The bike skidded but righted itself and came roaring after them.

Bea fumbled in her bag. Where was her mobile? Why couldn't she find it? She had put her smartphone back in her handbag after Benton's departure, hadn't she? 'Do I ring the police?'

'Just hang on.' He ran a red light and got a volley of abuse from tooting horns. He skidded out from under a bus and turned right on to the main road. The road which they had left what seemed like hours ago.

Bea screwed round in her seat. Where was the bike?

Yes, it was still there, two cars back.

She said, 'If they know my name, they know where I live.'

'I said, hold on!'

Down a side road, through an alleyway and out into a wider street . . . and swish, into a car park beside a local police station.

The motorbike drew up at the entrance to the car park, idled for a moment while the two visored heads consulted, and then wheeled off and away with a final burst of speed.

Bea tried to relax. 'They've gone.'

The driver was on his mobile. 'Police? I'm sitting in your car park. Spot of trouble. Got a lady in my cab, been followed by two men on motorbike. Kept trying to beat their way into the cab. She's not getting out of my cab without an escort, right? Can you send someone down to . . .? Ta.' He clicked off his mobile. 'So who have you been annoying, Mrs Abbot?'

TEN

Bea was in the kitchen, cooking for a guest, when she heard the key turn in the lock and looked up to see Maggie and Oliver closing the front door and resetting the alarm.

'We're having a fry up,' said Bea, taking a six pack of eggs out of the cupboard. She was so on edge that she felt she'd shatter into small pieces if anyone touched her. She knew her hair was a mess, her lipstick non-existent and her eye make-up smudged, and she didn't care. 'Midnight feasts a speciality. Oliver, Maggie: meet my bodyguard, whose name is Lucas.'

The big black man tried to get to his feet, hampered by the fact that he was nursing Winston. 'I said I'd leave as soon as you two got back.'

'Not till you've been fed,' said Bea, breaking eggs into a bowl and giving them a whisk. 'Children: Lucas has just saved my life.'

Oliver slapped his forehead. 'You caught the tiger by his tail, and he didn't just roar defiance, but went for you?'

'Laid a trap. At least, I think so. I can't bear to think that Dilys might have been there all the time, and I didn't find her. Have you two eaten, because if not, I can always do a second omelette? I got a phone call just as I was about to have some supper . . . and by the way, Winston ate the last of the ham I'd laid out for a sandwich for myself, but that's the least of our worries. Anyway, this phone call was from someone with a high, girlish voice, saying she'd escaped and would I come and fetch her. I assumed it was Dilys.' She pointed her whisk at Lucas. 'You know what they say, never assume. But of course I did just that. Silly me. Catch the toast, will you, Oliver? The toaster's misbehaving. I really must get a new one.'

Oliver reached out and caught two pieces of toast as they shot up into the air. 'A trap?'

Bea said, 'Maggie, you're gawping. Take a seat while I finish cooking. Yes, it was a trap. Now, if you two hadn't gone off in the car, I suppose I'd have rushed to the spot indicated, for which sufficient clues had been given, in the backstreets up above Notting Hill, not a very nice area. Fortunately for me I took a taxi and Lucas is one of the most resourceful, bravest men I've met in a long time. They were waiting for us, you see. Two men on a motorbike. I think the passenger was Benton, though I can't be sure as they were both togged up in leathers and visors and gauntlets and boots. Quite scary, in a way. Yes, definitely scary.'

Maggie sat down with a flump. 'You're not easily scared.'

'This time I was. There was no sign of Dilys, and the men on the bike kept pace with us, calling my name, thumping the cab. Lucas tried to shake them off, couldn't, but fortunately he knew what to do. He drove straight to the nearest police station, and there the motorbike left us.'

She divided the omelette into two helpings, slid them on to plates, handed one to Lucas, and said, 'Set to, before it gets cold. Toast on the side. Butter over there, if you want it. Tea for both of us, or would you prefer a beer? I think we've got some, somewhere, and you're off duty now.'

'I'll get the beer,' said Oliver. 'You're not hurt?'

Maggie clutched at her head. 'They called your name? They knew who you were?'

Oliver uncapped a bottle of beer and poured the contents into a glass for Lucas. 'I ought to have realized you were putting yourself in danger. I ought never to have gone out and left you.'

'I've been well looked after,' said Bea, round a mouthful. 'Wow. I was hungry. Salt and pepper, Lucas? Yes, my dears. They knew. If I'd gone in my own car and stepped out of it to search for Dilys, I'd have been toast by now. Which reminds me, do help yourself to some more toast, Lucas. I like to see a man with a good appetite.'

Winston had been dumped on the floor when Lucas started to eat. Winston wasn't going to be left out if food were on the go, so he jumped back up on to the table.

Oliver removed the cat, despite his protests. 'What did the police say?'

'They didn't say much. They were ultra busy, with two Rapid Response vans full of football fans who'd been trying their best to kill one another, and we soon saw that we'd have to wait ages to be heard. Lucas got on his mobile and talked to his handler, or whoever it is who controls his time on the road. Lucas was due to finish his shift and was worried about the damage his cab might have sustained, which I said I'd pay for, and of course I've given him all the money I had in my purse and I've got his phone number. And I said, would he like to make a statement there and then, just for him and me if they were all so busy at the desk? And he did, writing it down at the back of my big diary, which luckily I had with me.

'Then I tried to ring my friend the inspector but of course he's off duty at this time of night so I left him a message. But we couldn't leave the station till we'd made our official complaint and that took for ever, because they were so busy. They did eventually get round to it, but said they thought it was just a couple of opportunists on the bike and that they hadn't really known my name but had called out any old thing to get me out of the cab, and had really been after my handbag and my earrings. And that pissed me off; sorry, children, I'm rather tired, but it did.

'They gave us a crime report number, which I think I've put in my handbag but maybe it's in my coat pocket, and when we came out Lucas was worried the bikers might have been waiting for us all that time, but fortunately they weren't. Although it was well past the end of his shift, he insisted on bringing me home and he didn't want to leave me alone, so I said had he eaten, and he said not . . . and here we are. Ice cream for afters? Cheese?'

Lucas wiped the last of the toast around his plate. 'I said, shall I ring round and get some of my friends organized to act as bodyguards, and Mrs Abbot said she didn't think she could feed the five thousand with what she'd got in the fridge, so here I am. But now you're back, I'll be on my way.'

Bea took both of his hands in hers and held them tightly. 'Thank you, a thousand times. Will you keep in touch? That sounds stupid, as you probably don't want ever to be reminded of . . . Sorry, I'm rather tired, not thinking straight. But you'll let me know if there's been any damage to the cab, or if you think of something—?'

'There was one thing. I told the police the make of the bike and though, as you said, the licence number had been dirtied so we couldn't read it properly, I think I got part of it. But I didn't write it down for you, so if you'll let me have a piece of paper, I'll do it now, before I forget. And let me know if you need me again as a bodyguard, any time. I'm not working tomorrow, for a start.'

'Thanks.' Oliver handed Lucas the board on which they left messages for one another, and he neatly wrote down the details and his telephone number.

Bea followed Oliver into the hall as he let Lucas out. She watched him scan the street for passing bikers, but clearly there were none. She double-checked that the alarm had been set and leaned against the wall. Maggie was clearing away the remains of their late supper. Winston jumped on to the table to get at the butter dish, only to be shooed off.

Maggie clashed plates into the dishwasher. 'That Benton! Does he really think he can frighten you into forgetting what he's done?'

'Oh yes, I should think so,' said Bea, not moving. 'He believes in fear. And he holds a number of good cards.' She wouldn't refer to the ace he'd just made Max play that evening. What did Benton have on Max? Photographs of him kissing some redhead? Blondes used to be Max's weakness, but this time it's a redhead. The idiot!

Suddenly, she felt her knees give way and had to stiffen them to remain upright. 'Sorry, folks. It's just beginning to hit me. Those two men following us . . .' She shuddered.

Maggie put her arm around Bea. 'Nothing can happen now we're back. Let's get you up to bed, shall we?'

Oliver said, blankly, 'If he called you by your name, he knows where you live. Maggie and I won't leave your side tomorrow, but what happens when I go back to Cambridge?'

Bea said, 'It's true. I'm exhausted. But once the inspector learns what's happened tonight, he can arrest Benton, and that will be the end of it.'

Maggie and Oliver exchanged frowns. Bea wondered what she'd said to worry them, but was too tired to enquire.

'Up to bed, sleepy head,' said Maggie, helping Bea along. Even when they'd got upstairs Maggie helped Bea to undress, despite her protest. 'Into the shower, and I'll fetch a nice hot drink for you, right?'

By the time Maggie returned, Bea was letting herself down on to the bed. And was weeping. 'Sorry, sorry. So stupid.'

'Not stupid at all.' Maggie pulled the duvet over Bea and sat beside her, stroking her hand.

'Nothing like this ever happened to me when my dear Hamilton was alive and all I had to worry about was keeping the agency afloat. Since he died it seems that I keep getting involved in other people's problems, which I never did before, not to mention . . .' No, she wouldn't mention Max's latest problem, not even to Maggie. 'It takes it out of me. Look at me, all of a tremble. If Benton could see me now!' She tried to laugh. Failed.

Maggie said, 'If you hadn't held out your hands to Oliver and to me, we'd have been lost, wouldn't we? Oliver would probably be sleeping rough, with no hope of ever getting to university. I'd have sunk into a decline, like those Victorian heroines who didn't know what else to do with their lives.'

Bea managed a faint smile at the idea of Maggie sinking into a decline. And yet, and yet . . . yes, Maggie might have well have got so ground down that she'd have lost her way.

Maggie nodded. 'What's more, I can think of half a dozen other people you've helped since you took me in, including Zander, who might have gone to prison and would definitely have lost his job if you hadn't stirred yourself to work out what had gone wrong where he works. One or two other people might have died if you hadn't gone out of your way to help them. You go the extra mile, and it makes a difference.' She sought for the right words. 'Look, I'm no regular churchgoer, but didn't you say once something about God not letting anything happen to you that he wouldn't give you the strength to cope with?'

'That's not what it feels like at the moment.' Tears slid down Bea's cheeks.

Maggie brushed them gently away. 'You think Dilys is dead, don't you?'

Bea nodded, too choked up to speak. Yes, she did think just that. Benton had whisked her out of the hospital and dumped her somewhere. She was an inconvenience to him nowadays, and he had his sister looking after the boys. If Dilys wasn't already dead, she would be very soon.

Maggie said, 'You saved Bernice. We'll ring her in the morning, shall we? Find out if they've given her a pony to ride yet.'

Bea tried to smile.

Maggie said, 'Sleep now,' and left her alone.

Bea closed her eyes and prayed. And, praying, fell asleep.

Sunday morning

Maggie woke Bea with a morning cup of tea.

Bea produced a smile and said she was fine, had had a good night's sleep.

She lied. She wasn't fine. She'd hardly slept at all. Her eyes wouldn't open properly. Her body felt sluggish. Her head felt muzzy. When she looked in the mirror she recoiled in disgust. Her bruises were all colours of the rainbow except blue.

Would careful make-up help to disguise her frailty?

It was too much trouble to take the trouble.

She dressed in casual clothes, put on her watch and then – in a gesture of defiance that she couldn't rationalize – decided to put on her most expensive earrings and to wear her diamond engagement ring. The jewels looked out of place when she was wearing a sweatshirt and jeans, but she didn't care.

When she got downstairs, she found Oliver already hard at work with his laptop on the kitchen table. Winston was sitting nearby, paws tucked beneath him, now and then waving his tail to indicate that he was still hopeful of being fed, or rather, of being fed again.

Maggie banged about the kitchen, making a large cafetière of coffee and baking croissants. For once she hadn't turned the radio or the television on, and the only sound was that of Oliver tickling the keys of his laptop.

'Morning,' he said, not raising his eyes from the screen. 'Having drawn a blank with Ginevra and Benton, I'm turning my attention to the mysterious Leon and his sister. Plenty of information there.'

Bea sank on to a stool and nodded. She hoped Oliver wasn't going to ask her to use her brain because she didn't think it was in good working order at the moment. And, what was she going to do about Max? If Benton really did have evidence of Max playing away then that would definitely be the end of his marriage. If . . . if . . .

How to stop Benton in his tracks?

Would it be right to pay Benton off, in order to save Max?

Was it ever right to pay blackmail . . .? Which was what this amounted to.

Maggie placed a cup of good black coffee in front of Bea and asked if she'd like a couple of boiled eggs and soldiers for breakfast.

Bea shuddered. 'No more eggs. A croissant would be lovely, though.'

Oliver swung round. 'Sybil Holland. Married three times, twice divorced, now a widow. All three of her husbands were million-aires – or billionaires. American. The last husband was Hiram T. something or other the Third, who specialized in Manhattan real estate. She is on the board of various important and socially acceptable charities such as the Metropolitan Museum. She collects Renaissance art. She must be worth as much as or perhaps even more than her elder brother. Has dual nationality, British and American. Has never had any children, so far as I can see. Homes in all the sort of places you'd expect, including a flat in Venice and a condo in Manhattan. I can't find that she has any property in the UK.'

Maggie said, 'Which explains why she's taken refuge with her brother.'

'Mm,' said Bea, closing her eyes as a signal that she wasn't exactly 'with it' at the moment.

Oliver was frowning at the screen. 'Sybil told you she'd returned to the UK because her dividends at H & B had been cut? With that background, why should she bother about the dividends from such a small organization as Holland and Butcher?'

Maggie said, wisely, 'It's looking after the pennies which makes people like her so wealthy.'

'Mm,' said Bea, not caring why. And then, 'That's a good point. Sybil's got into a right flap about H & B. Why? That company really is small beer to her. It crossed my mind earlier that there's something wrong, not just at H & B, but at Holland Holdings. Didn't I pick up a reference to some other trouble there . . .? Now that would bring her over in a hurry, and that would make them drag Leon in . . . and Leon, ignoring whatever it is that's wrong with Holland Holdings, has gone after Benton, which is why . . .'

She rubbed her forehead, wishing she could think straight.

'Leon.' Oliver returned to his laptop. 'That family has a talent for making money, don't they? He started small, dry-cleaners . . . took on a second . . . got some backing from somewhere, prob-ably a bank . . . ended up with ten, no, eleven shops. Bought the long leases of some luxury flats in a new development, rented them out . . . Looks like it was a good move. Diversified into hairdressing of all things, somewhere along the line. Four, no five of those. Sold the dry-cleaner's shops to a national chain recently, must have walked away with a packet. The beauticians – mm, I think he's still got those. Managers in each shop, I suppose.' More clicks.

Bea reached for her coffee. She wanted to say she couldn't care less about Leon and his businesses, but it was too much trouble to do so.

Oliver said, 'Picture of Leon's house here. Devon. Very smart. Gated entrance to drive, six beds en suite, swimming pool, cinema and so on and so forth. On the market for, yes . . .' He gave a whistle. 'Now that's a respectable amount.'

Maggie said, 'Where's he living now, then?'

Bea moved reluctant lips. 'Hotel, down the road here. He said he was renting a service flat somewhere and also that he's buying a flat in the Barbican.'

Oliver shrugged. 'Retiring from hands-on management? Going to live on his rents? Wonder what he's planning to do with his money?'

Bea said, 'He's told me he's refused to help Holland and Butcher out. He says the family has never been close, that they didn't give him a helping hand when he left school, that he made his fortune without them and has had minimum contact over the years. So, he says, why should he buy into an ailing business now?'

Oliver was still on the scent. 'Leon doesn't work the charity circuit like Sybil. Never married. One long-term partner. She had a strong face, handsome rather than beautiful. She part-owned and ran a string of beautician's shops until she died. I suppose that's the chain he invested in . . . Yes, it is. She died not so long ago. I wonder if she left her shares to him. I'll see if I can find her will.'

Bea groaned, putting her head in her hands. 'Why did I ever get mixed up with that lot? The Hollands were using me to fish Dilys out of that unpleasant man's hands, weren't they?' And now Max . . .

'You couldn't have stood by and watched while Benton killed his wife. And we don't know for sure that she's dead, yet.' Maggie produced her mobile. 'It's a bit early, but in a minute I'm going to ring Bernice, see how she's getting on. You'll feel better when you've spoken to her.'

'No,' said Bea, pushing herself to her feet. 'Enough is enough. I'm out for the day. Absent. Gone missing. Not to be found.'

Oliver abandoned his laptop. 'You're not going anywhere by yourself till Benton's been locked up. He's assaulted you once already and, now that you've threatened him, he'll be on the warpath again. He tried to get at you last night, and the attempt failed. He's not going to produce his wife, is he? So he's got to silence you before you can do him any more damage. Today is his last chance, right? So I'm coming with you.'

She felt stifled. If she didn't get right away and find a quiet place in which to think, she'd explode . . . and wouldn't that be a sight for sore eyes, never mind the mess it would make.

She tried to explain. 'I need to think. I need to be by myself for a while. Oh, don't worry, I'm going to be very careful where I go. I'm not going to take the car because it may be difficult to find parking where I'm going. I promise to take taxis everywhere, and I'll have my smartphone with me all the time in case I'm accosted by little green men from Mars or an assortment of drunks and psychopaths. First I'm going to church. I doubt very much that I'll be followed there. Then I'm going to take a taxi down to a pub at Isleworth and have a steak for lunch. After that, I'm going to pop across the river to Kew Gardens and saunter around there and sit and think, followed by tea across the road at the Maids of Honour. In the evening I'll take another taxi to the Waterman's cinema down by the river and will probably fall asleep, provided there's not too much gunfire on screen. After that I'm coming home and going to bed, and I don't need a minder for any of that.'

'I'm still coming with you,' said Oliver, shutting up his laptop. 'I can drive you, and then if you fall asleep it won't matter.'

'I'm coming, too,' said Maggie. 'With one of us on either side of you, you can fall asleep whenever you wish.'

'Thank you, but no. I mean it.'

Maggie and Oliver exchanged frowns. The front doorbell rang. Maggie went to answer it and returned carrying a splendiferous white orchid in a pot. Expensive. 'Leon. He wants to know if you'd like a drive out to Richmond Park, and then lunch.'

Bea shook her head. 'Don't let him in. Tell him I'm otherwise engaged.'

Maggie relayed the message and came back looking troubled.

'He said there's to be a family discussion about Dilys and Bernice, and they would greatly value your input.'

'That's their affair and not mine,' said Bea, feeling only a little guilty about it.

Maggie retailed the bad news to Leon and closed the front door on him with a click. She returned to the kitchen, getting out her smartphone. 'Tell you what, just to make sure you get a good start on the day, I'll ring Zander. You like the church he goes to, don't you? He can pick you up in a little while and take you there. Agreed?'

'Fine,' said Bea, yawning. 'That'll save me one taxi fare. And yes, children, I'll dress up warmly and make sure I've got my keys and my hankie with me before I leave the house.'

Oliver said, 'You'll need some more cash. You gave the taxi driver all yours last night, didn't you?'

'So I did. Well, Zander can drop me off at a cash machine before I go to church. And Oliver, if you have to get back to Cambridge before I return—'

'No, I don't plan to leave till tomorrow morning. So while you're out, I'll have another go at finding the elusive Bentons.'

Zander, Maggie's boyfriend, was an intelligent, almost-handsome man in his early thirties. Bea had known him for a long time and sincerely hoped that one day Maggie and he would marry and set up as a family. Now that Maggie had decided he was off limits, it was a puzzle to know what to talk to him about . . . and yet it was Maggie who'd asked him for help that morning, and he'd responded to her call. Which meant . . .? Bea couldn't work out what it meant.

As Zander helped her to do up her seat belt, Bea decided the safest thing to talk about was his work. 'How's everything at the office?'

Zander worked for a charity which had been sinking under the weight of free-lunching non-executive directors until Bea intervened. Subsequently, he'd been a major influence in improving the organization's efficiency and had been promoted.

A brief smile. 'I still enjoy it, which must say something about the new blood on the board of directors.'

'And about you.'

A wider smile. 'They seem to think I'm there to stay.' He was not going to talk about Maggie? Well, good. Probably.

He said, 'Maggie tells me you need a quiet day. Don't blame you. You need to take out some money first, then come to church with me? Sounds good.'

After a quick visit to a cash machine, Zander delivered her to the church he attended and saw her settled before going about his own duties. Even on a dark winter's morning, this particular building seemed full of light and air. Bea liked the atmosphere. Her own parish church was over-ornate for her taste and on a dark day could seem oppressive. She told herself such things shouldn't matter but acknowledged that, for her, they did. She told herself to relax. She wouldn't think about, well, anything, for a while, except worshipping God and being part of the congregation.

The sermon was a cracker, being all about gifts; the gifts the wise men took to the baby Jesus and the gifts that we ourselves have, which we can use in the service of others. Or not, as we choose. With a challenge to the congregation to think about what they have to offer, themselves.

'Well, I don't have that sort of gift to offer,' said Bea to herself, refusing to accept that the words also applied to her. She reminded God – as if he needed reminding – that she gave money to all sorts of worthwhile causes and, as Maggie had pointed out the previous night, she'd taken in two dysfunctional youngsters and helped them grow up. It had cost her something, but she'd done it. That was enough charity giving for the moment, wasn't it?

Zander offered to treat her to lunch. Bea was afraid he might want to talk about Maggie's attitude to marriage so she declined, but did accept a lift to a famous old inn down by the river, where she seemed to remember that Dickens had written one of his books. She wasn't sure which one, and in fact rather wondered if there was a pub within twenty miles which *couldn't* claim that Dickens Was Here.

Zander saw her settled at a table overlooking the river. It was low tide. Seagulls wheeled overhead, and the tide eddied around the odd beached houseboat as it fell. A splendid watercolour scene. Zander reminded her to call a taxi and not walk around on foot when she'd finished her meal. She nodded and thanked him for his care of her. The food was good, and she enjoyed a medium-rare steak. Every time she thought of Max, she turned her mind away. Not yet. Too painful. Too difficult.

Afterwards she hailed a passing taxi which took her on over the river to the main gates at Kew. A fine, bright day. Fortunately, she'd thought to wear good clumpy boots with thick soles and a padded coat which came down well over her knees. She'd even remembered to pull on a woolly hat, to wind a scarf round her neck, and to provide herself with gloves.

There was a good number of people taking advantage of the fine weather to wander around the gardens; earnest-looking women who knew the Latin names of everything, clumps of parents with small children running around, the odd walker striding out by themselves. Bea avoided them all. She didn't often go to Kew, but she remembered seeing a very tall slender tree in the middle of a wide expanse of grass. A loner like herself. There was something about that tree which echoed what had been happening to her.

The tree wasn't hard to find. It was stood all by itself, proud and tall. Stately. She found a bench on which to sit and study it. And at last she allowed her mind to skid back to the problem of Max.

ELEVEN

The arguments in her head went to and fro.

I know what you'd say about it, Lord. You'd say that it's never right to do wrong, even with the best of intentions. That may be so, in theory, but this is real life. Query: do I save Max's marriage and career at the price Benton demands of me?

Max is such an idiot! He doesn't deserve to . . . Well, actually, I think he deserves whatever he gets. No, I don't mean that. Or do I? Most people say they'd do anything to save their loved ones a moment's distress. They'd think I was being selfish to refuse.

But Max can't seem to resist . . .

Benton is not to be trusted. If I bail Max out now, Benton will soon be back asking for more. Successful blackmailers take just so much at a time, so that they can go on feeding on their prey. What would he demand of me next time? The agency? Yes, probably.

If Nicole has already decided to ditch Max, he's going to be the loser whether I meet Benton's terms or not. Which means that it would be doubly stupid to do as he asks. As I see it, whatever I decide, Max is going to lose his career and his marriage and everything that goes with it, including, I suppose, my grandson. I can't see any way out . . . Oh, my son, my son. I can't cope, and it's no good saying I can.

Listen to me, Lord. I'm a widow who's never really got over losing her husband. I'm in good health but I am in my mid-sixties and I have more than enough to do, keeping the agency afloat and looking after Maggie and Oliver. So why are you letting me in for this? I don't know how to help Max. I don't know how to combat psychopaths in biker gear. I know my limits.

I don't think you do know your limits. It may be painful, but stretch and grow.

That sounded like an exercise class. Ugh.

Consider the Leylandii. This particular specimen has been allowed to grow to its full height. Impressive, isn't it?

Look, Lord. My gift is for running the agency, for fitting round pegs into round holes. It is not for detecting and dealing with villains. I leave all that to Oliver, who has a flair for searching out information on the Internet.

He hasn't found Ginevra, has he?

And you think I can?

If you put your mind to it, yes.

The age-old question . . . Why me?

Silence.

She shivered. The temperature was dropping, and she felt chilled. She got up and took a turn round the tree. It was a splendid tree. It must be over thirty metres high, never been clipped.

Lord, it's true I've been in danger a couple of times, but it was all over quickly, before I had time to think. This business of watching and waiting for someone to come at me out of the blue, armed perhaps with a knife . . . Will he try again tonight, or tomorrow . . . or in a week's time?

She hung on her heel and looked about her. There was no one within a hundred metres. Some way off two small children were chasing one another around, the mother calling them back off the grass, the father bending over a pushchair containing a toddler.

No heavy-set bikers.

She smiled at herself. What, in Kew Gardens? Dearie me, not appropriate. If anyone had tried to approach her with evil intent, she'd have seen them coming. But, she had to admit that she was still afraid. Fear undermined her breathing.

I'm a coward. I hadn't realized it before, but I am. See how I've turned to jelly. I never thought I could be broken so easily, but I have been. And that's why I've got to opt out of this sort of thing. It's warping my judgement.

Feeling sorry for yourself, are you? I chose you in the womb. I know what you are capable of, even if you don't. The Leylandii tree grows fast. In a small garden where there are constraints on height, the tree is often cropped to a misshapen stub. In vain it tries to expand to the height it was meant to be. But where there are no constraints in the wider world, it grows to be a magnificent specimen.

I don't understand. I won't listen.

You do understand. But . . . the choice is yours.

Sunday, late afternoon

The shadows were deepening in the distance. Soon it would be time for the gardens to close for the night. Incredibly, she was hungry again.

She walked to the nearest gate, crossed the road, and made her way to the Maids of Honour restaurant. Lights shone in homely fashion from the small-paned windows. There wasn't a straight line in the place, but their teatime menu was out of this world. Only, they hadn't a table to spare and there was a queue of people waiting to be seated.

She stood outside for a while, thinking about that word, honour. A dry word. A word that didn't seem to have much meaning today. Honour. On our.

Wouldn't people laugh if she quoted 'honour' as a reason for doing something nowadays? Of course they would.

Courage was another word you didn't hear much about, either. It was expected of soldiers, of course. But not of middle-aged-to-elderly widows who thought they were going down with a cold. It was certainly chilly out tonight. She'd been sitting around on a damp bench in the park for far too long. She decided to forgo tea and take a taxi on to the Waterman's cinema.

There was a dearth of taxis, just when she needed one. There were a lot of buses, though. She decided to take one, rather than call up a minicab service and wait around twenty minutes or so for one to come.

Sitting in the bus, she thought about the many lives of the people who the Maids of Honour cafe must have seen pass before their windows. Some of the people who'd lived in the neighbourhood would have been stifled by the small-town lives they led, as the Leylandii trees were sometimes crippled into dwarfish shapes. Some of those who'd stepped over the threshold had been able to strike out into the bigger world, had grown to their full potential . . . and survived.

The question is, Mrs Abbot: are you prepared to risk a growth spurt, because you certainly aren't equipped to take on Benton at the moment?

She alighted at the cinema, took one look at the 'bang, bang, you're dead' film which was on offer and decided she couldn't face it. It had started to rain, and the only taxis which passed by were occupied. A lone biker drew up in the car park nearby, idling, waiting for someone.

A lone biker wouldn't be out to get her. Still, he made her feel uneasy.

A gust of wind and rain decided her to make a move, and she hopped on the next bus going north, trying to calculate where it would take her, where she would need to change, and what number bus she would then need to get back home.

She almost fell asleep, but roused herself to get off at the right stop and wait for a different bus which would take her past the end of her road. The rain had increased, and so had the traffic. Plenty of lone bikers about tonight, all looking exactly alike in the early dusk. She smiled to think how uneasy that one lone biker down by the river had made her feel.

An unoccupied taxi came along, and she flagged it down and gave her home address.

The house was dark and quiet. She dealt with the alarm, shed her coat and made for the kitchen. Oliver came in while she was feeding Winston his bedtime snack. Maggie followed soon after. Bea didn't feel like making small talk, so she said she'd had a lovely day and was off up to bed. As she climbed the stairs, she heard them conversing in low voices. Nice of them to keep the noise down when she was feeling so tired.

Monday morning
Shower and dress. The swelling on her face was going down nicely, and make-up helped to disguise her bruises. She told herself to pretend she knew what she was doing in destroying Max's future.

She reasoned with herself. Max had destroyed his own future.

True. But feelings didn't listen to reason, did they?

Maggie talked throughout breakfast on her phone. Today she was wearing full make-up. She had pink streaks in her hair, violet eye make-up, and a bright-orange cardigan, loosely belted over jeans. Gone was the dreary black she had been wearing. Perhaps she'd come to a better understanding with Zander overnight? If so, a cautious 'praise be' was in order.

Maggie shut off her phone. 'That was a call from a client who must be obeyed. Mrs A., promise me you won't leave the house while I'm gone? We can talk about yesterday when I'm back, which will be mid-morning. I've got paperwork up to here and stuff to run off.' She left with a kiss and an agitated, last-minute instruction to Bea to ring her if anything, but anything should happen!

What should happen, except the sky falling in? It looked like rain, anyway.

Breakfast. Avoid the exploding toaster. Must get another one.

Oliver, coming down the stairs after Maggie had left, said he'd get something to eat on the train as he was all packed up and ready to go. 'I did say I'd go back early today, but I'm worried about you. Will you contact that inspector friend of yours? I mean, Maggie did tell you what happened yesterday, didn't she?'

Had Maggie said something about yesterday? Bea couldn't think. She said, 'Don't worry, everything's under control.' As if she couldn't cope with minor problems such as ruining her son and fending off numerous baddies . . . which reminded her that if Oliver couldn't find Ginevra Benton, she'd better have a look herself.

As Oliver left the house, his last words were that Bea should ring him if anything, but anything at all, happened to worry her.

Alone in the house. Well, if you excepted Winston.

Feed cat. Clear away breakfast dishes. Make a shopping list. For the second time.

There were sounds of movement down below in the agency rooms. In a moment she must go down and pretend to be in charge.

The landline rang while she was picking up her handbag from

the sitting room, but stopped before she could get to it. Then her smartphone rang.

Max. 'You are going to help me out, aren't you?'

She sighed. Sat down on the nearest chair. Steeled herself. 'We have to talk.'

'Will you or won't you?'

'Not the way you want, no. But—'

She thought she heard a sob before he put the phone down.

She stared into space for a long time before, moving slowly and with heavy feet, she made her way down to the agency rooms, stitching on a smile. 'Morning, everyone. Morning, Carrie. Anything interesting in the mail this morning?'

Email. Not letter post. There wasn't much business done by letter nowadays.

She went into her office, booted up her computer. Her intercom buzzed.

Carrie, in the outer office. 'There's a policeman to see you.'

Inspector Durrell. Well, good. 'Send him in.'

It wasn't Inspector Durrell. It was a man she'd never seen before. Thickset, even fleshy, with the thickened nose of a drinker, and a streaming cold. He flashed his warrant card, blew his nose, asked her name, said he'd a few questions.

She was first puzzled, and then worried that this might be something cooked up by Benton to discredit Max. 'Of course, take a seat. Coffee? What did you say your name was?'

'Detective Inspector Robins.' Snuffle, snuffle. He shouldn't be out and about with that cold on him.

She pushed a box of tissues towards him across the desk. A social smile. 'Well, DI Robins, how can I help you?'

'You know a Mr Benton?'

She inclined her head. Wary. 'We've met. Discussed a business proposition.'

'It was a little more than that, wasn't it? Didn't you report an incident involving him on Saturday evening to the police?'

'Yes, I did.'

'In which you accused him of tailing you on a motorbike in menacing fashion?'

She frowned. 'Your sergeant asked if I knew of anyone who might have wanted to harm me, and I said I couldn't identify either of the men, but that one of them might have been Benton.'

'You two had had words?'

'You could call it that.'

'He assaulted you, I believe.'

'Slapped me. Yes. You can probably still see—'

'I can.' He caught a sneeze in his hankie. Sort of.
She winced.

He said, mopping up, 'That made you angry?'

'Of course. And, though I hate to admit it, scared.'

'Where were you yesterday?'

She felt herself lose colour, because she saw in an instant that she had no alibi for anything that might have happened the previous day. How unwise she'd been to refuse Maggie and Oliver's plans to stay with her! And what about their insistence that she contact them in case of trouble today? She smelled trouble with a capital T.

'Answer the question, please.'

'Is this where I ask for a solicitor?'

'If you wish we can continue this down at the station.'

'But . . . why? Whatever has happened? Why do you need to know what I did yesterday?'

'Mr Benton and his sons were found in his car in a country lay-by, late yesterday. Dead.'

Short of breath, she thrust back her chair. 'What?'

'So, I'm asking you again; where were you yesterday?'

'But . . . I can't believe it. Dead? And the boys, too? Oh no! That's terrible! What happened? A car crash?'

The inspector shook his head. 'I'm asking the questions here. So, where were you yesterday?'

She sank back into her chair. Benton dead? What did this mean for all concerned? What about Dilys? Where had he put her? Would they ever be able to find her again? 'What about his wife?'

The inspector trapped another sneeze in his handkerchief. 'She's in hospital, apparently. Keeps trying to commit suicide.'

'Yes, but where is she? What has he done with her? Oh, this is too much.'

The inspector was nothing if not dogged. 'We are informed that you threatened Mr Benton on Saturday and gave him some sort of deadline which he was unable to meet—'

'Humph!' Bea rolled her eyes. 'Well, yes. You could call it some sort of deadline, if you like. I sent him a message on the phone via his sister. I told him to produce his wife or I'd inform the police what he'd been up to.'

'A likely tale. I put it to you that you decided to revenge yourself on him for his behaviour. You broke into his house early yesterday, drugged the children and Mr Benton, put them in his car and drove out into the countryside where you left them to die.'

Bea put her hands to her head. 'That's so ridiculous that I can't even begin to—'

'You had stolen a spare key when you were at the house previously—'

'You mean when Leon Holland asked for help to rescue his niece from drowning?'

'And came prepared with sleeping tablets which you forced your three victims to take—'

'Me and who else? I can't believe this is happening.'

'Oh, you had accomplices, of course.'

'Really? I don't think I know anyone who would—'

'Leon Holland.'

'What! I've barely met the man. Why would he—'

'Money is the root of all evil. He's an undischarged bankrupt, isn't he? Do anything for a couple of thousand.'

'No, no. You've got it all wrong.'

'You also have two house guests or lodgers, who I'm told are completely under your thumb.'

Bea began to laugh.

The inspector was not amused. 'When you've recovered from your hysteria, suppose you tell me what you were doing yesterday. Unless, of course, you have no alibi to speak of.'

'No, I don't suppose I have. A friend collected me in his car after breakfast, I took some money from a cash machine, and we went to church. Then he—'

'Name, please? It wouldn't have been Leon Holland, by any chance?'

'No, it wouldn't. A friend of a friend. After church he dropped me off at a pub by the river where I had lunch, in a table by the window. The place was crowded but I think they'd remember me. I kept the receipt, I think.' She reached for her handbag to find it.

He stopped her, with a superior smile. 'Anyone can produce a receipt. You met your accomplice there?'

'Certainly not. I needed a quiet day. Then I called for a taxi. I suppose you'll be able to find whoever it was. The drivers keep records, don't they? He took me to the main entrance to Kew Gardens, the one off Kew Green, where I spent some time wandering around.'

'All by yourself?'

'Yes.'

'Do you make a habit of going to Kew Gardens at weekends? Are you, perhaps, a member?'

'No, but I needed to be quiet and to think.'

'It wasn't a very pleasant day for wandering around. It was cold, too. How long would you say you were there?'

'I don't know. About an hour, perhaps. I did get cold, yes; but I was well wrapped up. Then I tried to get into the Maids of Honour for tea, but they were fully booked, so I hopped on a bus to the Waterman's cinema, intending to catch a performance there. I didn't fancy what was showing, so I took another bus and then a taxi back home.'

'So from lunchtime onwards you have no one to vouch for you?'

'No.' She could see where this was leading. She had no alibi. 'But you don't seriously think that I . . . How did they die? Was it a car crash?'

'No.'

'Of all the people I've ever met, I'd have said he was the last one to take his own life.'

'That's what we've been told by his sister, too.'

'Oh, poor thing. She's only recently moved in with him, to look after the children. She must be devastated. But the person I'm most worried about is his wife. If she's as poorly as we thought, she might not be able to give a good account of herself, and if he's got her sectioned, and he's, well, not able to tell us where he's put her . . . she could be locked away for months . . . And that's if he hasn't actually done away with her. Oh, and his little daughter, and her grandfather! Have the Holland family been informed? There was supposed to be some sort of family conference yesterday, but . . . Someone has been in touch with them, haven't they?'

'I believe someone has gone to break the news to the Holland family. In the meantime, Mrs Abbot, I must ask you to accompany me down to the station for further questioning.'

She stared at him and through him. She could see the trap she'd walked into and sensed that someone had set her up. But with Benton dead, who could have masterminded such an intricate plan?

'Do you mind if I speak to Inspector Durrell first? I gave him all the background information on this case last Friday.'

'It's my case, Mrs Abbot.'

'Not if he's been working on it already. Which I asked him to do.'

He hesitated, and she drew the phone to her and pressed digits. Bother. Inspector Durrell was not picking up. She left a message for him to ring her, urgently.

DI Robins smiled, thinly. 'If you'd like to fetch a coat? It's chilly out.' He got out his hankie to sneeze into it, held his breath with closed eyes. Relaxed. And then it came, a monstrous sneeze. All over the place.

Bea recoiled.

The inspector muttered something which she could take as an apology or not. He fished a couple of tissues from Bea's box and mopped up.

Bea shuddered. She couldn't possibly get into a car with this man, who was shedding his germs all over the place. And for what? She was innocent.

She thought of defying him. She wondered what would happen if she did. Would he call for reinforcements to pick her up and carry her through the office and up the stairs into the street, and cram her into the back of a police car? How undignified.

A stir in the outer office, and Maggie came rushing in, out of breath. She slammed her tote bag on to Bea's desk and stood, arms akimbo, looking down on the policeman. Maggie in full fig was quite a sight.

The inspector blinked. 'Who are you?'

'I'm Maggie. Mrs Abbot's lodger. What's that nasty little toad been up to now?'

'Who?'

Bea said, 'You've got the wrong end of the stick, Maggie. It appears that Benton's dead. With his boys. In a car, somewhere in the country.'

Maggie took a step back. 'What? What the—'

'Yes, it takes some getting used to the idea. The inspector here thinks I broke into Benton's house, drugged and abducted him and the boys, drove them out into the country in his car, and left them there to die. Have I got that right, Inspector?'

'With an accomplice,' he said, eyeing Maggie's substantial form with interest. 'Do you have an alibi for yesterday, Ms Maggie?'

'Do I!' A short, sharp laugh. Maggie drew up a chair, sat, put her elbows on her knees and pointed a forefinger at the inspector. 'You listen to me, and you listen good. That slimy toad Benton thinks – no, if he's dead I ought to say "he thought" – that knocking women about was the right way to get what he wanted. You should have seen the state his poor wife was in when we fished her out of the bath! And the bruises on his daughter's arms and legs. Then his wife conveniently disappears from the hospital and no one knows where he's put her. He is a nasty piece of work, full stop. I mean, *was* a nasty piece of work.

'You heard what happened on Saturday night? Mrs A. told him to produce his wife or else, so what did he do? He lured her out of the house and, with an accomplice, followed her around on a bike, yelling her name and banging on the taxi in which she was travelling, putting the frighteners on her good and proper—'

The inspector tried to interrupt, but Maggie rolled right over him.

'So yesterday, Oliver and I thought we'd better take precautions in case he tried anything else. Oliver is Mrs A's adopted son. Sort of. And he was here for the weekend. Anyway, Mrs A. was desperate for a bit of peace and quiet so we – that's Oliver and Zander and Lucas and I – decided to act as her guardian angels for the day.'

'Ah,' said Bea, understanding at last. 'The lone biker. The little family at Kew.'

TWELVE

'Explain! Who are all these people? Zander? Lucas?' The inspector looked from one to the other. His eyes were watering, and he reached for another wodge of tissues. They waited while he sneezed and mopped up.

Maggie didn't want his germs either, thank you. She shoved her chair back a bit. 'They're friends. We, that is Oliver and I, thought that if anyone was out to get Mrs Abbot, they'd have to start from here. She was in such a tizz that she wasn't taking care to look both ways before crossing the road, never mind watching out for baddies, so I went upstairs when she left the house and watched her until Zander – that's my sort-of boyfriend – picked her up after breakfast in his car. As they drove off, I saw a lone biker peel away from the curb and follow them. The number plate wasn't easy to make out because it had been splashed with mud – if the police had caught him, he'd have been in for a fine – but I thought I'd got it, and as it turned out, I had.'

The inspector produced a painful smile. 'A perfectly ordinary man on a bike?'

'It might have been, but it wasn't. Zander rang me as soon as he got Mrs Abbot settled in church, and I gave him what I thought was the registration number of the bike, though I wasn't sure whether it was a five or a three in the middle. He went out to have a look and rang me back to say that a bike bearing that number – with a three, not a five – was parked outside. Zander said the biker hadn't come into church but was sitting there, watching people go in and out. So we knew someone was on her tail again. At that point I told Oliver, and he swung into action.'

'Oliver? Zander?'

Bea explained to the inspector, 'Oliver and Maggie both live here with me. Oliver's at university but was home for the weekend.'

Maggie said, 'Oliver contacted Lucas . . .'

'Who's Lucas?' The inspector was not following this very well.

'He's the taxi driver who'd saved Mrs Abbot's life the night before when his taxi had been followed and attacked. Check with your local police station as they have a report on what happened and took his details then. Anyway, he'd told us he wasn't working on Sunday, and when Oliver rang him, he agreed to help. To start with, we all exchanged mobile phone numbers so we'd be able to keep in contact with one another. We knew Mrs A. was planning to eat at a pub down by the river, so Oliver and I took her car and drove down there, parked in a side street and waited for Zander to arrive and take her inside. And, sure enough, they'd been followed by a biker with a familiar registration. He parked nearby and settled down to wait. We assumed he was going to keep on following her until he found her alone and defenceless.'

'Description?'

'We took photos on our mobiles – which you can have – but he never removed his helmet. A man, broad-shouldered, tall, about six foot, with hefty thighs. Wearing black leathers, the usual. The bike hadn't been personalized, which would have helped us to keep an eye on him, but there was a wing mirror on the roadside which looked as if it had taken a swipe. It wasn't correctly aligned, and he kept fiddling with it. You may find that helpful if you can track him down. Anyway, after a few minutes of waiting outside the pub, the biker got on the phone to someone, probably reporting his movements to date. We weren't close enough to hear what he said. We thought he must be phoning Benton. What time did the man die?'

'We can't be certain yet.'

'Oh, well.' She shrugged.

Bea held up her hand. 'I'm trying to remember what the biker who was chasing the taxi looked like. He sounds exactly like the person you described, above average height and weight. And yes, thick thighs. I think Benton was his passenger, as he had a slighter build.'

Maggie was all impatience. 'Let me tell you what happened next. While we were waiting for Mrs Abbot to finish her meal, we alerted Lucas to what was happening, and he set off for Kew in his own car with his wife and children. Meanwhile, Oliver got us three some takeaway food and we sat in Zander's car watching the biker, who was watching Mrs Abbot, who was sitting in the window above him, quite oblivious to his presence. As soon as she left the pub the biker started towards her. Fortunately, a taxi came along and she got into it without seeing him. Zander and I shadowed her taxi at a distance, while Oliver hared back to fetch Mrs A's car and follow on. The biker caught us up and cut in behind Mrs A's taxi, which dropped her off at the main entrance to the Gardens. Lucas and his family were waiting by the gates and followed her in. She was so bound up in her own thoughts, she didn't even notice them. Lucas loved the idea of taking the children to Kew while he kept an eye on Mrs Abbot because they'd never been there before. We said we'd pay their entrance fees, Mrs A. Hope that's all right.'

'Definitely,' said Bea, trying to keep up.

Maggie continued, 'There's not much parking on Kew Green, so Oliver and Zander went off to find a space while I got out to keep an eye on the biker, keeping in touch with Zander by phone all the time. And he with Oliver.'

The inspector pointed out, 'Someone must have had two phones.'

'Zander does,' said Maggie. 'One for work and one for play. The biker drew up outside the main gates but couldn't find anywhere to park, either. We could both see Mrs Abbot walking off into the distance, followed by Lucas and his family. The biker was stuck; he didn't want to leave his bike where there was no parking, and he couldn't take it down to the car park, or he'd be out of sight of the main gate and wouldn't see Mrs Abbot when she came out. He made another phone call, waving his arms around, not at all happy—' Maggie broke off to wonder, 'Who was he phoning for instructions if it wasn't Benton?'

The inspector shrugged, sneezed, blew his nose. 'How should I doh?' His voice was thick with phlegm.

Maggie frowned. 'Well, I expect it was Benton, before he met his sticky end, hurray. Anyway, we did wonder at that point if the biker might give up and go away, but he didn't. He took his bike round to the far side of the Green, squeezed in between a couple of parked cars and sat down to wait. And so did we.

'You see, as long as the biker stayed outside, and Mrs Abbot was inside and being kept in sight by Lucas and his family, we knew she was safe, but we didn't know which gate she'd leave Kew by. There's three that I know of and maybe more. We thought she'd probably stick to her plan to have tea at the Maids of Honour on the road to Richmond. If so, she'd leave by the gate nearest to the restaurant, and not the one she'd taken to get into the Gardens.

'So after Oliver found a place to park on the far side of the Green, he continued to watch the biker and the main gate, while I zipped back to rejoin Zander, and we drove round the corner to the Maids of Honour, where there is, luckily, some parking for customers. It was a long wait. Every now and then Oliver phoned to pass any news on to us. Oliver said the biker got very cold, started stamping his feet. The problem for him was the same as for us; he didn't know which gate Mrs Abbot would leave by.

'Eventually, the biker made a move. Oliver phoned us to say he'd left the Green, and in a couple of minutes he whizzed past where Zander and I were sitting outside the Maids of Honour. I think he'd lost his nerve because he disappeared down the road only to return at speed after a few minutes. We worked out that he was trying to patrol all three gates. At last Lucas reported that Mrs Abbot was also on the move, walking towards our gate. Lucas watched her leave the Gardens and then he took his family home.

'Luckily, the biker wasn't in sight when Mrs Abbot came out of the Gardens. We could see she was dismayed at finding a queue outside the Maids of Honour. She waited for a while but after a few minutes the biker came back and slowed down to scan the queue. This seemed to make Mrs Abbot uneasy, and she took the next bus going back to town. I phoned Oliver that we were on the move and we set off after the bus. The biker took no notice of us, but did a U-turn in the road and set off after her, too.

'When Mrs A. got to Waterman's, she got off the bus and walked down to the entrance. Zander and I went on into the car park, while Oliver tried to find a space further on. To our horror, the biker came into the car park after us. And then got out his phone again.'

She tugged at her hair. 'So who was he ringing? It must have been Benton, because the biker was obviously told to ratchet up the tension. He abandoned the bike and strode towards the entrance, only to see Mrs Abbot turn round and join a queue of people waiting for the next bus going north. It was getting dark. He was caught by surprise, left standing there as the bus pulled away. We could see him scrambling back to his bike as we left the car park and followed the bus. We were in a bit of a state, not sure what Mrs A. intended to do. The traffic was building up . . . but after a while the biker was there behind us, too. Oliver had to take quite a diversion to rejoin us, but managed it eventually.

'Mrs A. got off the bus at an interchange stop and stood there, waiting for another to come along. We had to overshoot. There was nowhere to park. Oliver was behind us and saw what happened next. The biker managed to park his bike by squeezing in between a couple of parked cars and was striding off towards her when a taxi came along and she took it. We followed her safely back home. Oliver got there before us. End of.'

'Ridiculous!' said the inspector, holding on to and then giving vent to another giant sneeze.

'God bless!' said Maggie, running her hands back through her hair. 'So who was giving the orders to the biker? It must have been Benton.'

Bea felt limp with gratitude to Maggie and Oliver, but ambivalent towards the inspector. The sooner she got rid of him, the better. 'Inspector, don't you think you ought to be in bed?'

'Wish I could be,' said the inspector, snuffling and mopping up. 'Now, Ms Maggie, are you prepared to give me a statement confirming—'

'I'll do better than that.' Maggie jumped up. 'We took photos on our mobiles every so often, and they give the timings, don't they? I transferred them to my computer but haven't printed them off yet. Half a tick and I'll get them for you.'

'Did Lucas, the taxi driver, take pictures, too?' Bea was fascinated. 'How thorough of you.'

'We didn't know what was going to happen. We thought that even with all our precautions, the biker might still find a way to attack you, and we wanted to have him on record, just in case.'

'But he didn't get a chance,' said Bea. 'You are quite, quite brilliant! Inspector, what happens now?'

But the inspector had had all the stuffing taken out of him. He'd set out to question a suspect in a murder and found she had an unbreakable alibi. His cold had got worse, and he was feeling sorry for himself. He blew his nose, noisily.

Maggie tapped her forehead. 'It wasn't Benton on the bike yesterday. It was a much bigger man. So who was it?'

'Perhaps,' said Bea, 'it was someone he'd hired to carry on frightening me even though he himself had other plans for the day?'

'Such as getting himself killed? We need to know when he died, don't we? Who else could the biker have been ringing?'

'He rang his girlfriend, of course,' Bea said, feeling that if she were not careful, she'd give way to hysteria. 'He was ringing to say he was going to be late for supper.'

'Flippancy,' croaked the inspector, 'is not helpful.'

The two women looked at him with sharp eyes. 'You really *ought* to be in bed,' said Bea. 'Why don't you phone in sick?'

He snuffled, took refuge in his handkerchief again. 'Might. Gib me dose photos.'

Maggie swept out of the office, saying she'd get them, pronto.

There was a commotion out in the main office. Some laughter, some cheers. What was going on?

The phone rang in Bea's office. It wasn't the landline. Bea fished around in her handbag and found her smartphone. 'Yes?'

It was Inspector Durrell. 'What now?' he said. 'I told you, I'm in the middle of—'

'The man I told you about has been murdered. Would you like to speak to Inspector Robins about it? He thought I'd done it, but fortunately I have an alibi.' She held the phone out to Inspector Robins, who made signals that he didn't want to speak to Inspector Durrell. Bea handed her phone over to him with one of her sweetest smiles. 'I'll leave you alone to take the call.'

She followed Maggie out into the main office. Leon was there. Of course. With a large box of fresh doughnuts, which he was handing out to all and sundry. He held the box out to Bea. 'I kept a chocolate one for you. Would there be a cup of coffee to go with it?'

She said, 'You've heard about Benton?'

'My sister phoned me. Have a doughnut. Carbohydrates are good for shock.'

She did as she was told. He was big and smiley and from another world. She didn't trust him, but she did like him. No, 'like' was the wrong word. She was attracted to him, but she told herself it wouldn't be wise to get into a dinghy with him without first donning a life jacket. 'Have the police been out to see the family already?'

'They have. First off they wanted to speak to Dilys. Sybil got my brother out of bed to talk to them. He was horrified by the news, naturally. Sybil then rang me. Complications all round.'

'But no tears, by request. Mm. I haven't had a doughnut for years.'

'Special treat.'

'What about my diet?' Was she really flirting with him? She was ashamed of herself. Slightly. Mentally, she checked what she'd put on that morning and was thankful that she'd reached for a business-like suit in her favourite oatmeal colour, and some brand new court shoes to match. She'd even put on the earrings she'd been wearing the day before. So, she wasn't badly turned out. And her bruises were beginning to fade.

'You've no need to worry about diets.' His eyes were warm with appreciation.

Mm. Well. A little admiration gets you a long way in this world. She refrained from running her hand back through her hair. No, that would be taken as too warm a response to his flattery.

'Lunch?' he said, quirking an eyebrow in what he must know was an attractive fashion.

She shook her head. 'I have one police inspector in my office, another on the phone, and an agency to run.'

'Can't you get rid of them? I really need your company.' He did his best to look soulful, and she found herself smiling.

Maggie erupted from her office, waving a sheaf of papers. 'One set for us, one for the police, right? Oh. Hi, Leon. How's Bernice?'

'I spoke to her on the phone this morning. She's enchanting. Asking when you're going to see her. She takes your little bear everywhere.'

'Oh, the poppet. I'll ring her this evening. I'll have to put my skates on now to catch up with what I was supposed to be doing this morning. Tell her I'll be in touch when you see her.' She handed Bea one set of photos.

Inspector Robins emerged from Bea's office, to hand her the phone with one hand while he stifled another sneeze with his hankie in the other. 'Someone will be round, wanting a statement from . . . Er-ashoo!'

Everyone took a step backwards. Bea took her phone, thinking she'd better get it disinfected before she used it again.

Maggie handed the inspector the second set of photos. 'For you. Oh, and by the way, I thought you'd like to know that I spotted the biker outside in the road when I came back a few minutes ago. Yes, it's the same registration number, and he's parked halfway along the road, looking this way. Can't you do something about him, arrest him for loitering or something?'

He growled something about being off duty and that he'd send someone to look into it. And made his way through the office and out.

Bea realized her phone was making quacking noises. Inspector Durrell was still on the line. 'Mrs Abbot, are you there?'

'Sure.' Handling the phone gingerly, and not too close to her ear.

'I've got enough on without being asked to chase up non-existent deaths.'

'What!'

'I took time off from the case I was supposed to be working on, to follow up your request. I need my head examined. You wanted me to find out if a girlfriend of Benton's had been killed in a traffic accident. Guess what! There is no record of any woman being run down and killed in the timescale you mentioned. Yes, there were some accidents resulting in death, but none for a young or youngish woman. Only for children and elderly people.'

'There must be!'

'No "must" about it. It was a complete waste of my time and of police resources. Please think twice before contacting me again.' He broke the connection.

Bea stared at the phone, bewildered. And then almost dropped it, realizing how contaminated it must be. 'Excuse me,' she said, rushing back into her office. Somewhere she'd got a bottle of disinfectant. Ah, there it was. She used the gel liberally on the phone and on her hands. And then, making sure, on the chair the inspector had been sitting on, and on the desk which he'd sprayed with his coughs and sneezes.

'Better now?' Leon had followed her, looking amused.

'I don't need to catch a cold on top of everything else. I was so sure that I'd worked out what happened, and it turns out I don't know anything at all. Benton did not have a girlfriend whom he had to pay off with the diamond from Dilys's ring . . . Well, I suppose he might have had a girlfriend, but not one who's died in a road accident. I thought it was him who'd been following me around on a motorbike, and I suppose he might have been the passenger on the bike on Saturday, but it can't have been him yesterday because Maggie says it was a much bigger man, and anyway, it turns out it couldn't have been him because he was dead . . . and his sons with him.'

She shuddered. 'Who would kill two small boys . . . even if they were not the most lovable of children? I suppose he had some other enemy who . . . If I didn't know Dilys was in hospital, I'd have wondered if she'd had enough gumption to kill him herself, but . . . No, that's a fantasy. She hasn't the guts nor the strength, I suppose . . . Although how much strength it would take to drug her husband and children and . . . No, let's start again. Dilys would never have harmed her children.'

'Agreed.' Leon took the chair the inspector had vacated and made himself at home.

'Besides,' said Bea, distractedly, 'no one knows where he's put

her. Dilys, I mean. Some private clinic somewhere? And if so, how
are we going to find out where she is, now he's dead? I suppose
the clinic will keep her till they find the bills aren't getting paid
. . . or perhaps, looking on the bright side, she'll be able to convince
them of her sanity.' Exhausted, she sank down into her own chair.
'What a mess.'

'I have a suggestion to make,' Leon said.

'Ah. Will you excuse me for a minute? There's someone who
needs to know what's happened.' She dialled Max's mobile.
'Max? I don't know if you've heard already, but there's some
rather tragic news. Benton was found dead in his car yesterday
with—'

His speech sounded slurred. 'It's not funny.'

He hadn't been drinking, had he? At this time of the morning?
'It's true. I suppose it will be on the local news. The police have
just been round to talk to me about it. They thought at first that
I—'

'You didn't, did you?'

She blinked. 'Don't be absurd. In any case, I have an alibi. I
suppose the police may ask where you were yesterday.'

'What? How . . . No, that's ridiculous. How you could even
think . . .!'

What she did think was that he was protesting too much, that
the whole tenor of this conversation was skewed. It was almost as
if he'd known about Benton's death before she rang. But, how could
that be? 'Did you know that whoever killed Benton also killed his
children?'

'What!' No, he hadn't known that. He said, 'That's terrible.'
Heavy breathing. 'I have to go. I'm in the middle of something.
Speak to you later.' Click. Off went the phone.

Bea switched her own phone off, trying to think. Max was hiding
something. But what? Surely Benton's death must bring him a sort
of relief . . . mustn't it?

Leon was sitting at ease in his chair, eating the last doughnut.

She passed her hand across her eyes. 'I can't stop thinking about
those boys. I hope they were drugged, wouldn't know anything, but
. . . How awful for Dilys, when she hears. And little Bernice, poor
kid. There's Benton's sister, too. What's more – I shouldn't laugh
but – looking on the bright side, it's going to play the very dickens
at Holland and Butcher.'

Leon brushed crumbs off his hands. 'That's why I need your help. My brother's going spare. World War Three has broken out at Holland Holdings because, just to complicate matters, his chief accountant – who's been with him for twenty years or so – has committed suicide after sacking her deputy. As if that weren't enough, the staff at Holland and Butcher are running around like headless chickens. Looking at it one way, it's a small matter who takes charge of Holland and Butcher, but as it affects the smooth running of my brother's household it's become the most urgent of his problems . . .'

Bea froze. The chief accountant of Holland Holdings had committed suicide? Ah-ha. Was this the missing piece of the jigsaw? If there'd been some major jiggery-pokery on the part of said accountant, then that explained why a multi-billionairess like Sybil had abandoned plans for a cruise to fly to London . . . and why she and her brother were leaning on Leon to sort things out. This needed thought. In the meantime . . .

Leon was still talking. 'Benton had well-advanced plans for a major reorganization at H & B. Some departments might disappear and others expand. He'd made verbal offers to this man and that, contingent upon refinancing – is this where Max was due to come up with some capital? – but there's nothing on paper, and no one knows how to proceed.'

'There'll be emails to show—'

'He put all his notes on his iPad and took it around with him but, according to his PA, he also backed up everything by putting it on to a memory stick at the end of each day. I spoke to his sister, who says the police have removed his iPad and all his paperwork and she doesn't know anything about a memory stick. Sybil shouts at our brother. He shouts back, and nothing whatever is done to sort out the mess.'

The accountant was definitely up to something. And Benton was involved?

Bea said, 'Naturally, your brother can't stomach his domestic arrangements being upset by such trivial matters as murder and suicide.'

Leon acknowledged the hit with a wave of his hand. 'Don't forget that the firm of Holland and Butcher employs upwards of thirty staff, all of whose jobs are at risk.'

'Why don't you take over?'

He grimaced. 'You know I don't want to get involved. But I did agree to look for the memory stick. I've stayed at Benton's and can make a guess where he might have left it. His sister says she'll have a look for it. I said I'd drop by to pick it up, but I'd very much like a witness because I don't trust her.'

Bea couldn't believe her ears. 'You want me to help you find Benton's memory stick in order to keep your brother provided with three meals a day and a warm bedroom? Ridiculous. Besides, the police won't allow us to take anything from the house of a murder victim.'

'They've got the iPad. They don't need the memory stick as well. If by any chance we do find it, they can have a copy. But at least we'll then have enough information to keep the company afloat.'

'Which company? H & B, or Holland Holdings?'

His eyelids contracted. 'That's a ridiculous suggestion. Holland Holdings is as safe as houses.'

Yes, but he would say that, wouldn't he? This hunt for a memory stick is about more than a reorganization at H & B, isn't it?

She didn't want to do it. No way, Jose. But, a thought. 'I wonder if he's left a clue on the memory stick as to where he's stashed Dilys.'

'A good point. If we can only find it. I'm hoping that Benton was secretive enough to hide it somewhere it wouldn't be found too easily.'

'It'll be on his key ring, and the key ring will be in his car.'

'His PA says not. She says he used to put it in the breast pocket of his jacket every evening. She says he also used to back up to the Cloud, but without his password she can't access anything.'

His passwords. That's what Leon was after, wasn't it? Bea was silent, thinking that if Oliver hadn't had to go back to university, he might have been helpful in sorting this out. 'People usually keep a record of their passwords somewhere, especially if they use more than one. I suspect Benton might have used several. He probably kept the list somewhere in his diary, or on a calendar? We could look for that.'

He hid a smile. 'Or on his memory stick? Shall we go?'

Bea hesitated. 'I can't leave the agency, just like that.' She checked her desk diary. She had two appointments that afternoon, but she might be able to defer them . . . Oh, yes. There was something else that she'd been going to tackle that day. She must talk to Carrie about it . . . Not the sort of thing Carrie usually dealt with, but she could have a go at it, and if she couldn't straighten it out Bea could give the client a ring tomorrow. Then there was a query from a long-time customer who needed plenty of soft soap, but that didn't have to be dealt with that day, did it? The monthly figures, yes, they could wait till tomorrow. But, um, there was that tangle over a bill which . . . No, she'd better deal with it when she got back.

Bea said, 'Give me half an hour and I'll be with you. There are some things I can pass to Carrie and others which can be postponed. I can give you a couple of hours, if that's enough? Do you want to wait for me here, or meet me there?'

'I'll wait for you. Remember, there's a bogey man on a bike outside, waiting for you to surface.'

She'd forgotten all about him. Ouch. Yes. Hm. She didn't particularly want Leon eavesdropping on her conference with Carrie. No real reason, but . . . She stood up, thinking rapidly. 'Perhaps you'd like to wait in Maggie's room next door? I expect it's a bit untidy but it will be better than waiting out in the cold on the doorstep. Maggie's gone out on a job and you can be comfortable there. I'll get someone to send you in a cup of coffee and be ready to leave in –' she looked at her watch – 'thirty-five minutes, all right?'

She showed him into Maggie's room. There was a comfortable chair to sit in and a view of the garden outside. He took out his smartphone as he sat down and started to look at his emails.

Before she talked to Carrie, Bea went upstairs to the sitting room and looked out on to the street. No biker. Well, what had she expected? Maggie had been mistaken, that's all.

She was just about to leave the window when a biker came idling down the road, looking up at the houses as he went. A black visored, leather jacketed, anonymous hit man? He parked a little way down the road and walked off. Only then did Bea see that this was a small, thin man, and that he had a sunrise or similar logo on the back of his jacket.

Relief. How absurd to be frightened of a man who probably had a wife, a mortgage and two point four children.

It occurred to her for the first time that the man who'd been following her around the previous day must have been an amateur, because he'd had no back-up. He'd been nowhere near as efficient as Oliver and Maggie, Zander and Lucas.

An amateur? Hmm. This would bear thinking about, but not yet.

She went back down the stairs, wondering who it was Leon had been emailing. Well, it was no business of hers, was it? Or was it?

THIRTEEN

Monday noon

Leon handed Bea out of the taxi at their destination. 'Have you any idea how we should handle this?'

A wind straight from Siberia whipped around her ankles, and she drew her coat more closely around her. 'You've met the woman. I haven't. What do you think?'

He grimaced. 'She'll try to hit on me. I don't know whether to let her, so that you can do the searching, or ask you to protect me.'

He didn't look as if he needed protection so that amused her. 'Let's play it by ear.'

In daylight Benton's house looked less prosperous than it should, given its owner's position in life. 'Neglected' was the word that sprang to mind. A paint job would have helped.

Bea tried to work it out. Benton earned a good whack at H & B but it hadn't been enough because he'd gone on to steal Dilys's diamond. He'd kept Dilys short of spending money so that she had to buy clothes for herself from charity shops, and Bernice had been reduced to wearing the boys' cast-offs. The two boys had been pampered, and there'd been money spent on electronic games and equipment for them, but very little had gone on the house itself. So where had the shortfall gone? Perhaps he'd been something of a miser, squirrelling money away against a rainy day? Well, if he had, the rainy day had caught him unawares.

The police would investigate his bank accounts, but would they uncover a lead to where he'd put Dilys?

Benton's car had become his hearse. Bea wondered what happened to cars in which people died. No member of the family would want them afterwards, would they?

In any case, if they didn't find Dilys soon . . . Bea didn't want to think about that.

Leon rapped on the door and rang the bell. Bea remembered that he'd given his house keys to Ginevra so couldn't let himself in.

A glamour puss in a crackerjack of an outfit opened the door. At first sight she looked eighteen, all curves and long, straight, shining hair. Perhaps the curves were a little too obvious and the eyelashes artificial but the package was aimed to appeal to men and presumably did. Blue eyes, pouting lips, a good complexion. Reddened eyelids and a trace of cigarette smoke were the only items which didn't match the image.

Bea worked out how much Ginevra's clothes had cost. They had not been bought from a market stall. They were from Harvey Nicholls, from an exclusive range by one of the best of today's British designers. This was not the sort of outfit in which you washed the floor. It might be black, but it wouldn't be suitable for a funeral. A dangerously low neckline revealed a deep cleavage. A cropped top gave a glimpse of a taut, flat stomach – in this cold weather? – and the regulation piercing in the navel. A minimalist skirt. Black tights on long, long legs. Tiny black boots with a four-inch heel.

Ah-ha. Is this where Benton's money has been going?

No, I'm being uncharitable. Ginevra may have a top-flight job and be able to afford her own private jet for all I know.

The vision swung the door open. 'Oh, it's you. I'd forgotten you were coming.' A throaty, Lauren Bacall voice. Fake sexy? 'You wanted some memory stick or other of Benton's, right? Something he ought to have left at the office? Well, I haven't found anything like that and the police have taken all his paperwork away. What's more, I don't want you poking around and stealing anything that was his, right?'

'Would we?' Leon's look of sorrow was superb.

Ginevra was calmed by his manner. 'I've heard that people descend on the family of a murdered person looking for mementoes, so they can sell their story to the press. I don't want any of that, either.'

Bea revised Ginevra's age upwards. Thirty if she was a day.

'Promise,' said Leon, lifting both hands. 'No press.'

'Well, now you're here, I suppose it will save me a phone call. I need to know what insurance the firm might have had on Ben's life.'

Leon was avuncular. 'I'll find out for you, shall I? Anything to help. In the meantime, perhaps I could have a look, see if I can find the missing memory stick?'

Ginevra managed a smile – at Leon. 'Oh, all right. Fancy a coffee? Drop your coat here.'

Bea looked to see if Leon was impressed by their hostess. He was smiling at her. Warmly. So perhaps he was impressed? Bea thought Ginevra was overdoing it slightly, then chided herself for being a jealous cat. She dropped her own coat on top of his on a chair in the hall. The house was warm enough to do without.

'And you are?' Ginevra looked at Bea without interest. Too old to be any competition for her?

'Mrs Abbot,' said Leon.

'What?' The girl's eyes narrowed to slits. 'You're the woman who—'

Bea cut in: 'I didn't kill your brother. I had people with me all day, so I can prove it.'

Leon added oil. 'Benton was having talks with her about merging his Training College with her domestic agency. A Holland and Butcher matter. Nothing for you to concern yourself about.'

Ginevra shrugged. She was not interested in H & B, nor in Bea. A washing machine in the kitchen went into whine mode. 'You catch me in the middle of clearing up, or trying to.' She gestured to a pile of black plastic sacks. 'The boys' games and toys. It's heart-rending but I thought I'd better make a start. They'll have to go to the charity shop, I suppose.' Her lower lip quivered, tears rose to her eyes.

Leon said, in a deeply caring voice, 'Could you bear to tell us what happened?'

Ginevra wrung her hands. 'At first the police thought someone must have had it in for him, perhaps someone he'd upset at work. I said from the beginning that there was no getting away from it, he must have killed himself and the boys. I know he was depressed about work, things not going well. Dilys's trying to commit suicide must have tipped him over the edge.'

With tears in her big blue eyes, she looked helplessly up at Leon. 'I can't bear to think of it, but there's no other explanation, is there?

He took the boys out for the day with sandwiches and a flask of tomato soup, and there were enough sleeping tablets in the soup to finish them all off!'

Either she was sincerely mourning the boys' death, or she was an excellent actress. Bea withheld judgement, while Leon patted the woman on her shoulder, peering down her cleavage.

Shoulder pads. And she's had a boob job, too. Possibly Botox around the chin?

Leon put his arm around Ginevra. 'You've had a terrible shock. Be kind to yourself. You shouldn't try to do too much, too quickly. I'll take the bags to the charity shop for you, if you like.'

'Thanks.' Ginevra rested her head on Leon's shoulder for a moment, then rubbed her eyes with a man's handkerchief. One with the initial 'B' in one corner. 'It's just so awful. I keep thinking, what if I hadn't left them alone that day? When he said he was going to take the kids out for a run in the car I took the opportunity to zip back to the shop. I have a boutique in Wandsworth, and though we don't normally open on a Sunday we'd decided to do a stocktake, so I wasn't here when he . . . I keep thinking that if only I hadn't decided to go in to work, if only he'd confided in me . . . But he didn't. Every time I think, what if I hadn't gone? I start to shiver and . . . The policewoman was so understanding, she said he might have tried to take me with them, too, if I'd stayed around. Oh, how could he have done such a dreadful thing?' Hankie to eyes.

'There, there,' said Leon, pulling her closer to him.

She sniffed. 'The police asked if I had anyone who could be with me, but I said "no" because my partner is needed at the shop if I'm not there. I'll be all right. Only, sometimes I find that I'm not.' She looked up at Leon with her blue, blue eyes, leaning towards him till she was pressing herself against his broad chest.

Poor ickle me. And if you believe that . . .!

Leon seemed to do so, but he released Ginevra long enough to say, 'I'll start shifting the bags now if you like.'

Hang on a minute. I'd like to see what she's throwing away.

Bea said, 'We'll take them in a taxi when we're finished. Which charity shop were you thinking of, Ginevra?'

Ginevra gave Bea a millisecond of a glance and turned her eyes up to Leon again. 'I don't know. I've never lived around here. I only came because Benton wanted . . .' Her lips quivered and twisted, and she put her handkerchief to her eyes again. 'Sorry,' she said in a muffled tone. 'He wanted me to look after the children and keep them safe, and now they're . . . Oh!'

'There, there,' said Leon, pulling her back to him again. 'There, there.'

'It's just so . . .' She gulped, prettily.

Was she going to burst into tears? A rather heavy perfume.

'The thing is . . .' Ginevra looked up confidingly to Leon. 'I don't know what to think, what to do. I mean, is the house mine? Can I put it on the market, because I wouldn't want to live here. I have my own sweet little flat in Wandsworth, which is so convenient for work, but . . . what am I supposed to do?'

Leon was looking down her cleavage again. 'Surely you can't do anything much except clear up a bit, because when Dilys comes back—'

'I think –' another gulp – 'I think he must have killed her, too, because she's disappeared off the face of the earth.'

'She may still be alive. You'll have to ask your solicitors what the position may be. Do you have a solicitor yourself? Would you like me to come with you to see them?'

Hm. Overplaying your hand, aren't you, Leon? Because every-thing depends on who died first, Dilys or Benton. If Dilys died first, Benton inherited all her worldly goods, and yes, Ginevra might well inherit the lot. It all depends on what has happened to Dilys.

Ginevra held on to Leon's arm with both hands. 'The police took his address book because at first, until they'd worked it out that it was suicide, they thought he must have annoyed someone . . .' And she cast the quickest of glances in Bea's direction. Yes, it was defin-itely Ginevra who had primed Inspector Robins to suspect Bea of Benton's death. 'And then they tried to find Dilys and could only contact her father . . .'

'Which is where I came in,' said Leon, smiling down at her. 'I'm her uncle.'

Bea kept her face wooden. 'Do you mind if I just . . .?' She gestured to the stairs.

Ginevra's eyes sharpened again. 'Perhaps you'd care to leave that big handbag of yours down here? We don't want there to be any misunderstanding about removing saleable items from my house, do we?'

Bea meekly laid her handbag down on her coat. Ginevra dried her eyes, looking up at Leon. 'I do feel so alone. Would you like a coffee or something? Or some food? I think there's some in the freezer which . . . Mostly fish fingers, I'm afraid. Dilys wasn't much of a cook, was she?'

Leon followed Ginevra into the living room, while Bea went up the stairs to see what had been happening there.

The small bedroom – Bernice's – was more or less as Bea had seen it last. An empty black plastic bag had been draped over the door of the cupboard containing the child's scanty wardrobe. No doubt those clothes would be next to go, but that wasn't important because Bernice was being given a whole new wardrobe now. Perhaps there might be a stuffed toy or two which the child might want to keep? Yes, there was a cardboard box in the corner containing some aged children's books and a few toys.

The bed had been stripped. Was Ginevra sleeping here? If so, where were her clothes and, more importantly, her make-up and haircare items?

The boys' bedroom at the back looked stark, the beds stripped, the cupboard doors hanging open, the shelves inside empty. Some posters had been pulled off the wall, torn up and stuffed into a black plastic bag. No clothing or toys remained. A cardboard box contained a stack of comics and a few annuals.

The washing machine must be directly below the boys' bedroom. It thumped, whined and sighed. Presumably, the children's bedding would be in that.

The bathroom. Bea ran the tap and flushed the loo while taking note of what had been removed and what was still there.

The bathroom cupboard had been cleared of its contents. Yes, it would have been, wouldn't it? There was a slight taint in the air from the aftermath of Dilys's near-drowning. One clean towel on the radiator. No beauty products.

Bea tried to remember what had been done with Leon's overcoat, shoes and trousers which had been ruined when he'd worked on Dilys's inert body. Had he taken them to be dry-cleaned? Well, not the shoes, of course.

So, where was madam sleeping?

One guess. The master bedroom.

The king-sized bed had been made up with fresh linen, a peach negligee hung behind the door, and there was an attractive nightdress neatly folded on the bed. Ginevra was here.

There was a plethora of beauty products on the dressing table and in the en suite, including a phial of expensive perfume. The mirror had been cleansed of the word 'Sorry!' and there was no sign of Dilys's few items of make-up. Ginevra was not expecting Dilys back, was she?

The built-in cupboard space confirmed Bea's guess. An expensive holdall had been slotted into the space at the top, replacing two scuffed suitcases which now stood on the floor by the door. The wardrobe space and drawers contained some expensive clothing, far too bright and showy for Dilys. Designer shoes and fashionable boots had been laid out below. Underwear – Bea quickly opened and riffled through the drawers – also expensive. Also not Dilys's. So where had the previous occupant's clothes gone?

Ah, in the bay window were two bulging black plastic bags which proved to contain Dilys's clothing. Bea recognized the girl's black winter coat and the unsuitable silk dress she'd worn at their first meeting. Boots and shoes had been included. Also a plastic bag containing her few toiletries. A hurried glance into a cardboard box revealed a few pieces of jewellery in a tangle.

Ginevra must be very sure that Dilys was not coming back. Which meant that she must know Dilys was dead.

Bea felt despair close around her. Oh, this was dreadful.

She told herself not to waste time in crying when she could be searching for a clue as to what Benton had done with his wife.

She'd looked everywhere except . . . ah, Benton's clothes must be in the suitcases.

Bea crept back to the top of the stairs. The washing machine was still humming away, mingling with the sound of frying chips. Ginevra understood that the way to a man's heart was through his stomach, right?

Bea told herself to hurry. Any minute now Ginevra would realize Bea had been gone too long for a quick visit to the bathroom.

Bea laid the first suitcase flat on the floor and tried to open it.

It was locked.

She thought of cursing, decided it was a waste of breath.

She laid the second one on top of it and tried to open that. Failed. Where would Benton's keys be? Probably with the police.

Ah, but wait a minute. The police had searched the house and taken away what they needed yesterday. Ginevra wouldn't have started to pack up the house till they'd gone, would she?

Which meant that the keys must still be somewhere around.

Bea sat back on her heels. Where would Benton have kept keys which he didn't need on a day-to-day basis? Probably not on his key ring. Bea herself kept the keys for her luggage items in a small box in the top drawer of her dressing table.

Bea investigated the dressing table. More items which undoubtedly belonged to Ginevra. Costume jewellery, belts, hair ties. The woman had moved in for the duration, hadn't she?

So, if Ginevra had cleared out these top drawers, where would she have put the keys?

Leon put his head around the door. 'How are you doing?'

Bea jumped. 'You gave me a fright.'

'Found anything?'

'Not yet. Have you?'

'No. I've been through dozens of CDs and computer games. Ginevra thinks she can sell them. Maybe she can. She wondered what you were doing. I said I'd see if you were OK.'

'Tell her I've got a touch of the runs.'

'You won't want any food, then.'

Bea wrinkled her nose. 'Not fried food, anyway.'

He laughed and withdrew.

Think, Bea, think! Was Benton wearing a watch? Yes, but he would have had that on him when he died. Collar studs, no. Cufflinks, yes. A smart businessman wore shirts with cufflinks. And Benton had been well-turned-out. Gold ones? Undoubtedly. But, he wouldn't have worn those for an outing to the country, so what had Ginevra done with them?

Answer: put them aside to sell separately.

If so, they'd be in her handbag, which must be downstairs where she could keep an eye on it.

So where had she put the keys to the suitcases? The answer must be staring her in the face. Think, woman!

She sat on the edge of the bed and studied the cases.

Presuming Benton's clothes were in the suitcases, what had Ginevra intended to do with them? If meant for a charity shop, why lock them? The charity shop wouldn't take locked cases, would they?

Was she planning to sell them or to give them to a friend? Benton's clothes had been expensive and worth passing on. But to whom? And if there was such a friend, then he'd have to be able to unlock the cases, wouldn't he? Or she? A second-hand clothes shop might be glad to take Benton's clothing.

Ho, hum. If Bea were Ginevra, planning to pass the cases on to someone else, she would put the keys in an envelope, possibly writing the name of the person on the outside . . . and put the envelope in her handbag, ready to hand over.

That wasn't a very helpful scenario. Bea couldn't very well ask Ginevra to turn out her handbag. No.

Start again. Stand in the middle of the room, with the imaginary keys in your hand, and look around. There was no safe in the house, was there? So where would Ginevra leave the keys for the time being?

This was an elderly house which had originally been provided with fireplaces in the larger bedrooms. The fireplace in this room had been bricked in and wallpapered over, but the mantelpiece still existed. Some of Ginevra's beauty products had drifted there, and a couple of china ornaments. Bea wondered which of the two women in Benton's life had chosen them: Ginevra or Dilys? There was a figurine of a lady holding up her skirt with one hand while smiling, unfocused, into the distance. The other was a pottery lamb in pink. Pink! Dilys's choice.

The top half of the lamb lifted off. It was, in effect, a small pot, intended to house the odd safety pin.

There were two small keys inside. Eureka!

Bea knelt down by the first suitcase and managed to unlock it. Clothing, casual; underwear; shoes. The scent of aftershave. Bea sniffed, half closing her eyes. No, no scent of cigarettes. She hadn't thought Benson was a smoker, and his clothes confirmed that. She'd noted a trace of cigarette smoke in the hall when they first entered. Presumably, Ginevra was the smoker? Must check.

No paperwork or diary. Some well-polished shoes. Bea could imagine Dilys polishing her master's shoes every morning before he went off to work.

Bea locked the first suitcase again and tried the other one.

Ah. Business suits. Yes!

Ginevra had probably gone through the pockets . . .?

Trouser pockets: yes, she had. Nothing in the first pair.

Benton was supposed to have kept a memory stick in the breast pocket of his jacket, wasn't he? Nothing in this one.

Time was marching, etcetera. If Ginevra came up to find Bea searching through her brother's things there would be an unpleasant scene. Ginevra had given Leon permission to look, but she'd wanted to see anything which they might find. Ginevra was capable, in Bea's estimation, of demanding a king's ransom for a memory stick which might have a cash value, and Leon needed it to find Dilys and to sort out the affairs of H & B. Maybe more than H & B. Maybe he was really interested in what was happening at Holland Holdings . . .

Bea began to sweat. What had Benton been wearing last time she'd seen him? She couldn't remember. Navy with a pin stripe, perhaps? Might be. Ah. Something small and hard at the bottom of this last pocket.

She drew out the memory stick with a sigh of relief.

Now, what to do? Tell Ginevra?

Um. There arose a question of right and wrong. Ginevra didn't want anything taken out of the house without her permission, and her brother's memory stick must be high on her list. Had she the right to make such a demand? Probably not. Of course, if it turned out that Ginevra did indeed inherit the house and its contents, then Bea would have to own up and give it to her. On the other hand, if it had H & B business on it, then Ginevra had no right to it whatever.

The question was how to get it out of the house without Ginevra seeing it. If she tried to put it in her handbag downstairs, Ginevra would be on to her like a ton of bricks, and she had no pockets in her skirt.

Possibly, she was overreacting. But instinct screamed not to let Ginevra have it . . . yet.

Oh well, every woman knows that, in times of stress, the bra is the best place in which to hide something.

There were sounds of movement down below. The washing machine had finished its programme. How did Ginevra propose to dry the bedding? Over the banisters? In which case, she'd be coming upstairs any minute now. Perhaps she had a drier downstairs as well as a washing machine? Bea couldn't remember, but fervently hoped so.

Trying not to rush, she refolded the clothes she'd taken out of the suitcase and replaced them. Turned the key in the lock.

She'd been kneeling on the floor. Got up, wincing. Knees . . .

She hobbled over to the mantelpiece and replaced the keys in the lamb's pot.

Now for the loo. She really did need to go, now. Into the bathroom. Yes, it did still smell of that dreadful night.

'Bea, are you all right up there?' Leon, calling up the stairs.

'So sorry, Leon. I can't seem to . . . Just one more go and I'll be right with you.'

Flush the loo. Wash her hands.

Tidy her hair. She was having a bad hair day. She was overdue for a cut and blow dry, and for a manicure. The skin around her left eye was still yellow rather than peach. Oh well, let Ginevra preen herself in the knowledge that she was both beautiful and young, whereas Bea was neither . . . today. Tomorrow, Bea told herself firmly, was another matter.

She made her way down the stairs, holding on to the banister, and into the living room.

'Feeling better now?' Ginevra didn't even bother to meet Bea's eyes.

'Sorry to be so long.' Bea avoided answering the question.

'All right, now?' said Leon. 'I've called a minicab so that we can take these bags off Ginevra's hands. All right, my dear?' He smiled down at Ginevra, who managed to blink tears into her eyes as she drew his head down so she could kiss his cheek.

Bea registered the fact that Ginevra was perfectly willing to make a conquest of this much older man, but was not going to allow him her lips or to think he could take advantage of her, ahem, body.

They retrieved their coats and Bea's handbag before loading the boys' clothing and toys into the taxi. A tight squeeze. Leon got out his smartphone, frowning at the emails which appeared on it.

Bea didn't approve of people using their phones in company, so gave a tiny cough.

'What did you find out?'

'Mm?' He gave her half his attention. 'No paperwork to be seen. Diaries, everything gone. She says they even emptied the waste paper basket. You've got the memory stick, though?' He held out his hand for it, his eyes still on his emails.

'I'll have a quick look at what's on it first, see if there's anything which would help us find Dilys, and then I'll let you have it. I know you need the information straight away so I'll put it in the post to you tonight, or forward you the contents by email if you wish.'

'Mm?' His eyes were on his smartphone. 'My brother is sending a car to pick us up. He wants to see you, straight away.'

Bea was not amused. 'You forget, I have an agency to run and –' a glance at her watch – 'I have people coming in to see me this afternoon. What's more, I haven't had any lunch, even if you have.'

'I'm sure he can get someone to rustle up a sandwich for you. I'll tell him we're on our way, shall I?'

Words such as: 'Tell him to stuff it,' hovered on the tip of her tongue, but she bit them back. 'Tell him I am otherwise engaged. Which I am.'

He raised his eyes from his smartphone for a second. 'He won't like it.'

'I dare say. Now, what did you learn from Ginevra?'

'Mm? Just let me text him . . .' He did so and looked up, but kept the smartphone in his hand. 'Not much. She says she's twenty-three years old—'

Twenty-nine?

'But I'd add a few more years to that. Shrewd businesswoman on a small scale, a partner in a fashion boutique, doing well, she says, even in these difficult times. They have a van for deliveries. Not married but keeping her eyes open for a "significant other". Rents a one-bedroom flat over some shops. Probably not above cheating the Income Tax people if she can. She had her laptop up and running. Her spreadsheet looked competent enough. Says she hasn't seen much of Benton in recent years, owing to some disagreement about dividing the assets when their parents died. She didn't think much of Dilys, whom she'd only met a couple of times.'

'Does she smoke?'

'What? No, of course not.'

Hm. So she'd had a visitor who smoked? The partner? 'What did you make of her personally?'

'Some bodywork has been done, particularly breasts. Maybe

bottom as well. She's a natural blonde but not as fair as she makes out. Some Botox. Not above using her body to influence people.'

That was a pretty acute judgement, and Bea gave him full marks for it.

He held up his smartphone again. 'My brother wants to make you an offer you won't wish to refuse.'

'To pull his chestnuts out of the fire? How many times do I have to say I'm not interested in taking on H & B? Anyway, why isn't he trying to get you to do it?'

'I have other fish to fry.'

'Such as?'

He ignored that. 'He's not going to give up, you know.'

'Tough.' They turned into the street in which Bea lived. She leaned forward, scanning the parked traffic for a biker. None in sight. Good.

He held out his hand. 'The memory stick.'

'Do you promise faithfully to tell me if there's anything there to indicate what's happened to Dilys?'

'Promise.'

She wasn't sure she believed him, but undid the top two buttons of her coat and fished inside layers of clothing for the memory stick. And handed it to him.

His eyes had followed her every movement. He grinned. 'Do that again!'

She had to laugh. 'Certainly not.'

His phone rang. He listened, shut it off. 'There's a hire car waiting outside your house to pick us up.'

'I've got to get back to work. Toss out the bags, and I'll get one of the agency girls to help me get them down to the office. I'll see they get to the nearest charity shop in due course.'

Surrounded by plastic bags, she watched him get into a luxurious car and be driven away. For a fleeting second, she wished she'd gone with him . . . and then she picked up the two largest bags and hauled them to the stairs which led down to the agency rooms.

FOURTEEN

Monday afternoon

'What do you think you're playing at?'

Someone – a man – sounded really angry.

Panting, Bea drew the two bags down the stairs and dumped them in the big office. She didn't bother to see who was shouting at her, but gestured to Carrie. 'Can you help me with the rest?' She was tired and cold and hungry and whoever it was who was shouting could jolly well wait!

Before she'd reached the top of the steps, Carrie had caught up with her. 'It's the inspector, the nice one, except that he's in a temper today. He's been waiting for you. Let me help you.'

Bea nodded her thanks, holding tightly on to the railing as she descended the stairs once more. 'Can you find somewhere to put these for the time being, Carrie?'

'Sure. There's been some phone calls, but they can wait. I put—'

'A bag lady is it now?' Inspector Durrell, normally of an equable temperament, was spitting mad. 'I've been waiting for—'

Bea lost it. Pushing the inspector before her into her own office, she rapped out, 'You want to know where I've been? I've been trying to find out where a poor abused girl might have been dumped by her bastard of a husband. That is, if she's still alive, which I know you couldn't care less about, but *I* do because someone has to care about the defenceless ones of this world who drop through the net. And yes, I know her husband's dead. Although I'm not usually one of the Hang 'Em and Flog 'Em brigade, and I am quite aware that I ought to be wailing over the death of his sons – though, if you'll pardon my French, they were the sort who could have done with the birch being applied to their pampered little bottoms – I would very much like to . . . Oh!'

One of her most august – and elderly – clients was sitting on Bea's settee, reading a magazine, with a pot of tea on a tray beside her. This was a client you would normally speak to in subdued tones, remembering to use the correct form of address. She opened events, was a patron of this and that, worked hard for various charities. She and her husband were national treasures. Normally, the lady would have had her personal assistant telephone Bea or email her if she required attention. So why had she arrived, unannounced and without an appointment?

Carrie was wringing her hands. 'Her Ladyship understood you had an appointment elsewhere, but said she'd wait.'

'Thank you, Carrie.' Bea tried to haul back her temper and return it to the box in which it was normally kept. Only, there was the inspector on her heels, looking thunderous, consulting his watch. Bea closed her eyes, counted to five, opened them again. Was she under control? Halfway.

The inspector exhaled. 'When you have a moment, Mrs Abbot?' And to the visitor, 'Detective Inspector Durrell, requesting the favour of an interview with Mrs Abbot, which is –' he bared his teeth in what was meant to be a smile – 'rather urgent.'

Her Ladyship seemed amused, rather than annoyed. 'Please, don't mind me. I've been out shopping all morning and would be delighted to rest quietly until Mrs Abbot is free. I'd heard she champions people who have no voice of their own. Who knows when any one of us might need her?'

Bea's antennae registered that Her Ladyship had something personal to discuss. 'Half an hour?' Her stomach was rumbling. She said to Carrie, 'I'll be upstairs if anything catastrophic happens, such as the end of the world,' and took the stairs to the kitchen, knowing the inspector would follow. Which he did.

'Food,' she said, opening the fridge. 'I'm desperate. Do you want feeding as well?'

'I suppose it would improve both our tempers.' He picked up Winston and went to stand at the window overlooking the back garden. He'd calmed down a bit now.

What could she produce quickly? 'How about a BLT? I have bacon, tomatoes and, yes, also some lettuce. On toasted brown bread.' She threw ingredients on to the table. Winston abandoned the visitor to wind around Bea's ankles, knowing she'd probably feed him even though it wasn't the right time to do so.

By way of accepting her offer, the inspector drew up a stool to the table.

She put the kettle on and got out the frying pan. 'You realize I'm exhausted?'

'You aren't the only one. I have been taken off a really

interesting case and told to take over from Robins because first he cries "murder", then he cries "suicide", and finally he goes off sick. The post-mortem results are not yet through, but someone high up is pressing for the whole affair to be swept under the carpet as quickly and quietly as possible. This would be fine by me if I could only be convinced that suicide is the right verdict. So, before you start spinning me a line, do tell; have you murdered anyone lately?'

'I've considered it. But, no.' Oil into the pan. Bread into the toaster. 'You'll have to catch the bread as it pops up out of the toaster.'

'What? Why don't you get a new one?'

'I will when I've got a minute. Here, take this knife and cut up some lettuce and tomatoes for me.'

He obeyed. 'I'm told this man Benton slapped you about, and you didn't retaliate? Pull the other one.'

'It's complicated, but the short answer is no, I didn't retaliate. Or not in the way you mean. I was going to get at him another way.' No need to mention Max's involvement. 'Thanks to Maggie and Oliver and their friends, I have an alibi for the day in which Benton and his sons were done to death. Or committed suicide. Whichever. So if you're looking for a possible murderer, please look elsewhere.' Lay the bacon in strips in the pan, turn the gas up.

He pointed the knife at her. 'His sister accused you of having done it at first. According to Robins, that is.'

'His sister is now aware that I didn't. I went out to see her this morning to clear the air. By the way, she could do with investigation herself.'

'Really? Why?'

Bea sighed. She didn't really know why. 'She's got such a silly name.'

The inspector didn't laugh, for which she was grateful.

'Sorry,' she said. 'I'm overtired.' She turned the bacon over. She could hear the toaster getting ready to eject the bread and cried out, 'Catch!'

He muttered something rude, but managed to catch both slices as they flew up into the air. He dropped them on to the table and blew on his fingers.

'Put two more slices in,' said Bea, reaching for the butter in the fridge. 'You want your toast buttered, I suppose?'

'Heart attack, here I come. Now look, you can't go around accusing people of . . . whatever, just because they have a silly name. Why did you go to see her, anyway?'

'We were looking for a memory stick which Benton carried round with him. It appears that he backed up his emails every night, and since the police took away his laptop and other documents when they thought he was murdered, the Hollands are desperate to have the stick so that they can sort out the mess his death has caused at the firm.' She shot him a sharp look. 'And, talking of suicide, were you aware that the chief accountant of the parent company, Holland Holdings, recently committed suicide? That's got nothing to do with Benton's death, I suppose?'

'I don't see why it should have.' A guarded tone. 'Why do you ask?'

'I have a suspicious mind. The Hollands are desperate to get hold of some information that Benton's supposed to have put on a memory stick, saying it's all to do with a reorganization of Holland and Butcher. But it crossed my mind to wonder – it's probably an absurd leap of imagination on my part – if Benton had got himself involved in murky doings at the parent company.'

'Really?' He was stonewalling. 'Now, why should you think that?'

She shrugged. 'No real reason. My chief interest in the memory stick is to see if it contains any information as to where Benton might have stowed his wife.'

'The girl in the bath? She exists?'

Bea suspended operations with her spatula to point it at him. 'You're thinking Dilys might be as fictional as Benton's previous girlfriend who was run over – or not – in a cul de sac, one October? Well, Dilys is real enough. As to the alleged girlfriend, are you sure there really was no such person?'

'There was no such *death*.'

'Which means Dilys lied, or was lied to. I tend to think the latter. Benton as a liar is a plausible thesis.' She slapped butter on to the first of the slices and cried, 'Catch!' as the toaster clicked, preparing to eject the next.

'Ouch!' He caught and dropped two more slices on to the table.

Bea said, 'What I want to know is, why did Benton lie about

having a girlfriend? I mean, it's the sort of story which is going to upset your wife, so why tell her?'

'He lied because he needed to account for stealing the diamond.'

'And lied about his girlfriend's death because he didn't want Dilys to go telling tales to the Hollands, who might have urged her to divorce him? Do you think he continued the liaison? It would account for the fact that he spent very little money on the house and on his wife and daughter . . . Although to be fair, he did seem to give the boys whatever they wanted. You'll have to look at his finances, I suppose. They'd show if he was keeping a mistress tucked away somewhere. A pity that Dilys didn't scream about it at the time as it might have saved her years of abuse and a dip in the bath.'

'She did tell *you* about it.'

'Only because her aunt spotted that the girl was wearing a fake diamond and I was able to get the truth out of her. Dilys's story was that it was all in the past.'

Bea built the sandwiches into a pile, used the big knife to cut them in two and slid half on to a plate for the inspector, keeping the rest for herself. 'Poor, lost kid. I wish I knew where Benton had stashed her. You can follow that up, though, can't you? Ask at the hospital who took her away?'

With a mouth full, he said, 'I'll try. My immediate concern is to decide between suicide and murder. Let's suppose it was murder. What's your take on that?'

Also with her mouth full, she said, 'It did cross my mind at first that the Hollands might have taken exception to his carryings on and decided to do something about it, but they wouldn't go in for infanticide. They'd do away with adults, yes; I wouldn't put it past any of them. Children; no. They would think that, with a strict education, Dilys's boys might be trained to be of use to the family business. Nurture overcoming nature. I'm not sure that I agree with them about that, but that's the way they'd think. Also, they'd be conscious of the bad press they'd get if they were known to have done away with two small boys, however obnoxious. Just think what the rumour of two boys being murdered in the Tower of London did for the last of the Plantagenets. That story rumbled on for centuries.'

'You really think the Hollands capable of murder?'

'Who isn't? Mind you, they'd not soil their hands by doing it themselves. The old man would say to one of his underlings, "Get rid of that idiot, Benton." The order would be passed down the line until someone, somewhere, contacted a hit man and got the job done.'

'The Hollands are that ruthless?'

'The old man is, but I really don't see him getting rid of Benton at this point in time because it's left the firm in a right old state and not only is he very conscious of his profit and loss account but he relies on the staff at Holland and Butcher to keep his house and estate running smoothly. He wouldn't put up with meals being late on the table, or a chauffeur appearing for duty without his uniform. I may be quite wrong, as I've never actually met him. Want some tea or coffee?' She switched on the kettle without waiting for an answer.

'You don't think you are wrong?'

She shook her head, running her finger round her plate to collect stray crumbs. 'Tea would be best after that, I think. Shove the tea caddy over, will you?'

'What about the other members of the Holland family?'

She screwed up her eyes. 'The sister, Sybil. Tough as old boots. Lives mainly in the States. Judging by the way she behaved over the question of Dilys's diamond ring, I'd say she'd be pretty vocal about Benton's bad behaviour, but not put herself out very much to interfere. She'd arrange for Dilys to be put in contact with a divorce lawyer, perhaps? Yes, she'd do that. Would she have the contacts to find a hit man over here? I doubt it.'

'She's too old or too much a stranger to order a murder?'

'Sounds odd, but yes; I think that's about it. She might put herself out for Bernice, Dilys's daughter, but not to any great extent. Yes, she's taken the child in and bought her some new clothes, but as far as I can make out she's got a maid or nursemaid called Maria to look after the little girl's daily needs. As the child grows up . . .? Yes, I can see Sybil taking more of an interest in her then, perhaps even using her as a sort of companion.'

The inspector reached for some kitchen towel to mop himself up. 'Scrub Sybil, subject to further information. Yes, I'll have a mug of tea. Thanks. So how about Leon?'

'Hard to say. He's not a Londoner, and he refuses to get involved with H & B, but he's been running errands for his brother, popping up all over the place. I can't see him getting worked up over Dilys's disappearance. In fact, I've tried pushing him into action there, and he stonewalls. I query whether he gives a hoot for her or the child. Yes, he did his best to save Dilys's life, but rather as a passer-by might give emergency attention to the victim of a roadside accident. He did persuade his sister to look after Bernice, but I don't think he's had much contact with the child since.'

Bea made two mugs of tea, added milk, and pushed one over to the inspector. 'Are you allowed to ask a child as young as Bernice about these things?'

'In the presence of a suitable adult.'

'Does she know that her father and brothers are dead?'

'She should have been told by now.' He cleared his throat. 'You mentioned that the Holland's chief accountant had committed suicide. May I ask how you came by that information?'

'Leon, or his sister, mentioned it. So it is relevant?'

'Could be. The chief accountant had a second-in-command called Adamsson, who would normally have taken over when she committed suicide. Unfortunately, he'd been sacked the week before, following a major row involving her and Benton. We'd like to talk to Adamsson, as you can imagine, but he seems to have disappeared. We think he might have gone abroad, in which case it depends where. There's no extradition from some countries, as you know. Have you ever come across him?'

She shook her head. 'What's he like?'

'Pernickety, they say. Full of righteous indignation. An angry little man.'

'You think he might have killed Benton? But why? And why would he kill the boys?'

The inspector shrugged. 'I have to keep an open mind.'

They sipped tea in silence.

He said, 'You personally favour a verdict of suicide?'

A shrug. 'I haven't the faintest. You've got his laptop and his papers. They ought to give you an insight into his state of mind. If it were just him who'd been killed, I'd say it was odds-on he'd been done in by someone he upset at work, such as this man Adamsson. Benton wasn't a good boss, and I'm told he was in the process of reorganizing the firm, sacking some people, promoting others. A seething hotbed of conjecture and wounded pride awaits you at

H & B. But to kill the children as well . . .? Would an aggrieved employee do that?'

'So you would go for suicide?'

She stacked plates and cutlery in the dishwasher. 'I can't see any other way it could have been, but I'm not happy about it.'

'Neither am I.' He put his empty mug down. 'It'll be all over the papers, I'm afraid. "Devoted father kills himself and sons after wife's suicide attempt."'

Bea's mouth twisted into an attempt at a smile. 'You've missed out the "Shock, Horror!" element that's needed for a headline. How about, "Dad takes boys to join Mum in death."'

He tried to cap that. '"Mum's suicide prompts Dad's death?"'

'You've missed out the sons.'

He slapped his forehead. '"Mum's suicide prompts family's death."'

She tried not to laugh. 'What bad taste! Both of us.'

'Sometimes we have to make horrible jokes, or we'd start bashing our heads against the wall.'

Yes, she knew all about that. She checked the time. 'I have a client waiting downstairs for me.'

'And I'm due somewhere . . . Thanks for the tea and sympathy.'

Bea saw the inspector out and went downstairs to see how her august client was getting on . . . only to find her, glasses askew, fast asleep on the settee. Bea rustled papers on her desk, and the sleeper awoke, sort of.

Bea pretended not to notice that her client was going through the usual 'Where am I?' bit, resettling her glasses on her nose, checking that her skirt was straight. Her records were on the computer. Bea checked them out. The agency had supplied a well-recommended personal assistant some ten years ago, who had only left in order to nurse her mother through the last few months of her life. Afterwards the assistant had wanted a complete change and had asked the agency to find her a job abroad, which they had done. Bea had no record of supplying another PA to this client, but it was unlikely this august and busy personage would have been able to manage without help. Perhaps that was the reason for this visit? Except that such a request might have been made by phone or email. There was more to this than met the eye.

When she saw the client was sitting upright and knew where she was, Bea said, 'Apologies for keeping you waiting. May I offer you another cup of tea?'

'No, no, my dear. I'm sure it is I who ought to be apologizing to you.'

'Anything I can do . . .?'

'I know you can be discreet?'

Bea nodded, thinking that she ought perhaps to add 'moral' or 'ethical' to the agency's slogan on their letterheads and in their advertisements.

'A favour. We did not come to you for assistance when my last dear helper left, because my husband found someone through an advertisement in the *Telegraph*. He was very taken with the girl who, it must be acknowledged, is a comely creature.'

There was a slight pause while both women reflected that elderly gentlemen might occasionally be less than avuncular to pretty young things who came to work for them.

Bea nodded. She could read the future as well as her client. If the elderly husband fell too hard for the newcomer, there might be a distressing breakdown in a long and happy marriage, perhaps even a divorce and remarriage. Would that make the man happy? Sigh. Probably, for a fortnight or so. And then, not.

'She provided references, of course?'

'Written references,' said the lady, 'which he did not follow up with telephone enquires. He has been so accustomed to your vetting applicants for us that he failed to realize that not all written references are genuine.'

'You think they were faked?'

The lady was not prepared to go that far. She fiddled with her rings – very good rings, diamonds and sapphires. 'One never knows if they're telling the truth or not when they give their reasons for leaving their previous employment. It's not that she's been a disappointment in her work, though she's not a patch on the girl before her, and she's becoming increasingly apt to disregard anything I say. Almost rude, in fact. But I could deal with that if I didn't feel that by doing so, I might be shooting myself in the foot.'

Bea understood that the elderly husband was beginning to take the part of the PA against his wife. Oh.

The client produced some letters from her handbag and handed them over. 'She says she's worked for these people in Yorkshire and a couple in Kensington who all laud her to the skies. I don't know either of them or I would have had a quiet chat . . . and now, I'm so afraid that . . .'

'Say no more,' said Bea. She glanced at the clock. 'I have ten minutes before my next appointment. Could you bear to wait while I see if I can contact one of these people?'

'Thank you, my dear. I'd be grateful. The girl's got such a silly name. Baptized Christine, but now calls herself Christobel. As if!'

Bea froze. Christine to Christobel.

What name had Ginevra been born with?

She turned back to her computer. Yes, the people in Kensington were also clients of hers, silver service for an anniversary dinner party once a year and for a drinks party in their garden every Midsummer's day. Four children under the ages of fifteen. Why had this client needed a personal assistant? Well, there was only one way to find out. Bea dialled their number and was fortunate enough to find the client there.

Bea introduced herself and apologized for bothering the client, but . . . 'I've a client who was approached by a certain Christobel—'

A shriek from the other end of the phone. 'That tart! Don't give her the time of day, Mrs Abbot. She came to us as an au pair when I was having a problem with the twins, but she was nothing but trouble from the word go. She could hardly tear herself away from Facebook to fetch the kids from school, and then I had my husband drooling all over her because she's a pretty little thing if you like the sort who spends more time flirting with visitors than emptying the dishwasher. The last straw came when I found her trying to get into bed with my fifteen-year-old son. I shot her out of the door before you could say knife, and believe me, if I'd had a knife in my hand at the time, there would have been blood on the carpet.'

'So you didn't give her a good written reference?'

'I said if she went for another job and the employer rang me, I'd be happy to tell what I knew of the girl.'

'Would you be kind enough to speak to someone who had been given your name as a reference for Christobel?'

'Would I!'

Bea passed the phone over and accessed Facebook with reference to dear little Christobel . . . and there she was, the minx. Cavorting

– if that was the right word – with various young men in compromising fashion. X-rated, definitely.

'Thank you so much. Most kind.' The elderly client replaced the phone with a hand that shook.

Bea turned her computer screen round so that Christobel's activities could be shared with her client. 'Facebook. With a number of young men.'

The client blew her nose. 'What a silly billy my old man has been. When I show him this . . . I wonder if he knows how to access Facebook?' Even her voice quavered.

'Perhaps,' said Bea, in a dulcet tone, 'you could ask Christobel to show you how?'

An amused smile. 'That might indeed be sufficient to show her the game was up, yes. But I fear he will have to see the evidence for himself.' She straightened her back. 'Well, these things are sent to try us. I'm grateful, Mrs Abbot. I won't insult you by asking if you'll keep this to yourself, because I know that you will. So, as my assistant is about to leave, perhaps you can find me someone else?'

'Delighted. Fair, fat and forty?'

The client had enough spirit left to laugh.

Carrie knocked and put her head round the door. 'Your half-past three appointment, Mrs Abbot.'

Bea helped Her Ladyship into her coat and saw that she had collected all her belongings before accompanying her to the front door. 'Would you like us to get you a taxi?'

'Yes, dear. Thank you. I hate driving in London nowadays.'

Carrie said, 'I'll arrange it, My Lady. If you'd like to take a seat here for a moment . . .?'

Bea turned her mind to her next appointment with some difficulty. Business before pleasure.

This time the client had a different problem for Bea to solve. A daughter's wedding had had to be brought forward as her fiancé was due for another tour of duty in Afghanistan. Could Bea rearrange everything at such short notice . . .? Of course. With sympathy.

As soon as the second client had gone, Bea re-entered Facebook and typed in the words 'Ginevra Benton'.

FIFTEEN

Gotcha!

Ginevra Benton, cavorting. A good word, cavorting. 'See me dance, see me play. This is where I live. See how big my bed is. This is me on holiday, holiday, holiday . . . This is me with Ricky. Aren't I cute?'

Bea had assumed that Ginevra's partner was a woman, but he wasn't. Ricky was a big butch of a man with muscles out to here though possibly not as many brains as muscles. Ricky had a motorbike. See me perched on the pillion of Ricky's motorbike.

Yes!

Ricky must be the man who'd menaced Bea on his motorbike. So if Ricky had been the biker, then who had been the passenger on Saturday night? Ginevra?

Bea closed her eyes, the better to recall the image of the men who'd terrorized her.

No. Not Ginevra. Not a woman.

Are we back to thinking it was Benton? Yes. Possibly.

A shame one couldn't ask him now.

Return to Facebook. Ginevra in different outfits, referencing her boutique, which was also – surprise! – called Ginevra. Her poses were seductive, showing off not so much the clothes, as the body within them.

Ginevra had been on Facebook for some time. Bea scrolled back and back.

And stopped. The trail ended – or rather began – when Ginevra opened her boutique in Wandsworth, full address given. On Twitter, etc.

Bea googled Ginevra's Boutique and came up lucky.

Pictures of the shop's fascia, and of Ginevra. None of Ricky.

More pictures of Ginevra wearing different outfits. This time the clothes were more important than the body within them. So why wasn't the partner shown?

Perhaps Ricky had taken the pictures? They did look a cut above the average family photos.

Ricky . . . who? What was his other name? Did he live with Ginevra? Why wasn't his full name on Ginevra's Boutique page?

Mm. Try a different way in. Bea accessed the website which gave details of registered companies. She found the boutique, but no details. So it was not a registered company, and there were no shareholders or directors. Just a loose partnership?

How could you find out? Bea stared the screen, wishing Oliver were still around because he was better at sorting these things out than she was . . . although she hadn't done too badly, come to think of it.

She got up to pace the floor. Look at it from a different angle. Perhaps Ricky had another career somewhere and just helped out in the boutique when required? Or did his biker stunt when required?

Carrie tapped on the door. 'Your next appointment?'

Bea wrenched her mind away from the chase and turned a professional smile to her next visitor, telling herself to deal with life one step at a time.

A complaint this time. Justified? Mm. Faults on both sides. Apply oil in large quantities, promise to investigate. And if it could be proved that the chef had been tipsy that night, then Bea promised he would never be used by her agency again. If. By the end of the interview, Bea was pretty sure the client was complaining solely to get a reduction in the bill. To be dealt with on the morrow.

Back to Ginevra. Something her august visitor had said earlier struck a chord.

If Christine had turned herself into Cristobel, and Ginevra had previously had another name, then what might that have been? Bea could well understand that the girl would have wanted to give herself an extravagant name if she were to open a boutique. People often kept the same initial or a similar-sounding name when they wanted an alias. How about 'Jean'?

Bea typed in 'Jean Benton', and lo and behold, up came the details for a person of this name.

At least . . . No, it couldn't be. Yes, this Jean had been born in 1983, which would make her thirty years old. Jean was about the right age, but the rest was nonsense. This could not be the right person. Bea told herself that she wasn't as good at this lark as Oliver and that she'd made a poor guess when she'd gone for the name 'Jean'.

Carrie tapped on the door. 'Your son is here and—'

Max thrust past her into the room and slammed the door to behind him. He looked pretty dreadful. 'I've left Nicole!'

'What!'

He threw a sports bag down and slumped into a chair. He hadn't shaved with any accuracy, and the cuff of a shirt hung out of the sports bag.

'She's been having an affair!'

Yes. Well. Anyone else would have tumbled to that ages ago. Bea had heard that the injured party was always the last to know. But what about his own shenanigans? He'd previously gone for blondes in a big way, but this last time it had been a redhead, hadn't it? What was sauce for the goose was sauce for the gander. Not that Max would see it that way. Men didn't.

Bea frowned at the door, as there was something going on in the outer office; laughter, even a cheer or two.

Max was locked into self-pity. 'To think that I trusted him. And her. It never occurred to me, but all the time he was making up to me, taking me for a sucker, he was having it off with her behind my back, making plans to take my place—'

'Benton?'

'Who else! Did you know, too? Mother, I can't believe that you would know and not warn me—'

'You didn't want to know, Max. And any time I tried to tell you that Benton was not a saint, you bit my head off.'

He shouted, 'You should have warned me! Nicole says you knew all along, that you went out of your way to warn her . . .'

The door opened. Bea glanced across to see a shadowy figure let himself in, but she had no time to spare for Leon. 'Max, I was trying to save your marriage—'

'You never thought to warn me? You treated me like a small child who—'

'Enough!'

He was shocked into silence. 'Mother, you can't—'

'If you can't behave like an adult, then you will have to be treated like a child. Now, let's get this straight. I rang you this morning and you put me off, pretending that you didn't know—'

'Nicole had just that minute told me Benton was dead. I was in shock!'

'So Nicole knew before you did? I wonder how.'

'His sister rang her. Even his sister knew that Nicole was having

an affair with Benton before I did. Nicole had hysterics. I couldn't
understand at first what she was on about, and when I did, when I
realized what a fool she'd made of me . . . How many other people
know, I wonder? Are they all going to be laughing at me in the
House of Commons?'

'That's the least of your worries, Max. Have you signed anything
which ties you to Benton? Taken out a mortgage, or a big loan?
How far did you invest in him?'

'What? Oh. No, nothing's signed yet. We were going to . . . I've
been made a director of the firm, but . . . what's going to happen
there?' He put his head in his hands. 'What a mess!'

True. Did he know that if a private company went to the wall,
the directors would be responsible for any outstanding debts? Um,
well. Perhaps it wouldn't be a good idea to bring that up for the
moment. She leaned back in her chair, thinking hard. 'Benton's
death is actually good news for you, right?'

'What? No, of course not. Well, I suppose if you mean—'

'The redhead?'

He gaped. 'Oh. Well . . . Yes, if you mean—'

'Have the police been round to talk to you about him?'

A stare. 'Why should they? Oh. You don't really think I'd want
to kill Benton because he was having an affair with Nicole?'

'Or because he had proof you were playing away from home as
well?'

He coloured up. 'That was nothing! But for Nicole to sleep with
. . . That trollop! I'm well rid of her.'

'No, you're not. You know perfectly well that your best bet is to
make it up with Nicole straight away, or you risk losing
everything.'

'Make it up with her? Don't be ridiculous! After what she's
done?'

Bea lowered her voice. 'You know very well, Max, that she could
have divorced you several times in the past because—'

'Nonsense. They didn't mean anything.'

Bea let silence develop. She knew that at least one of his little
flings had meant a lot to him at the time. He had a weakness for
blondes. The most serious of his little 'flings' had been with Nicole's
sister. Fortunately, the girl had moved on and married into the aris-
tocracy. Nicole didn't know about Max's lapse in that direction.
Hopefully.

Max muttered, 'You don't know what it's like, living with her. She's always finding fault, picking at her food, not particularly good in bed.'

Bea subdued a sigh. 'She's given you a wonderful son. She's beautiful and clever with people. She understands exactly what a member of parliament's wife should say and do. She dresses the part and charms the pants off the Powers That Be. She brings you money and the backing of her influential family. She can help you climb the ladder, if you listen to her.'

'She doesn't want me any more. Things were said. She's thrown me out.'

'She was in shock. Didn't know what to do, or say, or think. Go back and tell her how much she means to you, that you'd do anything to make her happy. Take flowers. She'd like that. Tell her that she is the most wonderful woman in the world and you realize you're not worthy of her—'

'Humph!'

'—and that together you two can climb the highest mountain.'

'She's in love with Benton!'

'Not now he's dead and can't flatter her any more. Tell her you realize you've been neglecting her—'

'I haven't!'

'Suggest an expensive holiday somewhere, just the two of you. Somewhere romantic.'

He managed to take that on board. 'And if she's pregnant by him?'

'She won't be. Trust me, she wouldn't have risked that.'

More silence.

He said, 'I've been making a blinking fool of myself, haven't I?'

Time to mend fences. 'Benton promised you the world, but demanded too high a price for it. That's why you didn't actually sign up with him.'

'No, I didn't. That's right. I was tempted, but I could clearly see the difficulties and even wondered whether what he wanted was entirely legal.' He was becoming once more the up and coming member of parliament.

She added another brick to his wall of self-esteem. 'Nicole was taken in, as well. We mustn't forget that. Poor Nicole. She must be so distressed.'

'You're right.' He checked his tie, smoothed back his hair. 'I must reassure her. Everybody makes mistakes. We both did, and now we have to move on. One good thing: so few people know about it that we can deny it. Yes, that's what we'll do. Deny everything, go away on holiday, have some pictures taken of us with Pippin, hard-working family taking time off.' He got up, ready to depart.

'Don't forget your bag.'

'I'll forget my head next.' He went over to give Bea a somewhat damp kiss on her cheek and departed.

The shadowy figure, who'd tucked himself into a chair at the back, said, 'Brilliant.' He clapped his hands once, twice.

'I must have a word with Carrie about letting you in when I'm busy.'

'I paid my way in with cakes from the bakery. I hope they kept you one.'

'What's more, you ought to have had the tact to leave a mother and son alone when they're having, er, problems.'

'I sat at the back and didn't interfere. Tact is my middle name.'

'I would hazard a guess that your middle name is Gofer. You're acting as hatchet man for your brother, aren't you? Go here and do this. See if you can get Mrs Abbot to find the memory stick, and . . . ah, the memory stick's no good to you?'

'Password protected, and we don't have the password.'

'Really? Mm. Do you think Ginevra knew that? I wouldn't put it past her. Do you think she guessed what I was doing while I was upstairs at their house?'

'I think that if she'd known about the memory stick, she'd have held on to it and demanded a king's ransom.'

'The police have all his papers. Why don't you ask them to help you?'

'A detective inspector is with my brother now, asking questions, getting background.'

'Did he speak to you?'

'I left before he arrived.'

'So your brother has sent you back here post haste to ask me . . . what? He's in a great hurry to find out what Benton was up to, isn't he?' She remembered the rumours about a missing accountant. No, not a *missing* accountant, but a suicidal one plus a second-in-command's disappearing act. 'Ah, I wonder if the hunt for the information on the memory stick is not to do with personnel. Has Benton been fiddling the books, by any chance?'

He stonewalled that. 'We certainly need to find out what he's been up to.'

'I'm sure the police would be only too happy to cooperate if you asked them nicely.'

'Perhaps, but time is of the essence.'

'Then why are you wasting time, sitting here with me? If you won't ask the police for help, why don't you ask Ginevra? I'm sure she's clever enough to sort out affairs at H & B. And now, if you don't mind, I have work to do.' Bea turned back to her computer, but the screen saver was up, and she didn't particularly want to do any more research on Ginevra Benton in front of Leon.

'My brother really would like to meet you—'

'Why? Has the boiler broken down? Have supplies of his favourite ice cream run out?'

He sat back in his chair, fingers drumming on his thigh. 'I'm serious.'

'So am I.' She swivelled round to him. 'There is only one thing I would like from you and yours, and that is the news that Dilys is not dead, that you've found her, and that she's safe and sound.'

'We . . .' A hesitation. This was like pulling teeth. 'We have located her, and she is safe and sound.'

She stared at him, trying to work it out. 'So it wasn't Benton who whipped her away from the hospital, but you? Yes, of course it was. Or it was you who organized it? And when Sybil rang me, asking if I knew what had happened, that was at your instigation, covering your tracks. I don't know whether to applaud or kick you where it hurts.'

He raised his hands. 'Guilty as charged. You understand why?'

'I see that you didn't trust me with the truth.'

'Would you have done, in our place?'

She pulled a face. 'Possibly not. Has Dilys been told that Benton's dead?'

'Yes. She can hardly take it in.'

'Did you tell her about the boys?'

'No, not yet. She's not been well.'

'Is Bernice back with her mother?'

'Soon, we hope.'

'Can you assure me, hand on heart, that what you've said is true?'

'Yes. Don't you trust me?'

'No further than I can throw you.' She thought about it. 'All right, let's have a look at the boys' effects. I'm not sending anything to a charity shop till we know if Dilys would like to keep some of their things as mementoes. I'm not hoping for much as Ginevra must have gone through the lot with a fine-tooth comb but, sharp as she is, she must start making mistakes soon.'

Bea shut down her computer and cleared her desk so that they could lay everything out. The first bag contained casual clothing, underwear and nightwear, some of it still in good condition, and all beautifully clean. Dilys had looked after the boys' clothes well. 'Nothing here that Bernice would want, is there? But we'll keep the lot till Dilys can decide what to do with it.'

The second bag was also clothing, mostly outdoor wear, trainers, school uniforms.

Leon said, 'Sybil's getting Bernice enrolled at a small, private school nearby. It has a good reputation, and the chauffeur will take her and bring her back every day.'

Bea wondered what Dilys would make of that. Wouldn't it have been better to keep the child at her old school? Well, it was none of her business.

Third bag. School bags, wellies, football gear.

Fourth. Electronic games, mostly, but not the Wii boxes which Ginevra must have kept for resale. There were airplane kits, started but not finished; comics; a few books; masses of DVDs, separated from their boxes. Two Kindles, first generation, one with a smashed cover. Mobile phones, ancient and modern with a tangle of black USB cables for same.

'Ah-ha!' said Bea, pouncing on a netbook. 'I bet this was Benton's at one time. The cover's so scratched, I don't suppose it's worth anything. He would have got himself the very latest and handed the old one to the boys to play with. Batteries low. Can we recharge?'

He held up the mess of wiring. 'Take your pick. Surely, he wouldn't have left anything important on it when he passed it on to the boys?'

'Maybe. Maybe not. He might not have bothered to take everything off. I mean, the boys wouldn't be interested in a list of passwords, would they?'

'Unless they could use it to override parental controls so that they could access porn on the telly?'

'Cynic. Do you really think they would?'

'I've no idea.'

'We need the right cable.' She delved into the mass of wiring. Told herself patience was a virtue. Nearly threw the lot in the waste paper basket. Found the right one. 'Ah. Eureka.' She fitted the USB cable into the socket on her computer and booted up. 'Now what have we here? Mostly, the boys seem to have played games . . . emailed friends . . . an exchange of ruderies appropriate to boys of that age, I suppose. No, nothing there. I'll try the Recycle Bin. Mm. Give me a minute or two.'

He began to pack everything else back into the black plastic bags.

Bea concentrated. It was no good having a wild dash at this. Be methodical, Bea. Take it one icon at a time. She sat back with a sigh. 'There does appear to be some business stuff in the Recycle Bin. I don't know whether it's any use to you or not; it's six months old.'

'Emails to a bank, moving money around?'

'You think that's what he's been doing? Yes, I suppose . . . You'll have to check it with his bank. Lloyds Bank. And yes, here's another file for Barclays. And . . . Oh, a bank in the Cayman Islands. Is that what you've been looking for?'

He grimaced. 'No good without the password and account numbers.'

'I think you'll have to ask the police to let you have . . . ah.' She stood up, gesturing for him to look at the screen. 'You're looking for a list of passwords? There is a list here in an old recycled file marked Security which might fit the bill, but which password is for which account, and which for his memory stick, I cannot tell. They might be out of date, or again, they might not. That do you?'

He bent down to look. She could feel his excitement, though he was trying hard to conceal it. 'Can we print it out?' He was humming with energy, shifting from foot to foot, shooting glances at his watch. Aching to be off, to report his success back to his boss.

She printed the list out and made him stand still long enough to check that she'd got it right. Then she unplugged the cable and handed the netbook to him. 'Bon voyage.'

'Yes, thanks.' He was fretting to go. 'Have supper with me?'

She shook her head. 'Off with you, now. When you see Dilys, tell her that I'll keep all the boys' stuff till she decides what she wants to do with it.'

He disappeared, with the speed of a conjuror's vanishing act.

Ah well. Bea cleared the rest of the boys' things away, reinstated her computer and accessed the site which had thrown up 'Jean Benton'.

She studied the screen. No, it couldn't be the right person. Yes, the age was right, and it was coupled with the other name she'd been looking for, that of Benjamin Benton. But Ginevra – or Jean, if that was her birth name – was Benton's sister, and not his wife, so there must be some mistake.

Bea took another turn around the office. Dusk had set in. She checked that the grille was locked over the window and pulled the curtains. Considered making herself a cup of tea. Thought better of it. Went back to her computer. Started on another tack.

She found a marriage certificate which stated that Jean Marsh, spinster, aged twenty, married Benjamin Benton, bachelor, aged twenty-two in October, twelve years ago. Witnesses: George and Mabel Marsh, parents of Jean. Registry office.

There must be some mistake. She told herself that Ginevra was not the same person as Jean Benton. There must be dozens of Bentons with a similar or the same name.

Ginevra was Benton's sister.

Or so she said.

But if she was – or had been – Benton's wife, then everything Bea thought she knew about him changed.

She reached for the phone and got through to Oliver. 'Safe journey back? No, I'm all right, not been attacked recently. Can you tell me which website I need to find out if someone has been divorced?'

'What are you on about?'

'Someone called Jean Marsh married Benjamin Benton twelve years ago, and I have a horrid suspicion that this is the Ginevra Benton who's been calling herself his sister, and who has moved into his house. If she divorced him before he married Dilys, fine. But if she didn't—'

'His marriage to Dilys is no go, and Ginevra is still his wife and should inherit his house? Phew! What a turn up for the books. It's quicker if I do it. I'll ring you back in ten minutes.'

He killed the call, and Bea tried to shake her senses back into their proper place. She was so wound up, she couldn't concentrate on everyday life. She went through to the big office. They were packing up for the day, switching phones through to the emergency number, putting on coats.

Carrie produced a cream puff on a plate. 'Leon asked us to save this for you.'

'It looks delicious, but I couldn't eat it at the moment. Can you find a home for it? By the way, I don't like him barging in whenever he feels like it. In future, will you ask me before you let him in?'

Carrie was in a mood to be saucy. 'Don't you like him?'

Bea smiled and shook her head. 'Safe journey home, girls. See you tomorrow.'

Her phone trilled, and she rushed back to hear Oliver's voice.

'Nothing. No divorce. I've tried every year from the one in which they were married, to today. As far as I can see, unless it's been annulled . . . I could try that.'

'No. It makes a horrible kind of sense. They married young, perhaps stayed together, perhaps not. He got the job with H & B and saw how to climb the ladder by making up to Dilys. Perhaps he tried to get free of Ginevra, and she refused him a divorce? Then, oh dear, he got Dilys pregnant but couldn't confess to old man Holland that he was already married. And Ginevra was on his heels. He raised money to buy Dilys a huge diamond and paid Ginevra off by selling it again.'

She made a note. 'I must check to see if that's when she started up her boutique. The timing's about right. So she did OK out of it, but he was still in debt for the original purchase. Dilys spotted that the diamond had been changed but he calmed her down with the story about paying off a previous girlfriend. He told her the affair was over, that the girl had died. But we know there was no such death in reality. Did Ginevra continue to blackmail him throughout his marriage to Dilys? I suspect so. Well, well. That puts a different complexion on the matter.'

'I could come back at any time if you need me. Just give me a ring.'

'I'm all right for the time being, but I'll keep in touch, right?'

She turned off the lights and went upstairs to the kitchen, taking care to lock the door from the agency at the bottom of the stairs as she went. There were lights on in the hall and kitchen, and music. TV and radio. So Maggie was at home.

Also, surprise! Zander was in the kitchen playing with Winston, while Maggie was deep in conversation with someone on the phone. Maggie was dressed in a peacock blue shaggy top over tight black trousers, and there was a matching band of blue around her dark hair. And purple on her eyelids. Maggie was feeling happy again.

'Can I cook you something, Mrs A?' Zander looked slumberously content.

Bea knew the meaning of that look. Successful sex. Ah, but . . . She felt a little shocked. Had Zander . . . In spite of all his protestations? And Maggie had enjoyed it?

Whoops. No business of yours to interfere, Bea, or even to comment. Instead, think, Bravo, children! You've made up? Good!

'Food?' She shook her head. 'I was going to have a takeaway.'

Maggie said, 'You never!' into the phone. She was smiling.

Zander put Winston down on the floor. 'Maggie took a call for you on the landline just now. She said CJ – is that right? – was coming round to see you. She told him she thought that would be all right and that you wouldn't mind.'

Maggie was still on the phone, laughing at something she'd heard. 'Really? What fun! Yes, of course you have to get ready for supper. I'll ring you again tomorrow, right?' She clicked off her phone. 'Bernice has a new pair of wellies with pink stars on them, and tomorrow she's going to be taken to the Harry Potter experience, and next week she's starting at a new school. She sounds fine. I didn't like to ask if she knew about the deaths in the family, but she said straight off that her great auntie had told her about her daddy and her brothers, and they all agreed it was terribly sad, but that she was going to see her mummy soon, and that would cheer them all up. I think the Hollands are handling the situation rather well.'

Zander put his arm around Maggie, proudly grinning at Bea. 'She's gone all broody, wants a child of her own soonest, and I'm more than happy to oblige.'

SIXTEEN

'I'm delighted,' said Bea. And she was . . . for two seconds. Then she realized that Zander marrying Maggie was going to mean the girl moving away, leaving Bea all alone in her big house. She kept her smile on, though. 'I'm thrilled for you. Both of you.'

Maggie snuggled into Zander's shoulder. 'My mother won't approve, of course—'

'We'll manage,' said Zander. 'I've been offered yet another promotion, and I've been saving like mad, hoping that one day Maggie would agree to marry me. And now she has. We want to do the deed as quickly as possible. It'll have to be in a registry office because of Maggie's first disastrous marriage, but we can have a blessing in my church afterwards.'

Maggie said, 'We thought Oliver could be best man, and you're to be Matron of Honour, but—'

They looked at one another, and then at Bea. 'Would it be possible, would you mind very much if we lived here in the top flat till we've found somewhere else? All that's needed is to change my single bed for a double. What do you think?'

So they weren't going to leave her all alone, after all. They sounded really worried that Bea wouldn't agree, but she was delighted. 'Bless you, my children. I can't think of anything I'd like better. Please, don't be in any hurry to move.' Bea embraced them both. 'I'm thrilled. Does Oliver know yet?'

'Not yet.' They were flushed and laughing. 'We wanted to ask you first.'

The doorbell rang. Smiling, Bea went to let CJ into the hall.

'Are you all right, Bea?' He looked serious. Almost, worried.

'Why shouldn't I be? Maggie and Zander have just got engaged and are going to stay on here in the top flat. Isn't that good?'

'Excellent,' he said, in a tone laden with doom.

Bea twitched a frown at him. 'Come and congratulate them.'

'Does Oliver know?'

'You think he'd object?'

'No, of course not. He can always move into my son's old flat if he feels he's being squeezed out here.'

Trust CJ to put a damper on their high spirits. Bea was annoyed with him, though she conceded that he had a point. Oliver must not feel he was being pushed out of his home.

The happy pair accepted CJ's congratulations and went off to have a celebratory supper locally.

'Well, CJ. Shall I cook something for us?' said Bea, thinking it was the last thing she wanted to do.

'I have a table booked at that steak place up the road.'

Bea immediately felt she'd prefer to cook for him at home, but couldn't very well say so. She wondered what it was that made the men in her life always choose to take her to restaurants she'd just been to. All right, this particular restaurant wasn't bad, and it was nearby.

She fetched her coat, checked that the alarm was on and accepted CJ's arm to walk up the road to the restaurant.

Once they were settled and had placed their order, he gave a little cough. 'I was concerned about you. Those attacks. And, you're looking, well, not quite yourself.'

Bea, who had been feeling fairly perky, winced, remembering her slapped face and her terror at being followed by the biker. She forced a smile. 'I'm all right.'

'Good. Not everyone has come out of this as well. Defenestration, I believe they call it.'

'De-what? Out of the window? As in . . . Wasn't that the Czech way of disposing of inconvenient or redundant politicians? You mean someone's been thrown out of a window?'

'Top floor, twenty-something storeys. Not much left.'

'Pity the street cleaners!'

CJ did not care for levity. Bea reflected that Inspector Durrell would probably have tried to cap her comment. What might he have said? 'Another little job for the undertaker?' Or possibly made a reference to raspberry jam. She stifled a sigh. The trouble with CJ was that you couldn't take the horror out of a situation by having a giggle with him about it. 'I don't know anyone who's jumped out of a window lately, do I?'

'The chief accountant for Holland Holdings.'

Now there was a blow to the solar plexus. What was the matter with her? She ought to have seen that coming. 'Did she fall, or was she pushed?'

'Yes, that is the question. I see you already know it was a woman. White wine or red? It should be red with steak, but if you're tired . . .?'

Bea ground her teeth. Yes, she was tired. But she actually needed a full-bodied red wine at that moment. 'Red, please. I am happy to say I don't know anyone in that organization, apart from Leon and Benton. And Leon won't even admit to being in their employ.'

'Ah.' He folded long-fingered hands one over the other and produced his Cheshire Cat smile.

She could have hit him. Not that that would have done any good. 'I see you are big with news. Tell.'

'You must understand that I have access to information through my contacts which—'

'I understand. Nothing you say can be substantiated. It's all rumour. But true.'

'I believe so. You read the papers, don't you? Perhaps not the *Financial Times* . . .'

'Are you suggesting that I am unable to read more than two words a minute? Yes —' with sarcasm – 'I read one of the tabloids every day over breakfast. And *The Times*, too. Sometimes. When I have a minute to spare.'

He frowned. 'You must be aware there's been considerable public reaction to the fact that certain companies have, quite legally, been avoiding payment of tax to the British exchequer by claiming their registered office is overseas.'

'Big flapdoodle. It's not illegal, but it *is* immoral, right?'

'Quite. A factory based in Birmingham, for instance, may have its registered office in the Cayman Islands . . .'

'Ah.' She was adding up the column of figures faster than CJ could spit them out.

'Which is so they can pay a lower rate of tax there than they would have to do here.'

Bea said, 'Wait a minute. I understood the Holland mansion here was their head office.'

'Yes, but not their registered office—'

'Which is in the Cayman Islands. And there's a big scare on, which brought Sybil haring back from the States and drew in the younger brother willy nilly. Mm. Do you think their chief accountant has been caught diverting money from accounts in the Cayman Islands to . . . herself? Or to herself and partner?'

'All conjecture.'

The waiter plonked their plates down in front of them. Her stomach was queasy, for she could now put a different interpretation on Leon's quest for information. 'Was this chief accountant, perhaps, a susceptible woman, who might have been persuaded to depart from the straight and narrow by a much younger man?'

'So they say. This wine is almost tolerable.'

'Benton, of course. He had a habit of getting his own way through his attentions to women. So he seduced her . . . which partly accounts for his swift rise through Holland Holdings and his then being in a position to capture the eye of the boss's daughter. May I assume that the aforesaid chief accountant was old Mr Holland's tried and trusted right-hand woman? Been with him for ever and a day?'

'There is a hint that the partnership might have been very close in the past. Mistress *and* accountant to Mr Holland, a double whammy, as they say.' He allowed himself a tiny smile at his apology for a joke.

Bea acknowledged his quip with a nod. 'We know that Benton needed money, was in debt, probably being blackmailed . . . Yes, I have good reason to make that statement, but we won't go into details now. He needed money. She was in charge of moving it around the world. Might we not toy with the idea that he induced her to siphon some of it off in his direction? It would tally with what I know of him. But then something went wrong. Ah. An audit was due?'

He took another sip of wine. 'Such a very complex organization requires the services of a good accountant over a long period of time. Sometimes they can take years to agree the amount of tax due to HM Revenue and Customs.'

'Benton was Boy Wonder for Holland Holdings long before the eight or nine years during which he was married to Dilys. How long ago did the jiggery pokery start?'

CJ's nose whiffled at the use of 'jiggery pokery' but he said, 'My information would indicate that it is fairly recent.'

Bea descended to counting on her fingers. 'How many years would the accountants have been lagging behind, do you think? Three or four? No more than that. Probably less. Say two, possibly three. The conspirators realized that Judgement Day couldn't be

put off for ever. The great big wheel was coming nearer and nearer
to Vera.'

Did CJ know the old song about the wheel coming nearer and
nearer to Vera, which took Bea back to the flickering black
and white movies of old, in which the heroine was always being
tied up and threatened with an unpleasant death by some fiendish
villain or other? Bea couldn't for the moment recall whether or not
the wheel which was approaching Vera had been a part of a lumber
mill. And then there was the episode in which the train bore down
upon the heroine, who was tied up on the tracks. 'Vera' was always
saved at the last minute, of course.

'I regret I am not acquainted with Vera,' said CJ in his driest
tone, 'Nor am I able to tell you exactly how far the auditors had
got. Do eat up. You're looking tired.'

No woman feels better for being told she looks tired. Bea gave
him a glare which he declined to notice. She picked up her knife
and fork and managed to eat a couple of mouthfuls. Realized how
hungry she was, and tucked in. Only when she'd finished did she
speak again.

'Right. An audit was due, or something else alerted Mr Holland
to the fact that he was being bamboozled big time by people he'd
trusted for ever. Ah, I think I may know what triggered the catas-
trophe for the conspirators. The deputy accountant – a man called
Adamsson – is reported to have had a blazing row with his boss
and with Benton, in which he accused the pair of treason, inter-
national money-laundering and pilfering the petty cash. Righteous
indignation on the part of the chief accountant and Benton.
Adamsson is sacked and departs, muttering threats to all and
sundry.

'But Adamsson's words start a slow rumble in Mr Holland's
mind. The firm of H & B services his household, which is the main
reason for its existence as far as he is concerned. His daughter,
whom he doesn't see often, had been satisfactorily – as far as he
knew – married off to Benton and had produced a reasonable quiver
of children. Old Mr Holland has an acute financial brain. He hasn't
been using it much in recent years, but now Adamsson's words have
made him uneasy. He takes a look at the books of H & B. Shock,
horror! The firm is not doing well. Dividends are way down. But,
it's a piddling little firm compared to the might of Holland Holdings
so . . . perhaps a word of warning in Benton's ear? That should do

the trick. He still doesn't realize that H & B's been in trouble for yonks and that Benton's been taking increasingly desperate steps to refinance them.

'Once roused, Mr Holland can't rest. He begins to think the unthinkable; could Adamsson be right? Is Holland Holdings really in trouble? He demands an up-to-date review of their finances. The answers he gets are not to his liking. So what does he do next? He summons reinforcements in the shape of his sister Sybil. She's a rich woman in her own right but, like him, she's not one to sit back and let herself be cheated.'

'I have no information about her.'

'Take it from me, she's a formidable lady. She storms over from the States, drags Leon in, and there is a family conference. Red flags pop up all over the place. Mr Holland's trusted accountant realizes the game is up and jumps. When exactly did she do the deed?'

'Ten days ago.'

'She took the easy way out by falling out of the sky. End of. Leaving Benton to take the ensuing flack, and the money . . . I wonder where the money has gone to? Beyond the first drop to the Cayman Islands, I mean.' She also wondered how Leon was getting on, tracing Benton's accounts . . . and how long it would take to locate the missing millions and get them returned. If, indeed, it were possible to do so.

CJ said, 'You can't be drawn into this mess through Max, can you?'

'I sincerely hope not.' She shuddered. 'Yes, Benton was trying to build up the fortunes of the ailing firm of H & B by enticing me and Max on to their board of directors. And yes, Max was anxious to play at one time, but I think he's learned his lesson there. Perhaps it was a sign of desperation on Benton's part that he felt he had to rough me up and chase me around on a friend's scooter?'

'Scooter?'

'All right. Motorbike. And no, I don't know for sure who was on that bike, but I think I know how to find out. Trying to terrify a middle-aged woman by such tactics is a ploy born out of desperation, wouldn't you say?' She leaned back in her chair and took a sip of wine. 'Benton wasn't as clever as he thought he was. As witness his being taken in by the Joker. Leon Holland to you.'

'Ah. You do think he's taking a hand in the game, then?'

'I do. Let's look at the facts. Long-estranged younger brother. Financially sound through his own efforts in other directions. Currently at a loose end. The Hollands' solution was to bring him in as trouble spotter and hatchet man. Leon – out of curiosity, perhaps – does exactly what they want him to do. I think he identified Benton as the main conspirator straight away, which explains why he infiltrates Benton's household pretending to be an undischarged bankrupt. He observes what's going on there, he listens to everything, he sits in on meetings, he saves Dilys's life and he makes up to me as a possible saviour for H & B.'

'Did he kill Benton?'

'He's ruthless enough, but I can't see him killing the two boys.'

'Did Benton commit suicide because he'd been found out and was about to be prosecuted?'

Silence. Then, 'It feels wrong. It doesn't *feel* as if it's to do with money, but . . . No, I know that's no sort of answer. It depends on my instinct, and you are about to say that instinct is not evidence.'

'Agreed, but personally I value your instincts. Tell me what you suspect.'

'About Benton's death? I really have no idea. Well, I do have a vague thought wandering about at the back of my mind, but nothing coherent as yet. About Leon? He's a wolf in sheep's clothing. He got me to find Benton's missing memory stick, and then to find the password for it. The information on it will probably give him enough clues to trace where some of the money has gone. How much is missing?'

'Estimates vary from ten million to ten billion.'

That amused her. 'There *is* a difference. But even if it's only one million that's missing – hark at me saying *only* one million! – it's more than enough in my estimation. It's worth taking a risk or two.'

'Worth killing Benton for?'

She frowned. 'I'm struggling with that.'

'Coffee? No? Then I'll walk you home. Guard you from attack by bikers.'

Was he trying to make another joke? Possibly. She smiled her appreciation and thanked him. She was aware he would like to be invited in for a late night snifter of brandy, or whatever, and she didn't really want to do so. He was a very old friend, but lately he was sending her signals that he would like to take matters further, which she did not want to do. How to turn him down without offending him?

Perhaps the biker would magically appear on her doorstep? But it wasn't a biker who awaited her on her return.

Bea heard a plaintive wailing as they turned into her road and identified it with the antennae of a grandmother. 'That's Pippin, my grandson. What on earth . . .?'

It was indeed Pippin, struggling in his mother's arms, unhappy about being roused from sleep and taken out into the cold night. Nicole was muffled in a huge fake fur coat and Russian style hat. She was crying.

CJ stopped short. 'What's your daughter-in-law doing out with the boy at this time of night?'

'You may well ask,' said Bea, thinking grimly that she could probably guess. 'Come in, Nicole. Give me Pippin. There, there, little one. Thanks for the meal, CJ. It was good of you to spare the time, but I must just . . . Where's my key? And I'll turn off the alarm. Don't just stand there, Nicole. Come on in.'

Nicole was a wreck. Eye make-up smeared, hair coming down, one glove on and one nowhere to be seen. Pippin was smelly and upset. He knew her, all right, but he was uncomfortable in his wet nappy and had been crying for so long that he'd got into the rhythm of it, and it was going to take him time to calm down.

Bea kicked the front door to behind her, only to have it rebound. She didn't bother to look round, but said, 'You? Out!' The door closed quietly behind her. She could only hope the man who'd been lurking in the shadows was on the other side of it, but for now all her attention was on Pippin. She took him through to the kitchen, divested him of his outer clothing and changed his nappy. Before she'd even shed her own coat she made up a bottle of milk for him. He didn't always have a bottle at bedtime nowadays, but once he was warm, dry and fed, he'd probably drop off to sleep.

Nicole was going to need more attention than that, but a cup of coffee might help for a start. 'Take your coat off, my dear. Would you like to tidy up? You know where the bathroom is.'

'I'm all right.' Quite clearly she was not all right, but until Pippin had been attended to, Bea could do no more. Once the bottle had been popped into the toddler's mouth, he gulped, sneezed, and got on with it. Bea took him into the living room and propped him up in a corner of the big chair with his bottle. He was old enough to hold the bottle for himself, and did so. He settled down, then, and even managed a pearly-toothed smile. In a minute he would need burping, but so far, so good.

Bea relaxed for a moment. One problem down. Three to go? She braced herself for battle. 'Well, now, Nicole. Of course I'm delighted to see you at any time, you know that. But isn't it a bit late for Pippin to be out?'

The girl sank into another chair, still wearing her outer things. 'He –' sob – 'threw me out!'

'What!'

'Well, I threw him out first, and then he came back and said he was sorry, and then we argued and he threw me out instead. Tell him that it's him that's got to go, not me! I know my rights!'

Several responses jostled for attention in Bea's head. Nicole must know that in the case of a marital disagreement, she only had to ring the police to eject the offending partner. So why . . .? Ah, she hadn't wanted to ring the police because . . . because that would have made the tabloids with headlines such as "MP and wife in night-time tussle"? So it was still important to her to be an MP's wife?

Did she really want Bea to tell Max to leave the marital home? Oh, surely not. Which meant that Nicole was not willing to throw her marriage away.

The girl wailed, 'I loved him!'

'What?' Bea blinked. Then realized Nicole was not referring to her husband. 'You mean Benton?'

'Who else?' Another deep sob. 'I was going to leave Max and we were going to live on a desert island in the sun, and my parents wouldn't have minded because they'd have seen that Benton was miles better for me than Max, and Benton promised to take Pippin as his own, and his boys could go to boarding school and everything would have been perfect!'

Oh dear. Confirming Bea's worst suspicions. A desert island in the sun, indeed! How could Nicole have been so stupid? 'And how was he going to fund that lifestyle, pray?'

'You know I don't understand such things. Something to do with insider trading, I think.'

'Insider trading breaks the law.'

'Oh, I did tell him not to be so naughty, but he didn't listen to little old me.' Coyly. Pretending she was too much of a bimbo to understand such things. She sought for a hankie and didn't find one. Bea checked the Pippin was all right to be left for a moment and collected a box of tissues from the kitchen. 'Here. Could you do with a stiff drink?'

'No, no. Not when I'm . . .' She gestured to her stomach.

Bea sat down with a bump. 'You're pregnant? Whose is it?'

'Everything's such a mess. I didn't realize till yesterday, and all I was worried about was how Benton would take it, but I needn't have got so upset, need I? Oh, it's Max's, not that he cares. All he cares about is money and his career.'

'Now that's not true, Nicole. He cares deeply about you and Pippin.'

The girl wept. 'You don't understand. I'd have done anything for Benton. He loved me so much. I'll never meet anyone else like him.'

'I should hope not,' said Bea. 'He says that to all the girls, you know.'

'No, no. Only to me. His wife is a dreary little thing. He never cared for her, but she got herself pregnant by someone else in the office and begged Benton to marry her. She promised he'd be made managing director of the firm and—'

'You're overlooking the fact that it was he who was the father of her child. Of her three children, in fact.'

'Well, men have needs.'

Bea wanted to smack the girl, but refrained. With an effort. So Nicole was having another child. 'Does Max know you're pregnant?'

Sniff. 'Yes, I did tell him, and he said he couldn't be responsible for another man's brat. He thought it was Benton's, of course, and I did wish it was, too . . . at least, I would have done if Benton hadn't been killed. Oh, what am I going to do?'

'Face the fact that you're just one in a long line of women that Benton has lied to.'

'How dare you!' Yet her tone lacked heat. Whatever she said to the contrary, Nicole had known, deep down, what Benton was like. 'He loved me.'

'Be grateful that you're alive to say so. His partner in crime at work committed suicide, and he's put his wife into intensive care.'

'Lies. All lies.'

'Fact the facts, Nicole. He's dead, and you're alive. So what are you going to do with the rest of your life? Do you really want me to ask Max – the father of your children – to leave the flat so that you can live there by yourself? If you divorce him, you'd get alimony, but you know exactly how much money there is in the kitty, and that flat is expensive. I doubt if you'll be able to enjoy the same standard of living as you did when Max was beside you. Do you have any skills that you could use if you have to take a job? I remember how hard I found it when I divorced Max's father and had to go out to work to keep us. I'd married straight from school so hadn't had the benefit of any further education. I had to take anything I could get. Cleaning jobs, mostly. Not a happy time. And a divorced woman is such a drag on the marriage market, don't you think? Her social circle contracts, and friends take sides. I suppose your parents would be supportive enough, but going home to live with parents is such a confession of failure, isn't it? Not the same as being the wife of a rising young member of parliament. Not so many opportunities to wear evening dress.'

'I don't care about such things.' But she did, oh yes, she did. 'Benton was the love of my life.'

'The love of a number of women's lives, as far as I can make out. What do you know about his sister?'

'It was she who rang me early this morning, to say he was dead. She was horrid to me.'

Pippin let the bottle slide out of his mouth and start to mewl. Bea picked him up, put him over her shoulder and patted his back to bring his wind up. 'Ginevra was jealous of the attention he paid you, I expect. Oh, and by the way, she's his wife not his sister.'

'What nonsense!' Nicole didn't want to believe that. 'She said it wasn't clear whether or not he'd committed suicide. I don't care if he *was* caught fiddling the books, because he was only doing it so that we could marry. If he'd told me, I'd have stood by him.'

Bea doubted that. Nicole was a practical person when she wasn't indulging in a false dream of romance. A cream puff of a romance. A poisoned cream puff.

Bea picked up the phone and pressed buttons. 'I'd better let Max know that you're safe here with me. He'll be worrying himself stiff.'

'It would serve him right if he were worried about me.'

Bea ignored that. 'Max? It's Mother. I have Nicole and Pippin here, and we're having a good old talk. Since it's so late, they may stay the night and return to you in the morning. Any message for her?'

Max shouted, 'Tell her to go to hell!'

Bea winced. 'Very well, dear. I'll give her your love.' She put the phone down. 'He sends his love. He does love you, you know.'

Nicole inclined her head. Yes, she knew. With a sigh, she shed her coat and hat and ran her fingers back through her hair. 'I must look a mess.'

'It takes extra grooming to look good when you're pregnant.'

'At least I'm not being sick all the time, as I was with Pippin.'

'Max adores Pippin. Do you know yet whether the baby is a boy or a girl? I think he'd be a doting father for a little girl, but I don't suppose he really cares which it is.'

'I don't know yet. He'll probably want a DNA test to prove it's his.'

'Well, if that's all it takes . . . Will you stay the night here? I leave Pippin's cot ready in the spare bedroom for the odd day that he spends with me, and the bed is always made up. Or would you like me to summon a taxi for you?'

'I couldn't cope with another shouting match tonight.'

'Of course not. You need a spot of pampering, and I'll see that you get it. Max is a good lad, at bottom. Not perhaps as clever as you in some ways, but you've always known that, haven't you?'

A grimace. 'Yes, I suppose so. Daddy always said that Max would go far with me behind him.'

'A perfect partnership. Men like Benton come and go, but you can't rely on them to pay the bills every month.'

Nicole managed a smile. 'Benton might have accepted Pippin, but not a second child. The new baby would have been one too many.'

'You'll do,' said Bea. 'Now, let's get you up to bed. Did you bring a toothbrush with you? Do you want to borrow a T-shirt or nightdress? Luckily I keep extra clothes and nappies here for Pippin.'

She carried the sleeping toddler upstairs and saw her guests safely ensconced in the spare bedroom before she turned her attention to what was going to happen next. There was a light on upstairs, but no sound of music. Maggie must have come back and gone to bed. And Zander? Was he up there with her? Mm. Possibly. Better not to enquire.

Descending the stairs, Bea wondered if she'd imagined Leon slipping into the house after Nicole. Bea had told him to leave. She'd heard the front door shut, but on which side of that door had he been at that point?

Also, she must re-set the house alarm.

SEVENTEEN

Monday night

Bea reset the alarm and sniffed the air. Upstairs there'd been a trace Nicole's scent and Pippin's baby talc. Downstairs there was something else. Aftershave. Alcohol?

So Leon was still on the premises. Why?

She was afraid she knew the answer only too well.

She went into the living room and shut the door behind her. As she'd guessed, Leon was lounging in the big chair by the fireplace, one leg over the other, his overcoat thrown on the settee nearby.

He held his arms open in a welcoming gesture. 'What a partner you'll make!'

'Not I.' She went to check the phone to see if there were any messages. An unnecessary movement, but it took her to the opposite side of the room from him. No messages, thank goodness.

She said, 'I assume from your air of triumph that you've cracked the mystery of the memory stick and that your accountants are even now beavering away to get the stolen money back into your hands.'

'Mr Adamsson is back from his holidays, crowing with

triumph. Everything he's always said about our erstwhile chief accountant and about Benton has been proved true. He's working twelve hours a day to get everything shipshape and tickety-boo again. Yes, he really does talk like that. He puffed up his chest and smiled so widely when I reinstated him that I could have hit him. I can't think how I refrained. But there . . . He's indispensable now his boss is dead, and when he talks figures, we listen.'

'The police have cleared him of Benton's murder?'

'And of complicity in arranging his superior's dive off the roof. He really was out of the country at the time. I have to thank you for finding the password for us. Without it, and the details of Benton's overseas accounts, Adamsson couldn't even begin to untangle the mess.'

'I'm glad you're pleased. Well –' with a glance at the clock – 'it's getting late. I've had a hard day and need to get my head down. I thought you'd have left by now.'

'I couldn't resist. Your personal skills are remarkable.' Again, he opened his arms wide. 'Come here!'

She supposed most women would obey him. They would sit on his knee, and he'd go straight into seduction mode. There was a soft rug on the floor, and he would expect her to lie down there and strip off. She shook her head. 'You mistake me for a quick lay.'

'I don't make that kind of mistake. I've known since the moment we met that we'd end up in bed together.'

'Don't be ridiculous! I am not that kind of woman.' It had been a mistake to take that high tone with him, but she was tired and wanted to go to bed. Alone.

He sprang to his feet and had his arms around her and his mouth on hers before she realized what he intended to do. His arms were strong, and he held her so tightly she could hardly breathe. He was trying to get inside her mouth with his tongue, but she would not – not! – allow him to do so. She could smell whisky on his breath. So, he'd already been drinking. Bad news.

She thought of swooning away so that he would have to let her go. But no; he'd probably just pick her up and throw her on to the settee or down on to the rug to have his wicked way with her.

So she stood still, rigid in denial, waiting for him to come up for air.

'Come on, now. Loosen up!'

'I am not going to spit at you, or bite you, or scrape the heel of my boot down your leg. I am not going to pinch your thigh, which I am told is exceedingly painful and recommended for use on any man who tries to rape a woman, but—'

'I'm not trying to rape you! What do you think I am?'

'A man who's had everything too easy where women are concerned.'

'I've had only one partner for—'

'And how many one-night stands?'

'I'm offering you—'

'You don't have anything to offer which I'd wish to have.'

'You don't realize—'

'That the price of your helping your brother out of a nasty hole is that he retires and you take over?'

He loosened his hold but retained his grasp of her upper arms. 'Who told you that?'

She didn't reply that it was obvious, because to her way of thinking it was.

His eyes switched from right to left. He was the alpha male and not accustomed to being refused. In a moment he would switch from lust to rage.

She modified her tone in an effort to divert him. 'I'm too old for you, Leon. You need someone in her thirties, intelligent enough to argue with you but still young enough to give you children.'

'Do you think I hadn't realized you were too old to give me children? I want you for your bright mind *and* your admirable body. I want you by my side, sharing in my triumphs, advising me when I miss something important. I'm prepared to pay—'

She lowered her eyelids and turned her head away.

He shook her, hard. 'Don't you understand that I could ruin your precious son with the evidence Benton had on him and his love affairs!'

'You could try, though I must point out that the public doesn't seem to be all that troubled about the extramarital affairs of their members of parliament. But you can't force someone to love you. Also, I must warn you that my arthritis restricts bedtime acrobatics.' She didn't have much arthritis yet, but he wasn't to know that.

He threw her away from him. She staggered back, ending up on the settee.

He said, 'I need . . .' With jerky movements, he forced himself back on to his chair. 'Do you have any alcohol on the premises?'

'No.' She did keep some in the cupboard for the odd occasion when an old friend was visiting, but she considered Leon had had more than enough to drink already. 'Shall I make you some coffee before you leave?' She flicked a glance at the clock. Past midnight, Cinderella. Time for bed.

He ground his teeth. 'You think I'm drunk? I'm not, you know. I could make you—'

'If you touch me again I'll have you for assault and rape.'

'Who'd believe you?'

'Inspector Durrell, who is currently investigating Benton's murder and his links to the dead accountant.'

'She killed herself, and most of the money is on its way back to our coffers. As for your inspector, what action could he possibly take that would disturb me?'

'Leak information to the press which would cause a run on your brother's shares. That's why you didn't want to ask the police for help when Benton died, isn't it? That's why it was so important to find his passwords before the police did? You used me, Leon. I don't like that.'

A shrug. 'You proved your worth, yes.'

He *was* an arrogant so and so, wasn't he? She relaxed, as far as she could with a tiger in the room.

He started to pace up and down. 'Now you're going to say that a man who is in charge of others should first be in control of himself. I assure you, I do not normally drink more than one or two glasses a night, but today . . .'

She was, almost, amused. He did seem to know his strengths and weaknesses. 'As your hostess, I am happy to provide you with some coffee. I will even do you some ground coffee in a cafetière if you wish, rather than offer you a mug of instant. I am assuming you will then summon a taxi to take you back to your hotel, and that you don't intend to drive anywhere tonight.'

'Car and chauffeur waiting. I only have to make a call on the phone and he'll be here.'

Oh, the delights of being a multimillionaire. 'How late do you intend to keep the poor man waiting?'

He took out his smartphone, rang a number and said, 'You can go home now. I don't need you again tonight.' Switched off.

Which meant her hint that he should leave had fallen on stony ground. Before he could return to the attack, she said, 'Tell me. Did you and your partner never think of getting married?'

He winced. 'She brought the subject up now and then. I was always too busy . . . and then she got cancer. I asked her to marry me then, and she refused. Said she'd lived alone and would die alone.'

Bea understood that his partner had taken her revenge on him by refusing an offer of marriage when he finally got round to it. Now he was feeling guilty about not having asked sooner. Serve him right.

She said, 'When my dear husband died—'

'Don't pull that one. You're divorced.'

Did he think that entitled him to jump her? She sharpened her voice. 'One of the first things you should do when you take over your brother's organization is to sort out your information department. I've been married twice. I divorced my first husband, who was Max's father, yes. He was tom-catting around within a year of our marriage. We are now good friends and see one another regularly. Some years later I married Hamilton Abbot, who was my dear love and best friend for thirty-odd years till he succumbed to cancer. I still grieve for him.'

That gave him pause. He stopped pacing, leaned against the mantelpiece. 'What was he like, this Hamilton of yours?'

'Loving and caring, practical. Commonsensical, funny. He could make me laugh in the most difficult of situations. A good father to Max. He was a Christian, much further along the road than I.'

'She was, too.'

His partner? That was interesting. But not him, presumably?

He flung himself back into his chair, relaxed, staring at the ceiling. 'You don't think I'm capable of taking over from my brother, do you?'

'I have no opinion on the subject.' But, now he'd come to mention it, perhaps not. And was that really what he wanted out of life? She supposed he might want to take over from his brother to assuage some long-held resentment of the way he'd been treated in his early years, but was he really the stuff from which Captains of Industry are made? Had he the cutting edge of a good diamond? Could he put the trauma of his partner's death behind him?

On the other hand, he'd started a number of other projects and carried them through to a successful conclusion, and a man of principle could do a lot of good in the world if he took over a powerful organization.

She had a vivid memory of him working over Dilys's body, trying to save her life. 'Was it you who lifted Dilys from the hospital?'

'Sybil and I arranged it between us. We asked Maria, my brother's housekeeper, to collect Dilys from the hospital and take her to a private clinic. She needed peace and quiet. Sybil's been visiting her, and so have I. The doctors didn't think she ought to be told about Benton and the boys at first, but she's getting better, slowly. Sybil did tell her that Benton's dead. We hope she'll soon be strong enough to hear the rest, but for the moment we've let her assume that the boys are with their sister and that Sybil is looking after them all.'

'Bernice knows that the boys are dead?'

'She does. Sybil's taking Bernice to see her mother tomorrow, if she's had another good night. Bernice is an oddly mature little person, isn't she? Most impressive. It's almost as if Dilys is the child, and she the parent.'

'Does Dilys know that Benton might have been married before?'

'What! No . . . Was he? Who to? Ah . . . not Ginevra! I suppose . . . But how . . .? What other secrets are you keeping from me?'

Bea was silent. She'd uncovered evidence which seemed to point to Benton as a bigamist, but perhaps there had been a divorce after all. If he had divorced his first wife, then his marriage to Dilys was legal, and she would inherit the house . . . that is, if he hadn't made a will leaving everything to Ginevra and . . . Oh, let the lawyers sort that lot out. She said, 'I said "might". I'm not sure yet. Whether Benton was married to her or divorced or whatever, I don't think Dilys should have to face Ginevra yet.'

'No, I suppose not.' He closed his eyes. Was he going to go to sleep on her? How inconvenient. She said, 'I'll make you that coffee now.'

He nodded, and she went out to the kitchen to put the kettle on. Winston arrived to be stroked and given a late-night treat. She was so tired . . . Should she have some coffee, too? No, she'd never sleep if she did.

She took the coffee back into the sitting room to find Leon gently snoring. His chest rose and fell, rhythmically. She shook his arm, and he failed to wake.

Now what?

She didn't know whether to laugh or cry. If she let him sleep the night here, would he wake in a couple of hours' time and try to force his way into her room? She could lock her door, but would that stop him trying to break it down if he felt like it? Think again, Bea.

Oh, the inconvenience of having a man around!

Tuesday morning

'Mrs A! There's a man in your bed!'

Bea started awake. Where was she? This wasn't her bed, nor her bedroom.

Maggie's concerned face hovered over her. 'I took a cuppa into your bedroom, and there was this man – it's Leon Holland, isn't it? – in your bed. And not you.'

Bea rubbed her eyes. 'I thought he might try to join me in my own bed, and Oliver's was already made up so I came up here to sleep instead.'

Maggie danced from one foot to the other, subduing the giggles. 'I thought . . . Oh, wait till I tell Zander! I'll make you another cuppa, shall I?'

'Bless you, my dear. Is Leon still in my bedroom? I need a shower and clean clothes and, oh, my make-up. I'm not facing the day without war paint.'

'You'd best swap rooms. I'll rout him out and bring him up here. He can use Oliver's bathroom kit. What a carry on! And is it Nicole in the spare room? I could hear Pippin – at least, I thought it was Pippin – wanting attention. I'd better go and help her with him.' Maggie was dressed in black and lilac today, with a lilac band around her hair. The effect was tasteful, which wasn't always the case.

There was a prolonged peal on the front doorbell, and both women started. Pippin began to wail in earnest on the floor below.

Then the knocker went, bang, bang, bang!

'I'll see to it.' Maggie disappeared.

Bea could hear the girl progressing down the stairs, turning on the lights as she went, for it was a dark morning. Then the radio came on as Maggie reached the kitchen. The front doorbell continued to ring at the same time as someone used the knocker. Too much noise!

Bea put on her dressing gown, made a face at herself in the mirror, and went down the stairs to the first floor . . . to be confronted by a washed-out Nicole holding a smelly Pippin in the doorway to the guest bedroom.

Nicole was staring in disbelief at a large man wearing nothing but a pair of well-filled designer shorts, who was propped up against the door frame of the master bedroom.

Leon was holding one hand over his eyes. Did he have a hangover? Serve him right.

The front door banged open. 'Where is she, then?'

Max?

Maggie shut the front door behind him. 'No one's up yet. Do you want to go into the kitchen and make yourself a cup of coffee while you wait?'

The visitor was not listening. 'Where is she? Nicole!' In a bellow.

Maggie bounded up the stairs and said to Nicole, 'Max wants to see you. I'll take Pippin and feed him while you get dressed and go down to see your husband, right?'

Nicole recoiled. 'No, no! I don't want to see him.'

'Nonsense,' said Maggie. 'Fifteen minutes.' She took the child off Nicole and pushed Leon back into the master bedroom. 'Now, Mr Holland. Gather up your clothes. Take them upstairs to the top floor, bathroom straight ahead. Shower and shave. Coffee downstairs in half an hour, right?'

Leon grunted and obeyed. He didn't seem too steady on his feet this morning.

Bea floated past him into her own bedroom, had a shower, dressed and was putting on her make-up before Maggie returned with a second cup of tea for her and with Pippin on her hip. Sounds of marital strife could be heard from the rooms below.

'You did!' 'I didn't!' type of thing. Maggie and Bea ignored them.

Maggie seated herself on the bed and proceeded to give Pippin his bottle. 'I gave him soggy cereal and half a banana. Hope that's right.'

'Perfect. You're really good with babies.' Bea selected a pair of silver and topaz earrings to go with her grey silk top and skirt.

Maggie was pleased at the compliment. 'I did want to train as a nanny but Mummy said that was no kind of career for her daughter. I'm looking forward to having babies of my own. I must say, Mrs A., you look better, even without your face on, than Nicole does in full fig. I hope I look as good as you when I'm old. Are you serious about Mr Holland?'

Bea shook her head. 'He's not cost effective.' And I'm too old to tangle with tricky Dickies like him.

Maggie put Pippin over her shoulder to burp him. 'Zander wasn't sure he liked the sound of him.'

'Meaning that you don't, either? He's stimulating in small doses.'

Pippin obligingly burped, and Maggie popped his bottle back into his pursed-up mouth. 'You don't want to marry him then. What about CJ?'

Bea was amused. 'What do you think?'

Maggie wrinkled her nose. 'Would he ask you to clean your teeth before he kissed you?'

Bea laughed so much, it took her three attempts to get her wristwatch fastened. 'Have you time for breakfast before you start work? Where do you have to be today, and when?'

Maggie looked at her oversized watch and yelped. 'No, it's all right. I've got a late start today. Ten o'clock. I'll start cooking. By the way, Zander's seeing to a licence and a double bed today. We thought the sooner the better. You don't mind, do you?'

'Bless you, my child. I'm over the moon. It will be good to have a man about the house again. He can fend off my unwanted suitors, and I'm sure he's handy with a screwdriver. Perhaps he can even mend the toaster.'

Down the stairs they went. There was a significant silence from the sitting room. Bea and Maggie looked at one another, tried not to giggle and tiptoed past the door and into the kitchen. Winston was already there, waiting for his breakfast. Bea turned off the radio.

The doorbell rang. Bea set off to open it. 'I know that ring.' She opened the door. 'Inspector, do come in. You're just in time for breakfast.'

DI Durrell stamped his feet on the doormat. It was raining. 'I wanted to ask Ginevra Benton some questions, but she's done a bunk.'

Bea nodded. 'You thought I might know why she's disappeared? Well, I don't know all the answers – oh, we're just about to cook a full English, that do you? – but I think I can tell you where to look for the information you need. The trouble with this business is that there's so many sides to it. The missing money. Dilys's "suicide" attempts. Benton's death. But they're all so tangled up with his attempt to take me over . . . What does Ginevra's partner say?'

'Clodagh? Sleeping partner. She put money into the business but says she hadn't seen Ginevra for weeks until Sunday, when they did the stocktake together.'

'Clodagh? Wait a minute. Her partner's called Ricky.'

'Who's Ricky?'

'Don't you ever check on Facebook? Well, if there are two partners, one for business and one for pleasure, that explains a lot. Oh, come on into the kitchen and sit down. Does this Clodagh share the flat with Ginevra?'

'No, she doesn't. She lives on the other side of the Common in a nice semi-D.'

Maggie said, 'Can someone take Pippin off me while I make the coffee?' She turned the radio on again.

The inspector took Pippin out of Maggie's arms and jiggled him as to the manner born. 'My men report that Benton's house is empty, and there's no sign of Ginevra. Packed up and gone. Her flat, likewise. Also, the shop was closed yesterday. Clodagh is incensed that Ginevra should have left her in the lurch. Who, she says, is going to run the shop, in which she has invested good money? Who's Ricky?'

'Her partner for pleasure, according to Facebook. I think he may also have been the man who took the boutique's promotional photographs, and who was following me around on his bike. So what does this Clodagh do for a living?'

'Part-time at a garden centre. Divorced. Put her alimony settlement into Ginevra's boutique and claims to know nothing of her private life.'

Leon sleepwalked down the stairs, dressed but not altogether in his right mind. His eyes were half closed. 'Grrffgh?'

Bea stifled amusement. 'Try again?'

He cleared his throat. 'Coffee?'

Max wrenched open the door to the hall and pounded up the stairs, tugging Nicole along behind him. She didn't scream or yell for help, so no one intervened. The door to the spare room slammed shut behind them.

Maggie said, 'Domestic spat. Take no notice, Mr Policeman. Mr Holland, do you want a full English breakfast?'

He cleared his throat again, and this time sounded almost normal. 'I believe I owe you all an apology. My behaviour last night—'

Bea had her head inside the fridge, retrieving bacon and sausages. 'Accepted. Send round some flowers later. Now, what do you want for breakfast?'

'Er . . . half an avocado with a home-made dressing. Perhaps some smoked salmon and scrambled eggs afterwards?'

Bea slung ingredients from the fridge on to the table. 'Full or part English. I'm doing the lot, and you can choose which bits you want. Maggie, do turn off the radio, there's a dear. Inspector Durrell, can you sit over there by the toaster and feed it in the usual way? We will all eat and drink, and we will *not* talk business till we've finished. Winston; off the table!'

Max and Nicole did not reappear. Pippin was put in the walker Bea kept for him and given pieces of apple to eat. Winston sampled a bit of apple, decided it was not to his taste and spat it out. Pippin ate what the cat rejected and threw the rest on to the floor.

Leon ate what everyone else did, even polishing off a sausage that was going begging.

The inspector drained his third cup of coffee, squared his elbows and said, 'Now, Mrs Abbot. You didn't look surprised when I said Ginevra had disappeared. May I ask why? You said she could do with being investigated, but the only reason you gave was that she had a silly name.'

'I didn't think she'd been born "Ginevra", which is the name of her boutique. There's nothing wrong in that, but I did wonder what name she might have been born with, and I came up with "Jean". Someone called "Jean Marsh", who is the right age, does appear in the records as having married a man named Benjamin Benton some ten years ago.'

Leon quirked an eyebrow. 'And divorced, I assume?'

'I can't find that she was,' said Bea. 'I wish I could, but I can't. Inspector, you have better resources than I . . . Can you find that out for us?'

'Where did you look?'

'Oliver looked for me.'

'If Oliver looked, then I think we can take it that there was no divorce.'

Leon clutched his head. 'No divorce? But that means . . . Tell me I'm not going crazy. Was Benton a bigamist as well as a lecher and a thief? And where does that leave my niece?'

'If it's true,' said Bea, 'then Bernice is illegitimate. And if Benton was clever enough to get Dilys to sign over her share of the house and her shares in H & B, then it means your niece will have neither house nor income to her name when she comes out of the clinic. Unless, that is, Benton made a will leaving everything to her when he died. And somehow, I doubt that he did.'

Leon drew in his breath. 'What a mess!'

The inspector fed a morsel of bacon fat to Winston. 'It gives Dilys a nice motive for killing Benton—'

Leon intervened. 'It's a good thing she's been under supervision since the moment she was taken out of the house in an ambulance. Otherwise . . .'

Bea said, 'Yes, she might well have been tempted to clock him one. If she hadn't been so downtrodden. But she'd never have killed her own children. Fortunately, she has a solid alibi. As I have. As I gather Mr Adamsson has. But as Ginevra hasn't. And neither, come to think of it, has Clodagh, who may well prove to be one of the missing pieces of the puzzle. Or Ricky.'

The inspector said, 'You're giving me a headache. Is there another cup of coffee?'

Maggie put the kettle on again. 'Mrs A., why is Clodagh so important?'

'I think she and Ginevra lied about what they did on Sunday. Ginevra said they were doing a stocktake together, which gives her an alibi. Inspector, I suggest you lean on Clodagh. Break that alibi. I think it was Ginevra who killed Benton and his sons.'

The inspector groaned. 'I can't cope with this. Back to basics. Why should his sister – no, you say she's not his sister – why should his *wife* want to kill Benton?'

Bea sighed. 'She should have stayed put and denied everything.

Perhaps she realizes Clodagh won't confirm her alibi if checked? Her flight is an admission of guilt.'

The inspector held out his cup for another coffee. 'Start from the beginning.'

EIGHTEEN

'Ginevra – or Jean Marsh if you prefer her birth name – married Ben Benton. Both were very young. For some reason they went their separate ways but didn't bother to get divorced. Benton got a job at one of the companies owned by Holland Holdings. He got promoted and moved to H & B, which gave him the opportunity to chat up not only the chief accountant but also the boss's daughter. The old man came to think Benton was the bee's knees. Benton got Dilys pregnant by accident or design and – oops! – realized what a fix he was in. He asked Ginevra for a divorce, and she refused because she'd got pound signs in her eyes. He was too much of a coward to confess to the Hollands that he was already married and went through with the bigamous marriage, raising money somehow to buy Dilys a good diamond ring.

'Subsequently, he sold the diamond to pay off Ginevra and calmed Dilys with the story that he was settling affairs with an old girlfriend who later died. Dilys accepted this. But he still had to pay off his debt for the diamond, so he skimped and saved at home to do so. Proof: his house hadn't been painted or updated for years, and although the boys were given the usual toys, Dilys and Bernice were clothed from charity shops.'

'And Ginevra?' said the inspector.

'Was still hanging around. Successful blackmailers don't demand too much at any one time, but keep coming back time again. It looks to me as if Ginevra started her boutique about then, using the money from the diamond plus what she could get from Clodagh . . . who was a sleeping partner, though not a bedtime one, you understand? Ginevra used Ricky, the photographer and motorbike owner, for fun, but he didn't live with her. He was her bit of rough on the side. He doesn't show up on the boutique's website in pictures, but if you look closely you'll see the photographs there and on her

Facebook site are attributed to him. I expect you can find him easily
enough.

'Three children were born to Benton and Dilys. Benton had Dilys
well under his thumb but was still strapped for cash, and he was
beginning to realize that running Holland and Butcher was not going
to lead to a place in the sun. He'd continued to pay court on the
side to the old man's chief accountant and that was when he had a
vision of Shangri-La, because she was responsible for switching
large sums of money around the world to minimize tax for Holland
Holdings.

'I don't know whether he proposed the theft himself, or she
wanted to repay him for favours received, but the end result was
that a very large sum of money went missing from Holland Holdings'
account in the Cayman Islands. I don't know how she'd proposed
to hide the theft, perhaps by confusing transfers of money round
the globe, or fudging the accounts somewhere . . .? Unfortunately
for the conspirators, this irregularity was observed by the deputy
chief accountant, a man named Adamsson. He made a fuss. At first
old man Holland couldn't believe that his favourites had been
cheating him. He threw a wobbly and dismissed the whistle-blower
. . . but the damage was done and he began to suspect he'd been
diddled. Mr Holland went back a long way with his accountant. He
didn't want to hand her over to the police, partly because that would
send the wrong signals to his investors. I think he did what most
people would do under the circumstances. He told her to repay the
money and he would take no further action.

'But Madam Accountant had already paid Benton his cut – probably by transfer to a new account in the Cayman Islands – and
Benton had divvied up with Ginevra. I am assuming she was in on
this from the beginning, or at least knew what he was up to. I
suppose, Inspector, that you'll be able to find a paper trace of what
went on between the three of them in the Cayman Islands? I don't
like to think of the accountant's frame of mind. She probably pleaded
with Benton to return his share and he wouldn't, or couldn't, because
he'd already passed a chunk of it on to Ginevra. So she topped
herself.

'When old man Holland first understood he'd been robbed, he'd
no reason to suspect that Benton was involved except that he'd
been a protégé of the accountant's. But once suspicion had been
planted in his mind he soon discovered the hole in the accounts

was larger than a volcanic crater, which brought his sister Sybil screeching over from the States, demanding that something be done about it, immediately. At that point they roped Leon in, to work out what had gone wrong and how to put it right. Leon was at a loose end, and for various reasons, decided to help but to go under-cover to do so.'

Leon washed his face with his hands. Wiping away a smile?

Bea continued. 'Benton began to panic. Perhaps his "deal" with the accountant might not be uncovered, but his comfortable lifestyle was at risk because, although he'd once been old man Holland's blue-eyed boy, he'd failed to make H & B profitable. He could see his luck running out. He'd been trying for some time both directly and through Max to get me to take over the running of H & B so as to pull it round and make it into a profitable company. I'd failed to take the bait. He'd been using his fists on Dilys and Bernice as a matter of course, and he probably thought I'd be as easy to cow. He tried slapping me around, but that didn't work, either. The chief accountant had committed suicide and, at any moment, Mr Holland would discover his involvement with the affair of the missing money.

'He was making love to another woman – no, not Ginevra, and not another accountant, and for the moment you don't need to know who it was – and he'd promised her they'd run off to live on a desert island. Only, Dilys was in the way. If he could get rid of her, he could sell the house, put the children into boarding schools and go off into the blue with his new love. But his attempts to stage Dilys's suicides failed and got me further involved. Once she'd been whisked out of the hospital by person or persons unknown, I jumped to the conclusion that Benton had done away with her, so I phoned him to say that unless he produced Dilys alive and well, I'd go to the police. An empty threat as the police weren't interested in what I had to say about false suicide messages written in the wrong lipstick on the mirror. Crucially, Benton was out when I phoned, and Ginevra took the message.

'Now, neither Benton and Ginevra knew where Dilys was and they couldn't produce her. What to do? They panicked. They decided to lure me to a quiet part of town where I could be ambushed, perhaps beaten up, perhaps killed. I believe it was Ginevra's partner Ricky who took Benton on the back of his motorbike and did his best to scare me off. Fortunately for me, that ploy failed because

my taxi driver took me to the nearest manned police station. That
was on Saturday night.

'That same night the three of them, Benton, Ginevra and Ricky,
met at his house. Yes, I think there has been at least one other visitor
to that house. Neither Benton nor Ginevra smoke. Smoked. But I
smelt cigarette smoke when Ginevra opened the door to us when
Leon and I called there on Monday. Does Clodagh smoke? I'll lay
odds that Ricky does.'

'I'll find out,' said the inspector.

'Benton couldn't come up with any fresh ideas. He said Ricky
must keep following me till he could get me alone. Ginevra agreed.
And that's what Ricky did on Sunday, reporting to her by mobile
phone, and not to Benton. Fortunately, I was well protected. Now
consider Ginevra's position. Benton had given her a share of the
financial scam and that was fine, but he was going to become a
liability if I carried out my threat to go to the police. She knew him
well. Would he keep her out of it, if he were arrested? She thought
not. She was Benton's wife but not the mother of his children, who
were nothing to her. Less than nothing. So that morning I believe
she suggested that while Ricky was taking care of me, Benton should
take the kids out into the country with a picnic lunch. Perhaps she
said she'd meet them at a favourite picnic spot with their lunch. I
don't know that she *did* meet them there, but if I'd been her, I would
have done so, because I'd have wanted to make sure that Benton
and his children drank the drugged soup.'

'Wait a minute. How did Ginevra get there?'

'She had a van for work, didn't she? When you find it, you can
check for signs of mud or whatever which might show where the
van was taken on Sunday. Aren't there CCTV cameras on the
motorway? I'm sure you can trace her journey. Ginevra asked
Clodagh to give her an alibi in case anything went wrong. I don't
know what excuse she gave, but Clodagh agreed. The two of them
were supposed to be stocktaking. That actually raised my suspicions
because you usually stocktake as soon as possible after Christmas,
and this was the end of January. If they have used a computer to
do the stocktake, I expect it will give you the actual date on which
they did it – and it won't have been this last Sunday. I have no idea
how much Clodagh knew of what was going on, but I think she'd
break down pretty quickly if she were confronted with a charge of
conspiracy to murder.'

Maggie cleaned Pippin's face and hands, to his intense displeasure. 'To kill the children, though!'

'It costs money to bring up children, and they weren't hers,' said Bea, with an ache in her voice. 'They stood between her and money, so they had to go.'

Silence.

The inspector stirred. 'Anyone have any ideas why she should do a bunk now?'

Leon held up one finger. 'Ah. I think that's my fault. Dilys has been fretting about some bits and pieces of jewellery that were her mother's. She wasn't sure that Benton had renewed the insurance policy, and she was afraid their empty house might be burgled in her absence. I didn't tell her that Ginevra had moved in. I said I'd call and collect them for her. Also, I thought it would help if I could scare Ginevra into leaving.

'As I arrived, I noticed a For Sale sign had been put up in the garden, and a man in biker's leathers – Ricky, I assume – was putting some black plastic bags and cardboard boxes out for the dustmen to take. Ginevra let me in. There were two dirty plates and two wine glasses on the table. And, yes, a saucer with some cigarette butts on it, no lipstick. Ricky is the smoker. I told Ginevra why I'd come. She said she'd put all Dilys's things out for the dustman to collect next day, but that I could take them if I liked. She said Benton's stuff had gone to a second-hand clothes shop. I said she'd no right to do that as the house and everything in it now belonged to Dilys. She fired up, said Benton had left every-thing to her and not to Dilys. I said Benton might or might not have left his personal effects to her – though the lawyers could argue about that one – but that the deeds to the house were still lodged with the company's lawyers and the house was in the company's name.'

Bea gaped, as did Maggie. 'Was that true?'

'I checked. As a wedding present, Dilys – not Benton – had been given a repairing lease on the house at a peppercorn rent. The house is still owned by Holland Holdings, who can cancel the arrangement if the property is not kept up properly . . . which it hasn't been. Benton had not asked Dilys to turn the lease over to him, because it would have meant his having to spend money on the house. This instance of cheese-paring on Benton's part has actually turned out well as it means Dilys has a home to return to.

'When I explained this to Ginevra she was furious, spat out a lot of abuse. Ricky blustered, threatened to alter the shape of my face. So my chauffeur and I took the black plastic bags containing Dilys's things out to the car and left. I found the box which Dilys said she kept her few bits and pieces of jewellery in. Every earring, every necklace, every brooch had been smashed, probably with a hammer. Nothing terribly valuable. The pearls she'd been given for her eight-eenth, a gold locket which had been her grandmother's, that sort of thing. I was . . . shattered. I'm going to try to get the things restored, but they'll never be the same again.'

Bea breathed out a long sigh. So finding this destruction was what had made him take to drink last night? He really was the joker in the pack, wasn't he?

The inspector nodded. 'Ginevra must have realized that if she couldn't sell the house, she'd got as much as she was likely to get, and called it a day. We'll pick her up at the airport, I expect.'

But they didn't. It seemed she'd disappeared into thin air.

Preparations for Maggie's wedding

By way of apology, Leon had a huge basket of fruit from Harrods delivered to Bea, together with an invitation for supper. She declined. She resolved to put that troublesome man out of her mind even though events kept thrusting him back.

For one thing, Bernice and Maggie were on the phone to one another at least once a day. Bernice wanted to be a flower girl at Maggie's wedding. She'd thought this up all by herself, and Sybil had bought her an exquisite dress to wear, so whatever Maggie said about this being a quiet wedding for immediate family and friends, the Hollands would have to be invited . . . which meant a spruce-up for Bea's house in which they planned to host a small party after the church blessing.

The Hollands sent Maggie a magnificent cheque for a wedding present, which deprived her of words for quite half an hour.

Then Maggie's mother returned from her winter cruise and objected to all the arrangements that had been made. She tried to carry Maggie off to a select dressmaker to be fitted with a puffball of a dress with bare shoulders instead of the sleek coat dress she'd already picked out, and stated that *this* arrangement could not even be considered . . . and as for *that* . . .!

Hot words were spoken by the bride, by the bride's mother and even by Zander. Tears were shed by the bride *and* her mother, so that Bea had to intervene, suggesting a compromise here, a softened refusal there, and a graceful acceptance of some of the least important suggestions.

The celebratory meal was moved to the penthouse in which Maggie's mother lived, the guest list expanded: ditto the menu. This larger party wouldn't be such a relaxed occasion, but it was a compromise which they could all live with.

One blessing; Max and Nicole were not going to be around for the celebration, as they had taken Pippin off for a winter holiday in the sun. The tabloids sported pictures of the happy family, who were expecting another addition, etc.

Leon continued to send Bea a bouquet of flowers and an invitation to supper every few days. Bea binned the invitations and passed the flowers on to the girls in the office. One day there was no invitation, but a handwritten note from Leon excusing himself from attendance at the wedding, due to pressure of business. So that was that. Wasn't it?

Bea told herself it was no more than she'd expected.

Maggie developed pre-wedding nerves but Bea got her to the Registry Office in time. Two hours later Maggie danced down the aisle at church for a blessing on her marriage, while her mother cried neatly into a hankie, and Bernice threw rose petals around with abandon and total disregard for those who had to clear them up afterwards. The wedding breakfast started off rather stiffly, but people relaxed as soon as sufficient champagne had been poured down their throats. Sybil wore yet another fabulous fur coat and a hat decorated with feathers. Bea wore grey and caught herself wondering why Leon had opted out of the occasion.

In the Business section of *The Times* the following day Bea read that Holland Holdings had been split into two. Old man Holland would retain chairmanship of the overseas division, while Leon – pictured with colourful managing directors of various of his companies – took over the rest.

At the weekend CJ took Bea out for a meal, saying he'd heard that almost all the money stolen from Holland Holdings had been recovered, and that the stock market had been favourably impressed by the new CEO for the British division while reserving judgement on old man Holland's continuing to rule his overseas empire. She did not invite him back for a nightcap.

Still no one could find Ginevra, which was unsettling to say the least.

Midweek, Inspector Durrell arrived in time for supper. He said that Forensics had painstakingly fingerprinted Benton's car, and although Ginevra had sworn she'd never been anywhere near it, they'd found her prints on the radio button and on the back of a wing mirror. In addition, although they hadn't yet found where she'd bought the pills she'd used to kill Benton and the boys, they had found the empty packaging in a neighbour's dustbin and identified her prints on it.

Polishing off a large helping of pheasant pie, the inspector also reported that Ginevra's business partner Clodagh had been appalled to find herself implicated in murder and had admitted she'd given Ginevra a false alibi. The police had also traced Ricky, who was indeed a professional photographer. When arrested, he admitted that he'd seen nothing wrong in helping his friend Ginevra 'sort out' Mrs Abbot who, she said, had owed her a lot of money.

Inspector Durrell asked if Mrs Abbot would care to give witness against Ricky, and Mrs Abbot said that since Benton was dead and she was busy with a number of new clients, she'd prefer to let the matter drop.

Days passed without any more news.

Surprise! Sybil Holland rang to speak to Bea one afternoon. 'You have a minute, Mrs Abbot?' A throaty voice, used to command, but for some reason prepared to ask a favour.

Bea grinned to herself. This would be about Bernice. Maggie had reported – with some amusement – that Sybil considered Bernice spent too much time on the phone to Maggie. Sybil had ordered Bernice to stop phoning Maggie. The child had taken no notice, so Sybil had confiscated her phone. Bernice had got round Maria and used the house phone instead. Then Leon had intervened – apparently, he did his best to spend time with the child – and had given her a phone of her own.

So what did Bernice's great aunt want now? 'What can I do for you, Sybil?'

'My great niece is fascinated by Maggie's tale about having to catch the toast as it flies out of the machine. She wants to see it for herself and has asked if she may buy you a new one.'

'That's very kind of her, and you know she's welcome to visit at any time. As for the toaster, it's already been replaced.'

'Oh. Right. She's doing well at her new school. Mature for her age.'

According to Maggie, Bernice was looking after her mother, instead of the other way round.

'Dilys, you see,' said Sybil, every word being pulled out of her with pliers, 'is not doing so well.'

'It's early days, and you've provided the best possible care for her.' A statement, not a query.

'We've offered to buy her another house, or to take her on a world cruise. She has a therapist, and a flat for herself and Bernice in the guest quarters, but she wanders around like a lost soul.'

Dilys hadn't been a very strong character in the first place, and what had happened to her would have crushed a grown man.

Bea said, 'She was kind to me when I was poorly. Is there anything I can do?'

'Yes, well . . . Actually –' in a rush – 'I've got a meeting tomorrow morning that I can't get out of, and Leon's in Brussels, something to do with taxation. The only thing Dilys has set her heart on . . . We don't approve, but maybe it will help . . . She wants to revisit her old home. She imagines it as it was when she left, and she was distressed to hear that Ginevra had cleared out all the family's belongings. I said you'd kept all the boys' things and that you'd get them back to her. Perhaps, if she can pick out some mementoes and see the house as it is now, it will give her closure.'

Another little job for the hired help. 'You'd like me to meet her there tomorrow with the children's belongings?'

'Ten o'clock suit you?'

'Who's got the keys?'

'I'll see that Dilys has some. Our maintenance people changed the locks. They've been keeping an eye on the place. There was a leak, a broken downpipe at the back. That's been rectified and the whole house professionally cleaned. The furniture has been left there for the moment as we weren't sure whether to let the house furnished or not. Dilys thinks we've cleaned up so that she can move back in. We keep telling her that she's got other options, but she's not listening. She wants Bernice to take a day off school and go with her.' This was delivered in a flat, unemotional voice.

Tread carefully. 'Bernice as well? Is that wise? Hasn't the child suffered enough? Why remind her of the past?'

'I am entirely in agreement with you, and Bernice doesn't really want to go. I've told her to be brave and do it for her mother's sake.'

'In that case, shall I see if Maggie can come, too?'

A hesitation. 'Perhaps. The child does seem to rely on her, doesn't she?'

The next morning
A chilly wind. A spit of rain in the air.

Luckily, Bea found a parking space nearby. As they unloaded the plastic bags containing the children's belongings from their car, they spotted a chauffeur-driven limousine some way down the street.

And there was Bernice standing in the front door of her old home, looking anxious. Bernice hadn't wanted to come, had she? Poor child. She didn't run to greet them but, when they met, clasped Maggie about the waist and buried her head in her coat. Maggie dropped the bags she'd been carrying to give the girl a hug.

Bea dragged the last of the bags inside and closed the front door, grateful that someone had thought to turn the heating on.

Bernice whispered something to Maggie and tugged her up the stairs.

Bea called out, 'Hello? Dilys, it's me, Mrs Abbot. I've got the children's things.'

Dilys appeared in the doorway, a pale and thinner version of her former self. She'd had her hair cut in a becoming style and was wearing some pretty, warm clothing, but her eyes were unfocused. Bea wasn't even sure that the girl recognized her. Perhaps she was on heavy medication?

Dilys stared at the black bags, but made no move to open them. It took Bea two trips to cart them through into the living room. Yes, it was nice and clean in here now. And soulless. Stripped of all personal effects.

'Shall we have a look?' suggested Bea, opening up the first bag and spreading out the contents on the floor. Dilys sat on a chair and watched but made no move to pick anything up.

Bea could hear Bernice murmuring to Maggie upstairs and an exclamation from the older girl.

A seagull screeched.

Bea dropped the bag she was holding. 'What was that?'

A scamper down the stairs. Bernice, wailing, 'Mummy, the house is screaming!'

Maggie appeared behind the child, puzzled, amused. 'No, Bernice. Really!'

Dilys managed to focus on her daughter. 'Silly Bunny! Imagining things.'

Bernice's eyes were wild. 'Can't you hear it? We've got to go!'

'Silly Bunny,' said Dilys. 'That's what Daddy used to say, wasn't it? "Silly Bunny had a bad dream."'

Bea began to understand what was going on. She knelt by Bernice and caught her hands in both of hers. 'Bernice, where did you hear the screams?'

'In my room!'

'Were they in the walls, or in the air? Were they an echo in your head?'

The child thought about it. Nodded.

'You can hear yourself screaming?'

Dilys frowned. 'I always told her not to scream. It only made him worse. She never did. She never made a noise.'

'She couldn't scream out loud, so she made the noise inside her head. Is that right, Bernice?'

The child nodded. 'Inside my head. Inside Mummy's head, too, because she mustn't scream, either.'

Maggie wept. 'Oh, you poor things!'

Bea's own eyes filled with tears, but she realized how crucial it was to say and do the right thing. Dilys was poised between the past and the future and could tip either way. Bernice was the key to her mother's future well-being.

'Bernice, you are a little soldier. You saved your mother's life. Yes, she did, Dilys. Perhaps they haven't told you about it, but if it hadn't been for her you would have died, and neither of you would be looking forward to tomorrow.'

Dilys said, 'We need to get back to normal. Bernice must return to her old school—'

'Bernice has moved on. She has a new school now, and a loving family. The only thing she doesn't have is a loving mother.'

Dilys's face twisted. 'You don't understand. How can I think of anything but my lovely lost boys?'

'And your lovely lost girl? Who saved your life and who can still hear your screams?'

Dilys turned her head aside. 'How dare you!' Yet there was no heat in her protest.

'Do you want to lose her, too?'

'Don't be ridiculous! How could I lose her?'

'Very easily, the way you're going. Listen to me, Dilys. Children need to be loved. If they don't get that love from their parents, they'll get it elsewhere. From a great aunt or uncle. From Maggie. At the moment it seems to me that they all love her more than you do.'

'That's ridiculous!' She turned Bernice's face towards her. 'You love me, don't you, Bunny?'

'Of course I do, Mummy,' said Bernice, 'though I do wish you'd call me by my proper name, as Maggie does.'

Flecks of red appeared in Dilys's cheeks. 'Maggie, indeed! Come on, poppet, let's pick some things out of the bags to take home with us. We don't need Maggie or Mrs Abbot to tell us what to think, do we?'

Half an hour later, Bea and Maggie waved the chauffeur-driven car off and allowed themselves to relax. Maggie got into Bea's car and did up her seat belt, but kept her face averted.

Bea said, 'You think I betrayed you to Dilys? I didn't. That child will love you to the day you die, and you will soon have a child of your own to love. If Dilys thinks Bernice might love you more than her, then she'll value her more highly.'

'Yes. I know. I need chocolate.'

'Do you want hot chocolate, Dairy Milk, seventy per cent cocoa chocolate, or something made with powder in a plastic cup?'

'I could eat a whole bar of Fruit and Nut, but I'll settle for hot chocolate, properly made, with whipped cream on top. With a chocolate Flake in it.'

'For medicinal purposes, of course.'

'And a bacon sandwich. No lettuce or tomato.'

'God bless your tum. Now, where's the nearest good coffee shop?'

NINETEEN

Seven days later, Bea received not a food hamper nor flowers but a letter from Holland Enterprises (UK) stating that they were looking for an executive to fill the post of managing director at Holland Training College, salary so much with bonuses, accommodation provided. The successful applicant to be interviewed shortly. The letter was signed by Leon, who had scrawled at the bottom, 'Will you find me someone?'

She leaned back in her chair, smiling. So he'd accepted her decision not to get involved with H & B? Good. And yet. She had to admit to being a trifle disappointed. It had been . . . intriguing . . . to be offered more power, more money.

But, no. She knew her limitations.

Someone to run H & B for him? A name leaped into her mind. Anna was the events manager for a charity who had used the services of the Abbot Agency for many years. Anna could have run the Home Office if she'd been inclined to go into the Civil Service, but a career break for family reasons had hampered her rise in the world, and she'd reached a glass ceiling where she was.

Would she want the job? Bea referred back to the letter. Accommodation offered. That might mean a house move for the applicant or, if Anna didn't want to move, a not too difficult commute. The salary was attractive. Bonuses, too? Good.

Bea raised her hand to the phone to sound Anna out and dropped it again.

If Anna did take the job and Leon recognized her excellent qualities, would he also want to take her into his personal life? Propinquity, and all that, leading to a relationship?

How old exactly was Anna? Early forties. She'd been married once, had a couple of teenaged children. Was she still young enough to give Leon a baby?

Bea scolded herself. Did she have any right to influence such matters? Probably not. Definitely not.

It still took her an hour before she lifted the phone.

*   *   *

A week later – a whole seven days without hearing from Leon – she received a cheque in the post marked 'For Services Rendered', as Anna's application for the post had been successful. She would commute, starting at the beginning of the following month.

With the cheque from Leon came the usual invitation. Would she dine with him that night? Place and time to suit herself. He would send the car for her, and his chauffeur would take her home at whatever time suited her.

So he wasn't planning to jump her again? Mm. Oh well. Why not? She supposed he might already be wining and dining Anna, who was so much younger and more, well, eligible. This invitation was probably just by way of saying 'thank you' to Bea. Nice to have known you.

Well, it might be pleasant to meet him again.

With some hesitation, she said, Yes.

She chose a brand-new pale-green and silver outfit to wear and, with her evening coat thrown around her shoulders, was whisked away in Leon's car to a new and pricey restaurant. One she hadn't visited before.

Leon was waiting for her. He held both her hands in his but didn't try to kiss her. 'My behaviour last time . . . It's a wonder you're prepared to meet me again.'

She found herself smiling. 'Water under the bridge.'

There was a new air of certainty about him. He looked . . . more solid? . . . less hesitant? . . . than before.

She declined an aperitif, and they were shown to their table straightaway. The tables were not set close together, and the menu had been curtailed to A4 size. Two points in the restaurant's favour. He waited for her to choose what she wanted to eat. A point in *his* favour. CJ always wanted to tell her what she would like to have. White wine, or red? She noted that he had no need to push his own importance.

Unlike Max. Ah well, at least he and Nicole seemed to have accepted one another's limitations and were getting on better now.

Leon said, 'You've heard that I've taken over the UK end of Holland Holdings?'

'Wasn't it a foregone conclusion?'

He shook his head. 'I never wanted power. It amused me to think that I could help them out of trouble after their earlier rejection of me, but I had no intention of committing myself to the job. Gradually, I came to see that I'd been given an opportunity to make a difference, and that I did have some of the right skills for the job. I've been inviting the managing directors of each of the companies to meet me, to discuss the future. Already, I'm beginning to see where certain procedures could be tightened up, more emphasis placed on . . . well, on fair trade and honest dealing.' He laughed. 'Now there's a phrase that's frightening the life out of them!'

Bea applauded. 'Good for you.'

He sobered. 'There's no guarantee that I'll succeed, but there is a cold wind blowing about the ankles of those who cut corners and increase their wealth at the expense of the people they're supposed to serve. Perhaps I have a chance.'

'With all my heart, I hope you succeed.'

He raised his glass in a toast. 'I trust your judgement implicitly. Which brings me to another favour I need to ask of you. An even bigger one. I would like us to be friends. I know that I need your company and advice far more than you need mine. But there it is: I'm asking.'

She narrowed her eyes at him. 'You need a trophy woman to hang on your arm at functions. There must be hundreds of women who'd jump at the chance.' And what about Anna?

'Fake blondes are crawling out of the woodwork. Career women are throwing themselves under my car wheels every time I drive out. If I'm asked to dine anywhere, there'll be at least two beautiful babes vying for my attention. I need protection.'

'Use an escort agency. Or look among your executives.'

'You've taught me not to mix business with pleasure. And why should I when I could be enjoying the company of a wise and witty woman who knows how to behave?'

So he'd looked at Anna and decided not to go down that road?

Bea stared into the future, thinking that she could see where a friendship with this man might lead. She had plenty of friends in her life already, but it was a long time since her dear husband had died and left a void in her life. She'd become used to being on her own and bearing other people's burdens, but it struck her now that life recently had become somewhat . . . grey.

'You mean an occasional meal out, perhaps once a month?'

'I mean you and me. Telling one another our joys and sorrows, knowing our secrets would be safe with one another. For a start,

I'm invited to bring a partner to a Mansion House dinner. Would you care to accompany me? And that's only one of the invitations on my desk.'

Her first thought was: what should she wear? Which meant she'd already decided to accept. 'I'm too old for you. You must find a younger woman who will care for you, give you children.'

'I know exactly how old you are. I am two years and one month younger than you. So what! Yes, it is possible that I may some day meet someone I can love enough to marry. I'll bring her to you to vet, shall I?'

She had to laugh at that.

The future would be more colourful with him in her life, even if it were only for a few months. Yes, she might get hurt, but . . . live a little, Bea.

He lifted his glass in a toast to her.

She continued to smile, knowing that she was opening a door on to the future which might lead . . . anywhere.

'Agreed,' she said, and touched her glass to his.

Two days later

Bea put the phone down on a satisfied customer, and it rang again.

This time it was Inspector Durrell. 'Are you cooking?'

Bea laughed. 'At three in the afternoon? Try again when you've some good news for me.'

'Oh, I have. We've arrested Ginevra, stopped her at Heathrow as she tried to leave for the Caribbean. She'd dyed her hair black but had made a poor job of replacing her passport photo with one to match her new appearance. She's trying to make out she's as innocent as a newborn, and that any money in her account in the Cayman Islands is repayment of a sum she'd lent Benton earlier. Oh, and she denies all involvement in the deaths of her husband and his children.'

'You've got enough to hold her?' Bea was alarmed at the thought of Ginevra getting off on a technicality.

'There's more than enough forensic evidence to send her for trial, plus statements from Clodagh and Ricky. Rest assured, she's not getting away with it. So, when can I catch you in? I've told my wife about your toaster. She says I ought to get you a replacement, to make up for all the meals I've scrounged off you.'

'Zander fixed the old toaster and bought us a new one, but it would be good to see you. I'm out this evening. Tomorrow do you?'

'You can't find me a small window today?'

'You want something? The answer is "no". I'm too busy.'

'It's only a little thing. Won't take you half an hour to solve.'

'No.'

'I'll be round in five minutes . . .'

Lightning Source UK Ltd.
Milton Keynes UK
UKOW04f1031181117
312902UK00001B/15/P

Library and Information Centres

Red doles Lane

Huddersfield, West Yorkshire

HD2 1YF

This book should be returned on or before the latest date stamped below. Fines are charged if the item is late.

You may renew this loan for a further period by phone, personal visit or at www.kirklees.gov.uk/libraries, provided that the book is not required by another reader.

NO MORE THAN THREE RENEWALS ARE PERMITTED

800 694 360